# Downright Dead

Books by PAMELA KOPFLER

*Better Dead*

*Downright Dead*

# Downright Dead

## PAMELA KOPFLER

KENSINGTON PUBLISHING CORP.

www.kensingtonbooks.com

KENSINGTON BOOKS are published by

Kensington Publishing Corp.
119 West 40th Street
New York, NY 10018

All Kensington titles, imprints, and distributed lines are available at special quantity discounts for bulk purchases for sales promotions, premiums, fund-raising, educational, or institutional use. Special book excerpts or customized printings can also be created to fit specific needs. For details, write or phone the office of the Kensington sales manager: Kensington Publishing Corp., 119 West 40th Street, New York, NY 10018, attn: Sales Department; phone 1-800-221-2647.

KENSINGTON BOOKS and the K logo are Reg. U.S. Pat. & TM Off.

ISBN-13: 978-1-4967-1323-0
ISBN-10: 1-4967-1323-0

First printing: October 2018

10  9  8  7  6  5  4  3  2  1

Printed in the United States of America

First electronic edition: October 2018

ISBN-13: 978-1-4967-1324-7
ISBN-10: 1-4967-1324-9

# CHAPTER ONE

"I don't see dead people anymore and that's a good thing." Holly Davis swirled her latest attempt at a Sazerac in a Waterford lowball glass. The ruby color of the cocktail sparkled against the crystal. Maybe this effort would be guest worthy. She lifted her glass to Nelda, the best cook in St. Agnes Parish, her housekeeper and closest thing she had to family. "The only spirit at Holly Grove these days is in this glass."

"You sure 'bout that?" Nelda's brows flattened as she stared up at the steady glow of the milk-glass pendant light in the circa 1928 kitchen, which was modern compared to the rest of Holly's antebellum B&B. Nelda shoved her hands onto her generous hips. "That thing's been flickering like a lightning bug off and on all day."

Holly studied the light fixture and took a sip of the Sazerac. She shivered. Her taste buds offered a vague rejection. Too what? Too strong? Too sweet? Wrong whiskey? "Well, it's not flickering now."

"No. But Burl, God rest his soul," Nelda said,

making the sign of the cross. "He always messed with me when your back was turned or you weren't around." She snatched a cup towel off her shoulder and folded it into a pad. "You ain't been in here makin' gumbo and bread puddin' all afternoon with that light show."

Holly glanced at her Yorkie curled up sleeping in a sliver of what was left of the afternoon sun. "But you know Rhett yapped anytime Burl was around."

Rhett opened one sleepy eye when she said his name, but he didn't budge.

"That pup's been snoring all afternoon long. He wouldn't know if Jesus came in here."

"*He* hasn't been here either." Holly strolled across the cypress planks to the deep porcelain sink and dumped her failed Sazerac down the drain. "Hell evidently froze over in South Louisiana last week and bit back all the mint within miles. I always welcome guests with a Holly Grove mint julep, but that's out, and that Sazerac was nowhere near guest worthy."

"I hope all that flickerin' didn't make me mess up my bread puddin' like your Sazerac." Nelda shook her head then opened the oven. "Is your Jake really comin' this time?"

"He's not my Jake by any stretch of the imagination, but he swore he'd be here." *If he cancels this time, I'm done.* Since ICE sent him to Guatemala for a sting of some kind three months ago, he'd called her exactly three times, from three different numbers. Every call had been shorter than the last. *This girl can take a hint.*

"Humph. I'm gonna make it worth his while even if you don't. You know how he loves my bread puddin'." Nelda grinned and pulled out a pan of golden deliciousness from the oven. The sugary aroma wafted into the room and mixed with the savory bouquet of the gumbo simmering on the stove.

Steam curling from the gumbo pot reminded Holly of one of Burl's more memorable entrances. While it lasted, having a ghost at Holly Grove *had* been good for business, but not worth keeping the ghost of her sorry excuse for a husband for life.

Nelda's cooking was good for business, too, but Holly doubted it would bring Jake McCann back. It took him fifteen years to come back to Delta Ridge after the first time he left.

Nelda picked up her favorite wooden spoon that looked more like a paddle and stirred her gumbo. "It's flirtin' with ready."

The pendant light flickered.

Nelda spun around, wide-eyed. Gumbo dripped from her wooden spoon and splattered on the cypress floor. "I told you."

Rhett rousted and trotted to the splattering of gumbo. Just like a man—selective hearing . . . and sight.

"The bulb is probably loose." Holly shrugged. She'd witnessed her not-so-dearly-departed's dramatic exit. "Burl is gone for good."

Rhett licked his lips and stared up at the spoon as though he could will another dribble of gumbo to fall.

"You didn't make up that story for me just so I wouldn't quit on you, did ya?"

"I swear." Holly crossed her heart then gave the CliffsNotes version of the story she'd told Nelda too many times. "Bright lights. Trumpets on high. Better than any Hollywood movie. And poof. Burl was gone."

"And he's at rest 'cause—"

"In the end, he earned it." And she'd found peace in that too.

"Praise be." Nelda glanced over each shoulder as if Burl could hear her. "God rest his sorry soul."

"But remember, don't tell anyone our ghost is gone," Holly said. "All the most successful B&Bs have ghosts, and Holly Grove needs that edge to make it."

"I won't tell it but I won't lie neither. I'm plannin' on goin' through those pearly gates one day too." Nelda stirred her award-winning gumbo, then rapped her big wooden spoon on the side of the pot. She turned and eyed Holly. "The whole world is gonna think Holly Grove is haunted after tonight."

At nine, *Inquiring Minds* would air the episode they'd shot back in the fall about the haunting at Holly Grove B&B. Holly ran her finger under the high neck of her black cashmere sweater. She had been on the receiving end of that look Nelda had given her, practically since birth. Nelda knew her too well. "Technically, Holly Grove *had* a ghost."

"H-A-D." Nelda spelled out the word. "You know you're in for a hurricane of trouble if folks find out you're acting like you got a ghost and you know fool well you don't. That's all I got to say."


*Inquiring Minds* would air coast-to-coast, full-color proof Holly Davis's Louisiana B&B was haunted in less than an hour. *H-A-D a ghost my foot.* Holly swiped her hair from her face, then backed out into the entrance hall with her cart. *Trouble?* Nelda just couldn't see the value in keeping the ghost—in spirit anyway.

Holly's basic black stilettos clicked on the cypress planks as she rolled the cart down the twelve-foot-wide entrance hall that ran from her front door to her back door. The wheels wobbled under the weight of the one TV in her entire B&B. She only hauled the old thing out of storage for special occasions like the LSU-Alabama game, the Super Bowl, and . . . tonight. Otherwise, she kept her plantation home frozen in 1855 because that's what her guests paid to experience.

*That and the ghost.*

Holly could live with that lie, but it would be uncomfortable tonight. Her neck and chest heated. She had, no doubt, red splotches congregated under her black cashmere sweater like lie detectors.

No one—except Nelda and Jake—could ever know the ghost of her not-so-dearly-departed had checked out—permanently. The success of Holly Grove depended on keeping that a secret. She scrubbed a hand over an itchy spot on her neck, then straightened the pearls Burl had given her on their tenth anniversary.

Unfortunately, the ghost had top billing for the show tonight, but Holly Grove would still get nationwide exposure. She liked to think of it as alimony payments from beyond the grave. *Thank you, Burl.*

The steady thud of a hammer sounded from above. Holly and the whole town had done their part to keep Mackie McCann busy and sober until Jake could get back and keep an eye on his dad.

She'd hired Mackie to renovate the widow's walk and bring it up to code. Then she'd have an added attraction of stargazing from the top of Holly Grove. She'd even bought a special mounted telescope, which was a little over the top, but she loved it.

After the ghost buzz had died down and now in the dead of winter, business had slowed to a few guests here and there. That was to be expected and made this a good time to tackle the renovation. After tonight, she hoped she'd be booked for months and Holly Grove's future secured.

Portraits of five generations of the Lane women in her family lined the walls. She'd never let them down. They'd held on to Holly Grove through wars, yellow fever epidemics, floods, crop failures, and the Great Depression. Unfortunately, none of them could hold on to a man either.

The mystery portrait had hung across the hall from the family portraits and near the back door, until she moved it upstairs last week. It had always felt out of place. Mama and Grandma Rose had guessed the portrait was of some relative but neither knew for sure. With both of them gone, Holly would probably never know.

When tourists asked about the portrait, she had little to offer. After replacing the painting with recent ghost memorabilia, she had plenty to say at that stop on the tours. The display clashed with the period, but she could live with that infraction for the publicity.

She stopped and straightened a framed, glossy magazine article titled "The Ghost in the Grove." It was nestled between other articles and a collection of autographed photos of Holly with TV reporters and minor celebrities. The pics on a bulletin board of "supposed" ghost sightings by guests needed tidying too. Holly stood back and frowned. All the frames hung slightly askew.

She sighed and straightened the *Gazette* article about Nelda's Iron Skillet Award for her gumbo. Nelda's housekeeping skills didn't match her cooking skills. It seemed she could never dust and put things back exactly as they had been. But Nelda made up for that one flaw in so many ways it wasn't worth mentioning.

Nelda busted out of the kitchen and trotted down the hall waving Holly's cell phone. "Unknown number," she said panting. "Answer it quick. It might be your Jake."

Holly grabbed the phone and her heart took an involuntary uptick. "Or a telemarketer." She answered the call with a well-modulated *hello.*

# CHAPTER TWO

"Hey, sweetheart." Jake's deep voice hummed through the line in high-voltage charm and fine-tuned ease that gave her temporary amnesia about their rocky history. "Are you ready for your television debut?"

"I'm getting there," she said. Though she wasn't convinced she'd ever be ready to relive Burl's haunting by watching it on TV.

Nelda practically beamed. "It's Jake, huh? You tell him I made bread puddin'," She stretched across the table and straightened a frame in the display on the entrance hall wall.

*Now she notices her dusting chaos.* Holly bit back a grin.

"Nelda says hi and she made bread pudding for you." Holly leaned against the guest book table and caught her reflection in the pier mirror on the opposite wall. The sappy smile on her face said what she wouldn't admit. She brushed a stringy blond curl out of her face and looked away. "How far away are you?"

After a long pause he said, "Um, something came up down here. I'm not going to make it tonight."

"Down there?" She slumped against the table. "You're still in Guatemala, and you're just now letting me know you're not coming?"

"I'll explain when I get there. I promise."

*Another promise to break. He's not coming now or possibly ever. Take the hint, Holly.* "Don't bother. This is the third time you've canceled. I can't afford to hold a room and you not show up at the last minute."

Of course, she only had three rooms out of ten reserved tonight, but Jake didn't need to know that. She had to reframe her thinking to a strictly business relationship.

"I'll pay for it. Just hold a room until I can get there."

"For how long? Fifteen years?" It took him that long to come back to Delta Ridge after he blew out of town on graduation day.

"That could get expensive." Jake chuckled. "It won't be that long. You just keep a bed warm for me."

*In his dreams.* She wanted to reach through the phone and strangle him. "If you're lucky, I'll save Abe's cabin for you."

"The one without indoor plumbing?" he asked as though he didn't believe she'd put him out there.

"Yep and it's been unseasonably cold in Delta Ridge, too." She stared out the side panel of her front door at the winter fog rolling in off the river. Just like Jake, hard to predict.

"I guess you've missed me, since you're mad I'm not coming." He laughed again.

Muffled voices, speaking in Spanish, sounded in the background on his end.

"I missed you too, sweetheart," he whispered and ended the call.

She held the phone out and stared at it. *He missed me? Seriously?*

"Guess your Jake ain't comin'," Nelda said in a solemn tone and laid her hand on Holly's shoulder.

Holly didn't chance a glance at her. She didn't need that bless-your-poor-little-heart pity. And she didn't need Jake.

"Well, at least you won't be watchin' *Inquiring Minds* alone." Nelda held the kitchen door open for Holly to roll the TV cart into the kitchen.

"No thanks to Jake." As soon as Holly said his name she regretted it. The sooner she filed him away as a memory, the better.

"You should've had a big ol' party," Nelda said.

"I only want to watch the show with people who lived it with me." Even though they didn't know everything, they wouldn't question the haunting. Holly pushed the cart past the planter's table to the back wall. She'd carefully hidden her only cable connection behind a potted plant there.

"Me and Mackie are gonna stay and watch. You got Sam, Miss Alice and the Delta Ridge bridge ladies coming, too." Nelda clicked off the short guest list on her fingers. "Who else?"

"A couple has reservations." She slammed her

palm to her forehead. "I still have to find a decent Sazerac recipe to make welcome cocktails. That kind of thing gets me good reviews."

"Humph." Nelda wagged a finger at Holly. "You keep practicin' and sippin' and you'll find trouble. You know what happened last time you overserved yourself."

Holly shivered. How could she forget going from tipsy to facing the ghost of her not-so-dearly-departed materializing in front of her? And she had to relive a bit of that during *Inquiring Minds* tonight. Watching it stone-cold sober may not be her best option. "I'm going to sip until I get it right."

"Where you gettin' those recipes?" Nelda asked.

Holly unwound the cable wire from around the TV. "The Internet."

"Humph." Nelda shook her head. "Any fool can put a recipe up on that world-wide-waste-a-time."

"This fool is going to perfect a Sazerac and post pictures all over the Internet as soon as I get this TV set up." Holly connected the cable line then plugged in the TV at the end of the planter's table. "Everyone should be able to see the screen here."

"And eat my gumbo and bread puddin'."

Holly dusted her palms together. "Now back to Sazerac practice."

More banging came from upstairs. Holly hadn't noticed it had stopped until it started again.

"You mind if I turn on the cookin' channel since you've got the TV set up and all? Maybe it'll drown out some of that racket Mackie is makin' up there," Nelda said, thumbing toward the ceiling.

"Knock yourself out." Holly fired up her tablet and clicked on another bookmarked Sazerac recipe.

A loud pop sounded.

Holly jumped, then whirled around.

Rhett's nails scratched across the floor as he ran out the kitchen.

"What was that?" Holly asked.

Nelda stood with one hand on her heart and the other holding the remote control. "I 'bout caught a heart attack. All I did was turn on the TV and somethin' blew up."

"Did the TV come on?"

"For a second." She clicked the remote twice, but the screen stayed blank.

Holly flipped the light switch off and on. Nothing.

Tail between his legs, Rhett peeked around the kitchen door at them.

*Bless his heart.* "Scared the daylights out of me too, Rhett," Holly said.

"Just for my nerves, tell me one more time that ghost is gone," Nelda said with her hand still clutching her chest.

Holly studied the milk-glass pendant light. Soot dotted the bottom of the glass. *That can't be good.*

She sniffed. If there was smoke in the air, the scent of gumbo had won out. "This isn't a ghost problem. It's an electrical problem."

Nelda wagged a finger at Holly. "I told you somethin' was wrong with that thing."

"I hope it didn't blow out the TV too." Holly sighed. "An electrician after hours will cost a fortune. Maybe Mackie can fix it."

"If he can't we're gonna have eight folks sittin' around in the dark tellin' ghost stories instead of watchin' one on TV."

"Just peachy." Holly folded her arms and glared at the old light fixture. That repair wasn't in the budget either. "First Jake cancels. Now this. Bad luck always comes in threes. What's next?"

"Shush." Nelda pressed a finger across her lips. "Don't ask. You might get it."

Holly's phone buzzed again. Another unknown number. Couldn't be Jake. That left two choices. Telemarketer or potential guest, and she couldn't miss taking a reservation. "Hello."

"Holly Davis?" asked a smooth professional voice. *Totally a telemarketer. Fifty-fifty chance and I lose. Just my luck and a good reason I should never gamble.*

"Yes," Holly answered, her voice as flat as her mood.

"I'm Sylvia Martin's assistant, Megan Long," said the woman on the line.

"Sylvia Martin of *Inquiring Minds*?" Why would she be calling? Did they find out her ghost was gone? Cancel the show? The rash under Holly's sweater resurrected and marched across her collarbone in an organized protest of each scenario. She ambled into the hallway for privacy.

"Yes," Morgan or Meagan or whatever her name was said, but all Holly could think about was bad luck comes in threes. The rat-a-tat of fingers on a keyboard sounded in the background. "I'm certain you're getting ready for a viewing party, but Sylvia asked me to nail this down before you get a flood of reservations after the show."

Holly's internal thermostat kicked up a few degrees. "Nail what down?"

Rhett joined her and paced down the hall with her as though he sensed something wasn't right.

"She asked me to book Holly Grove for a follow-up, ASAP."

"Book Holly Grove? Follow-up?" Holly's throat tightened as she spoke. "On what?"

"Your ghost, of course."

Holly practically choked, then stood dead still. *The one that's gone.* "*My* ghost?"

Rhett sat in front of her. He cocked his head to the side as though he couldn't believe what she'd said. She could hardly believe what she'd heard.

"He was quite a hit with our test audience. They rated 'The Ghost in the Grove' best episode of the season," Megan continued at an excited clip. "'Return to The Ghost in the Grove' will open *Inquiring Minds*'s next season."

"But . . ." Holly rubbed the back of her neck. What could she say? *I don't have a ghost anymore?* Then go back to running just a B&B in the middle of nowhere and go broke. *Not happening.*

"This is quite an opportunity for your establishment. Our viewership is up to three million and growing."

"I'm sure it is, but I'm renovating right now." She pinched the bridge of her nose and plopped down on the bottom step of the staircase. "And after the show, I hope to be booked solid for a while. It's just not a good time." *Ever.*

"We'll work around the renovations and pay you for your trouble. I've booked your available rooms Wednesday through the weekend for the shoot as well as the formal rooms downstairs."

A riff from "Sweet Dreams (Are Made of This)" rang out from Holly's computer in the kitchen—her alert for online reservations. Holly launched herself from the steps. "No! You can't."

Rhett's nails tapped the wood planks as he trotted to her side.

*Oh, Rhett. This isn't good.*

"Excuse me," what's-her-name said, but she'd surely understood no.

Holly could live with the little lie that Holly Grove was still haunted, but she would never allow anyone to prove it wasn't. "No offense, but I'm not interested in being on the show again."

"Sylvia will not take this well." The assistant's tone turned sour. Holly had firsthand experience with Sylvia and didn't need round two. That woman was a force to be reckoned with.

"Give her my apologies," Holly said. *And tell her to butter my biscuit and take a bite because that show ain't gonna happen.*

"That won't be necessary. Please hold for Sylvia Martin."

*Oh, crapola.*

Almost instantly Sylvia said, "Holly, my dear friend." She coated her pitch-perfect voice in enough artificial sweetness to clog the line.

*Gag me.*

"Sylvia." Holly gushed. Not to be outdone, she faked it too. "Thank you so much for thinking about me and Holly Grove. It would have been so much fun to be on another episode of *Inquiring Minds.*"

*About as much fun as digging up her almost-ex for old times' sake.* "Unfortunately, as I told your charming assistant, we're in the middle of renovations. Maybe another time?" *Like next February 30.*

"Holly, dear, I've booked the rooms for the crew. I've contacted that incredible medium, Angel, to lead another séance. This *is* the time."

"Sylvia, dear, no offense, but I just can't make that commitment right now." Holly rubbed muscles knotting in her neck.

"May I be perfectly honest?" Sylvia asked.

*If possible.* "Always."

"I report on the strange, the unusual," Sylvia said, repeating the promo line from her show. "I'm very good at what I do."

*Modest too.*

"It's not all real," Sylvia said. "I report and the fans decide what's real and what's not."

Holly rolled her eyes. Most of it was questionable in her opinion, but Nelda and millions of others were true fans of the show.

"The Ghost in the Grove is real," Sylvia said emphatically. "I know it. You know it. And my viewers will know it after tonight, right?"

"Right." The word squeezed through her vocal cords an octave higher than the truth would allow. *H-A-D a ghost.* Nelda's correction looped through Holly's mind. "Tonight's show can speak for itself. Why do another one on the same ghost?"

"Because I can win." Sylvia chopped each word with cool calculation.

"Win what?"

"I'm getting to that."

*Lordy. The long way, especially for a New Yorker.*

"There's this creeper, a debunker, who's been trolling me ever since the debut season of *Inquiring Minds.*"

"I've had a few trolls on my website." Some of them had a creep factor that gave Holly chills. She wouldn't wish trolling on even a frenemy. "Just ignore him and delete his posts."

"I've blocked him several times. He *was* a nobody. Now he's got a huge following on his blog and YouTube channels. The little troll calls himself Tru, the truth teller." Sylvia huffed.

*That does have a ring to it.*

"He's questioning my credibility. My integrity." An edge crept into Sylvia's voice. "A few hours ago, I was promoting *Inquiring Minds* on a live radio show and that little troll had the nerve to call in."

Holly pitied the guy for taking on Sylvia live.

"He said he could debunk any of my hauntings—anytime, anywhere."

*Oh, crapola.* "And you called Tru, the, um, truth teller's bluff?"

"Of course. I challenged him to come to Holly Grove to attempt to debunk your ghost on *my* show because I know he can't. The whole thing is going viral. My producers are loving it. The sponsors will love it. Plus, your ghost is going to silence him once and for all. That troll is going down."

Holly cringed. *My ghost was real, but he's gone—and I can't tell her or anyone else ever.* A twinge of guilt lolled about in her gut but so be it.

"There's just one teeny-tiny problem," Holly said in a singsong voice. "Burl and I are, um, going through a rough patch. You know. Marital trouble. To tell you the truth, we're not speaking right now." *A proper lie is always partly true, right?* "He may not even show up if I want him to. He's spiteful like that."

"No problem." Sylvia said. "My undergrad is in theater. I'll act as if he's there even if he doesn't show up."

"Wouldn't that be lying?" *And if she could actually act wouldn't Sylvia be acting?*

"No. That would be great television."

"What if that's not enough to convince the debunker?"

"Holly, dear. Cameras fail. Hard drives crash. I wouldn't be the first to lose footage." Sylvia gave an exasperated sigh. "Believe me, nothing will air that makes me look bad."

"But without proof of the ghost, the debunker wins."

"*I* don't have to prove there *is* a ghost at Holly Grove. The show tonight proves that. *He* has to debunk the ghost on the follow-up show and he won't. I guarantee it. My career is on the line here."

"Mine too. I just can't chance anything that might ruin the publicity Holly Grove will get after the show tonight." Holly took a fortifying breath. "I'm sorry. I can't do another show."

"There's just one tiny problem, Holly," Sylvia said. *Is she mocking me?*

Papers rustled. "I'm looking over the contract and releases you signed with *Inquiring Minds* back on October 27."

Holly's mouth went dry. She'd been so thrilled for the publicity, she'd barely read the darned things.

"Section 6A," Sylvia said. "It's called an option. An option for us to follow up on the show or retake the episode within one hundred days of the original shoot. You know, in case there was significant public interest or something went wrong, which we know can happen, right?"

Holly plopped back down on the steps. "And if I don't allow the shoot?"

"Legal tells me you'd owe the production cost of the shoot. Megan, can you draft an estimate of the flight costs for the crew, rental cars, labor, etcetera?"

"I'll have my lawyer call you." Holly didn't have a lawyer. Delta Ridge hadn't had a lawyer since Bill Benoit retired, but they had a bail bondsman who'd lost his law license. At least he could read legalese. Holly closed her eyes and sighed. Proof positive. Bad luck does come in threes.

"Holly, dear." Sylvia's words dripped with smugness. "There are only two choices here. Pay or play."

"You better have a good reason for messin' up that bed you made this mornin'." Nelda's brows creased over her brown eyes as she peeked in the bedroom door. "What's the matter? You sick?"

Holly sniffled and shook her head. "I'm so screwed, and it's all my fault."

"Says who?" Nelda crossed the well-worn antique rug and propped a hip on the side of Holly's four-poster bed. As the mattress sagged under Nelda's weight, Rhett slid next to her.

"This." Holly waved the contract.

"A piece of paper made you crawl up in bed and blubber like a baby?" Nelda cocked her head to the side. "Must be some humdinger of a piece of paper."

"It's the contract I signed to have Holly Grove on *Inquiring Minds* back in October."

"And it's making you cry three months later?"

"I would have signed a deal with the devil to get publicity from *Inquiring Minds* back then." She flung the contract across the bed. "Evidently I did."

"I'm guessing Miss Sylvia Martin is the devil."

"Pretty much." Holly blew her nose, then wiped at her eyes. "There's an option in there that forces me to agree to a follow-up show if they ask and Sylvia did. She called a while ago to schedule another show on my ghost."

Nelda scrunched up her brows. "The one you've been telling me is gone?"

"And worse, she's challenged some debunker to try to prove Holly Grove isn't haunted on her show. I can't tell her it's not haunted anymore!" Holly fell back onto the bed and pressed her palms to her skull to ease her brewing headache.

"Don't *option* mean optional?"

"Yeah. For *Inquiring Minds*." Holly rubbed her temples. "Not for me."

"You sure 'bout that?"

"As sure as I can get without hiring a lawyer. I called my old roommate, Sarah. She's a lawyer in New Orleans now. Her free," Holly drew quotation marks in the air. "Legal advice was to comply and buy her a drink next time I'm in the city." Holly blew her nose again. "I even asked Purvis."

"That bail bondsman?"

"He used to be a lawyer until he got disbarred." She couldn't remember why, but he was the closest thing Delta Ridge had to a lawyer. "He said the same thing and offered his bail services if things got ugly."

"What happens if you don't do the show?"

"Sylvia said I had to play or pay." Holly held her hand up and rubbed her thumb across her fingers. "Paying is not happening. I can't. Then they'll sue and put a lien on Holly Grove."

Nelda shook her head. "There goes your credit, again."

"And maybe Holly Grove if reservations drop off." *Debt. Taxes. Nonstop maintenance.* "I was so close to making Holly Grove a success, and now, I'm one stumble away from losing her. If I play and do the follow-up show, I could be exposed as a fraud." Holly flopped her hands on the bed. "There goes my business and Holly Grove." *Pay or play.* "I'm so screwed."

"You're only screwed if you keep wallerin' and blubberin' in that bed. If you're gonna get screwed, it outta be fun, right?"

"Nelda!" Holly landed a teasing slap on Nelda's arm. "I guess that means I've got to play this thing like a boss."

"Now you're talkin'." Nelda picked up Rhett and stood. "What you gonna do?"

Holly eased off the high bed and slipped on her stilettos. The four inches of height always fortified her confidence. False confidence was better than none. "Whatever it takes."

"What ya got in mind?" Nelda asked, leaning in to Holly.

"It may take an unholy alliance with the devil, aka Sylvia Martin. No matter what it takes, there will be a Ghost in the Grove if I have to manufacture one."

# CHAPTER THREE

Three practice Sazeracs later, Holly ventured into the dark kitchen to check on Mackie's progress repairing the electrical problem. "You sure you can get the power back on before the show starts?"

From his perch on the ladder below the blown-out pendant light, his headlamp shined down on Holly like a stage light in the candlelit kitchen. "I'm sure I told you I'm not an electrician."

Mackie's reddened face mapped years of alcohol abuse that couldn't be erased by a few months of sobriety. He licked his lips and eyed her Sazerac like it was a sacred elixir.

*Poor Mackie.* She not so subtly covered her lowball glass with her hand. Even though he'd insisted he had to get used to being around whiskey, or the demon as he'd called it, she wasn't so sure about that plan.

"I miss my old friend in the bottle, but not enough to go through gettin' sober again," Mackie said. "You're lucky the breaker only blew out in the kitchen."

"Unlucky my only cable connection is in here."
She motioned toward the TV. If he couldn't get the
power back on, she'd miss the show because she
couldn't leave. The two confirmed reservations for
tonight could ring the doorbell any minute. She'd
have to call everyone else and tell them the party was
off. Why had she been too cheap to pay for stream-
ing cable to her tablet? *Priorities. That's why.*

"Yoo-hoo!" Miss Alice pushed through the kitchen
door. She carried an ancient Samsonite suitcase, a
knitting basket, and her dead husband's doctor's
bag that went everywhere with her—just in case her
nursing skills were required.

Holly forced a smile for the ringleader of the Delta
Ridge Bridge Society. The Deltas rented the parlor
every Thursday morning for bridge. Miss Alice never
knocked, and her orthopedic shoes made her footsteps practically silent. "You're early."

"I need to settle in before dinner." Miss Alice's
glasses dangled from a beaded chain around her
neck as she surveyed the kitchen. "You do realize
*Inquiring Minds* starts in an hour?"

"Yes, ma'am," Holly said. "We're having a little
electrical, um . . ."

"Snafu." Mackie's long gray ponytail swayed with
each twist of his wrist as he worked on the light fixture.

"Believe me. Compared to termites, this is small."
Miss Alice put her suitcase down near the kitchen
door. "Today, I had sixty years of accumulation
moved into some contraptions called pods, so the
exterminator could tent and fumigate my house. I'll
be staying here for a week."

"Bless your heart." *And mine too. I love her but in small doses—not a week at a time.*

Holly took a big swig of her so-so Sazerac for comfort. Smoother. Maybe it was the top-shelf bourbon that made it go down easier. Or maybe her taste buds were getting a little loose.

*Nah.* She'd only had a taste of each attempt.

Miss Alice positioned her glasses on her nose. "Is that a Sazerac, dear?"

"It's supposed to be." Holly lifted a shoulder. "But it doesn't taste like the ones Grandma Rose used to make."

"Ah, her secret family recipe."

Holly swirled the Sazerac in her glass. "You mean lost family recipe if there ever was one."

"My father said there was an art to the Sazerac. He made one that tasted just like Rose's. We often thought they had the same recipe, but we'll never know. He carried that to the grave with him as well."

Holly took another sip. "They're getting better, but still not right."

"Are you going to throw that one down the sink too?" Mackie asked. He shined his headlamp on her like an interrogation light. "Drinkin' in front of me is one thing. Wastin' another half-full glass of perfectly drinkable whiskey may drive me to drink."

"Not with me standing right here." Miss Alice planted her feet in her orthopedic shoes at the base of the ladder. "You just earned your one-hundred-day chip."

Mackie grumbled. "It feels like a hundred years."

"You've got to be tested." Miss Alice's mouth

formed a firm line as she gave him a steady stare. "The nature of man is to want what he can't have."

"Are you sure man needs this much temptation?" Holly asked.

Miss Alice turned to Holly. "He can't be coddled, young lady. He must live in the real world where there *is* and will always be readily available alcohol."

"Big Brother tried a little thing called prohibition back in the twenties." Mackie capped off a few wires. "About as effective as bailing water with a sieve. I don't like to admit it, but she's right."

"Of course, I'm right." Miss Alice lifted her chin a fraction. "Have you found the problem with the electricity?"

"What's left of this lightbulb is rusted into the socket. The bulb blowing out probably tripped the breaker. I won't know until I finish and flip the breaker back on." Mackie shined his headlamp on Miss Alice and she tented her eyes.

"I've got confidence in you." Miss Alice, like every other widow woman in Delta Ridge, thought Mackie could fix anything. And usually he could, even in his drinking days.

"Where's Jake?" Miss Alice asked. "Didn't you say he was coming today?"

Holly shook her head. "Something came up with work."

A pair of pliers clattered to the ground. Mackie's shoulders slumped and he just stared at the pliers.

"He called a little while ago." Holly had been so wigged out by Sylvia's call and the contract, she didn't think to tell Mackie. She picked up the pliers and handed them to him after he took a few steps down the ladder. "I'm sorry. I should have told you."

"Don't matter." He wiped his sleeve over his eyes and climbed back up the ladder.

But it did to her.

"Not your fault," he said but didn't glance her way. His hands shook as he tinkered with the guts of the fixture. "Can't change someone who don't want to change."

"Whew," Nelda said as she entered the kitchen. "Good thing I got Miss Alice's room ready early. I've got the carriage house all toasty for ya."

"Thank you, Nelda." Miss Alice hooked her over-sized purse over her arm. "I think I'll get settled in before the show."

"If there is a show," Holly added. She picked up Miss Alice's suitcase. "I'll walk you to the carriage house. It's getting dark."

"No need," Miss Alice said. "You have the outside of this place lit up like a lighthouse."

"But there's a dark patch between here and there."

Miss Alice pulled an ancient twenty-inch flashlight from her bottomless purse. "You need to stay here and get ready for your guests. The table isn't even set."

Mackie backed down the ladder. "I'm goin' outside to turn the breaker back on. I might as well carry your bags to your room."

"I don't need doting on. I'm perfectly capable of carrying my suitcase and a flashlight. I'll get my knitting and medical bag after dinner."

He tapped his headlamp. "My light's better than yours and I can carry everything at once."

Miss Alice huffed. "If you insist."

Mackie picked up her bags and walked out the back-porch door. She trailed behind him, industrial flashlight in hand.

"That woman is a piece of work," Nelda said as she took a stack of blue willow china out of the cabinet.

"Yep." Holly laid eight placemats around the table. "I just hope I have as much spunk when I'm her age."

"And not as much pee and vinegar." Nelda giggled. "But that's probably what keeps her tickin' along."

"I hope whatever Mackie did fixed the problem and we're not setting the table for nothing." Holly opened the silver drawer and counted out eight Gorham Chantilly silver spoons.

"Don't use those stingy spoons." Nelda pointed a finger at Holly. "Use the gumbo spoons."

The TV blared. The old refrigerator motor cranked out a steady hum. Holly ran to the light switch and flipped it on. Light flooded the room and she squealed. "He did it!"

Nelda slapped her hands together. "Sure did. TV works too. Looks like the party is on, girl."

Mackie stepped into the kitchen from the back porch, and Holly rushed across the room and hugged him. "Thank you. Thank you. Thank you."

He gave a sheepish grin. "Yeah, well, you better get a real electrician in here to check it out. Those wires are older and more worn out than me."

"I will after the reservations start pouring in tonight." She bounced around the room blowing out candles. *I'm not going to think past tonight. This show is going to make Holly Grove famous. I'll worry about keeping her famous tomorrow.*

He gave a nod at the ladder. "I'll put that away after I collect the tools I left out on the widow's walk. It's been a long day. I'm gonna pack it in."

"You sure?" Holly asked. "I thought you were staying for the show."

He shook his head and pushed through the kitchen door like he had a sack of sorrow on his back.

"What's wrong with Mackie?" Nelda asked. "He's not himself."

Holly shrugged. "Jake's not coming. It didn't help that I forgot to tell Mackie until just a little while ago. He's not drinking, but his hands were shaking while he worked on the light. I'm worried about him."

"I'm gonna make him a care package of gumbo and bread puddin' to take home with him."

A crash and then another and another rang out from upstairs. In the eerie silence that followed, Holly and Nelda stared at each other.

Holly gasped. "Mackie!"

"Lord have mercy." Nelda's eyes widened. "What if he fell off the roof?"

# CHAPTER FOUR

Holly charged out the kitchen. She should have never hired a man that age to install the safety panels on the widow's walk. Pounding up the three flights of stairs, she screamed his name.

All she'd wanted to do was help keep him busy and sober. She'd promised Jake she'd look after his dad. "Mackie! Mackie! Are you all right?"

Nelda lagged behind, puffing. "You don't think he was nipping the bottle up there, do you?"

Holly's stomach rolled into a tight knot. And if he had and took one drunk stumble . . . it'd be her fault. How would she tell Jake?

She reached the last step and bounded onto the widow's walk. Her heart thudded in her ears as she turned in a full circle alone at the highest point of Holly Grove.

Her mouth went dry. She swallowed hard and closed her eyes. There was only one other place he could be.

Holly held her breath and eased to the low banister around the widow's walk. The winter wind whipped through her hair. She looked over the railing and down the steep slope of the roof to the ground below. The high view sent a queasy jitter rushing through her gut.

No body. The air rushed from her lungs, but he could have fallen from any of the four sides.

"Lord have mercy. Is he down there?" Nelda stood frozen at the door of the small cupola in the center of the widow's walk.

"No." Holly dashed across the decking. "Help me look on the other sides."

"Uh-uh."

Holly glanced back at Nelda.

"I get dizzy lookin' down from anythin' higher than a short stool." Nelda took a step back.

Holly reached for her phone to call 911, but it wasn't in her pocket. She must have left it in the kitchen. "Then call 911."

"But what if Mackie just slipped out and all that banging was somethin' else? Somethin' we can't see."

"Nelda, don't start with the ghost crapola again." Holly carefully looked over the railing on the river side. He wasn't there either.

"You know 911 probably put us on the do-not-come list after what happened with the Deltas and the drug overdose that wasn't and all." Nelda cocked an eye at Holly. "Just sayin'."

She had a point. They couldn't even tell the operator if Mackie was alive or dead, much less his injuries. But where else could he be?

Holly walked behind the cupola to the street side of Holly Grove. Mackie's toolbox, a pile of lumber, and a couple of sawhorses lay across the decking to

her right. He must have been working there when . . .
Her heart took a deep dive into her gut. She braced
herself for seeing his crumpled body below. The
decking squeaked under her weight as she passed
his equipment. She took a long breath and inched to
the rail.

A moan came from behind her.

She wheeled around but no one was there. Then
she noticed a jagged hole in the floor in front of
Mackie's toolbox. She rushed to the opening.
"Mackie?"

"Down here." His voice came from the dark hole.

"Holy moly!" He must have fallen through to the
attic. She kneeled and leaned over the hole. "Are
you okay?"

"Don't know yet."

"Don't move." She scrambled to her feet. "I'll be
right there."

Holly nearly slammed into Nelda on her way
down the stairs. "Did you call 911? Mackie fell
through the decking into the attic." Holly pounded
down the stairs and flung open the attic door. She
felt for the cord that her grandmother had tied to
the doorframe years ago and yanked it. The single
bulb lit the attic space, which looked like an episode
of *Hoarders* in yellowish light. "Where are you?"

"Over here."

Holly stepped over toppled boxes and their con-
tents as she and Nelda followed his voice. It didn't
matter how many broken bones he had, at least he
was alive.

"Look." Nelda pointed to the soles of a pair of

work boots poking over an oak chifforobe that lie front down in the jumble of attic castaways.

Holly climbed over a rocking chair with a busted rocker and stooped beside him. A few scratches marked his hands and face. Most of his wiry gray hair had escaped his ponytail. No obvious injuries, but he could have internal injuries. "What hurts, Mackie?"

"I can't believe I didn't notice that rot and stepped right through it." He lay on his back staring up at the jagged hole in the ceiling. "I'm gonna have to fix that hole before the railing."

"You probably ain't gonna be fixin' nothin' for a while." Nelda stood over him with her hands on her hips. "At least you're among the livin', praise Jesus."

*Amen to that.* Holly shuddered to think of how awful it would have been to tell Jake if things had been worse. "Tell me what hurts."

"My teeth." He rubbed his jaw.

"Is that all?" She scanned his body for signs of injury, but he looked okay except for a few scratches.

"All I know of." He propped himself up on one elbow.

Holly's eyes watered. "I thought you—"

"Fell off the roof. Nah." He shrugged. "I caught myself on the edge of that rot I fell through, but the sides kept crumbling."

"We heard things crashing," Holly said.

He eyed the chifforobe. "I was dancin' on top of this old chest to keep from fallin' all the way through that hole. I almost got my footin', but then it was like someone pushed it right out from under me."

Nelda elbowed Holly but she didn't respond. She couldn't feed into Nelda's ghost worries right now.

"I heard everything fallin' out of the thing," Mackie said. "But when it fell, I guess it knocked over all this."

Holly glanced around at toppled boxes, bird-cages, old lamps, books, and papers scattered across the floor. *Well, at least he didn't knock loose any family skeletons.*

"The chifforobe landed front down, and I landed standin' up right on top of it. Thought I had it made, until I fell backward and got the wind knocked out of me." He rubbed his jaw. "Jarred me all the way down to my molars."

"Well, you just lay there." Holly patted his arm. "An ambulance is on the way."

"Um," Nelda said. "It may take a little longer."

Holly jerked around to look at Nelda. "You didn't call?"

"I've been busy helpin' you find Mackie. I don't keep a phone pasted to my body like you young folks do, so I've gotta go all the way downstairs to the house phone." Nelda shoved her hands onto her hips. "You know, I was built for comfort, not for speed."

"I don't need an ambulance." Mackie pushed up on both elbows. "If I can walk, I'll be long gone before it gets here anyway."

Knowing Mackie, he would. Her address was already flagged by EMS for the unfortunate incidents last fall. It didn't help that the operator knew Holly as Hurricane Holly from high school. "I tell you what, I'll get Miss Alice to check you out. If she says you're okay, I won't call an ambulance."

Mackie groaned. "I'd almost rather go to the hospital."

"You got that right," Nelda said.

"You stay here with Mackie." She wagged her finger at Nelda. "And don't let him move."


Holly raced down three flights of stairs and lost a shoe in the entrance hall. *Lordy.* She backtracked, then hopped on one foot to put the stiletto back on. If it wasn't forty degrees outside, she would run bare-footed to the carriage house. Maybe she should have called Miss Alice, but Holly couldn't chance her rushing over and twisting an ankle in the dark by herself.

She flung the front door open and smashed into something, bounced off, and stumbled backward.

A short pudgy guy with a mop of red hair and a beard to match blinked behind Clark Kent glasses, jacked up on one side from the blow. He adjusted the thick frames. "Holly Davis, correct?"

She nodded.

He hefted a grungy duffel bag on his shoulder. "I have a reservation."

Holly gasped and slapped her palms to her face. The Sinclairs. The reservation for tonight. She was supposed to meet him at the landing strip. "Oh, I'm so, so sorry. Yes, you do." She grabbed him by the arm and showed him to the parlor. "I have a bit of an emergency. Make yourself at home. I'll be right back."

*Mercy, I hope my next Sazerac is a good one because I'm going to owe that man a drink, big-time.*

She dashed for the carriage house. Holly's speed could make up for the slower pace she'd make getting Miss Alice back to check on Mackie. She beat on the carriage house door. "Miss Alice! Miss Alice!"

Swinging the door open, Miss Alice said, "What in the world?"

"Mackie fell through the roof. He may be hurt."

The old gal's face tensed like a battle-tested veteran. "I'll get my bag." She disappeared and returned with her doctor's bag and her industrial flashlight.

Arm in arm, Holly towed Miss Alice across the lawn, ushered her through the house, and up three flights of stairs. When they finally made it to the attic, Holly stood there stupefied.

No one was there.

She turned in a circle, then pointed to where she'd left Mackie. "He was right there."

"He must not be injured too badly if he walked away on his own." Miss Alice eyed the toppled furniture and the hole in the ceiling. "He works on old houses with rot all the time. How did Mackie manage not to notice the decking was soft up there? Did you give him any of your Sazeracs?"

"No ma'am." Though she could use one right now. Whatever buzz she'd had was long gone.

"Have you checked the level on your whiskey bottle?" Miss Alice asked, with a pointed stare.

Holly gulped. She hadn't.

"If his blood alcohol level is high enough, he may not notice his injuries immediately."

"I swear. I didn't give him a drop." *But he could*

*have taken a few swigs when I was out of the room.* Holly turned and headed back downstairs.

Miss Alice padded down the stairs behind Holly.

"The good news is he's walking." And not staggering, she hoped "Nelda was packing his dinner to go when we heard the crash. It'd be just like her to feed him to make him feel better. Maybe they're in the kitchen."

They stepped into the kitchen and the swinging door flapped behind them. Mackie was nowhere in sight, and Nelda didn't seem to notice they'd come in the room. She stood bent over with her elbows on the ceramic tile counter.

"Where's Mackie?" Holly couldn't keep the irritation out of her voice. All she'd asked Nelda to do was keep him put until she got back.

Nelda whirled around holding a bent-up, rusty biscuit tin. Scraps of aged ocher-colored paper spilled out of the tin and fluttered to the floor. "Good Lord. You 'bout scared the pee-willie out of me."

"That can happen as one gets older," Miss Alice said. "If you'd like, I can share some exercises that help with that."

Nelda crinkled up her nose. "It's just a sayin' Miss Alice. I'm high and dry."

Rhett ambled to the papers scattered on the floor.

"Doggone it. I dropped it," Nelda said shooing Rhett away.

*Lord, give me patience.* "But where is Mackie?" Holly asked again, this time slow and easy.

"I heard ya the first time," Nelda said. "He went home for a tub soak. I sent his to-go dinner with him, too."

"But Nelda," Holly took a breath. "I asked you to stay with him until Miss Alice could check him out." And relieve Holly's guilt about having a sixty-five-year-old man working on her roof and possibly injuring himself.

"He didn't walk outta here on broken bones carrying his toolbox and my cookin'-to-go." Nelda put the tin on the counter then squatted to pick up the rest of the bits of paper that had fallen out earlier. "What'd you want me to do? Sit on him? He's a grown man and gonna do what he's gonna do."

*Like father, like son.*

"I'll drive out to his place in the morning and check on him if he's too sore to work," Holly said.

"He may be," Miss Alice said. "He just doesn't know it yet."

Holly paced. "Lordy, all I was trying to do was keep him busy and sober, and I nearly killed him."

"But you didn't." Nelda picked up another scrap of yellowed paper. "If he hadn't fallen through the roof, I wouldn't have found that old biscuit box."

"I remember these." Miss Alice picked up the biscuit tin from the counter. Her old eyes stared at the box like it was a window to her past. "My father had one just like it. He hid things away in it for safekeeping. Before air-conditioning, humidity and bugs were a problem. We looked for it for years after he passed and never found it."

"Mackie and me were waiting for ya'll to come back, and the thing fell from the hole in the ceiling. Mackie thinks someone hid it there years ago and he knocked it loose."

Holly picked up one of the scattered scraps of paper, a receipt dated 1929, written in beautiful script, and signed with a name she didn't recognize. "Why would anyone hide receipts?"

"There's lots of those, but that's not what I'm lookin' for."

Miss Alice inspected the receipt. "Because selling alcohol was illegal in 1929."

"Right. Prohibition," Holly said. "You think these are from when Holly Grove was a speakeasy?"

"If bettin' wasn't a sin, I'd put my money on it." Nelda picked up another scrap of paper with the same beautiful handwriting. She dangled it between her sturdy fingers. "You know what else I found in this box?" She grinned. "And it ain't a receipt."

Nelda hid the paper behind her back. "You go get ready to pick up the Sinclairs at the airstrip. You ain't gonna believe it."

"Oh, crapola." Holly slapped her forehead. "He's waiting in the parlor. With all the excitement, I forgot to check him in."

# CHAPTER FIVE

Holly stopped outside the parlor to collect herself before she apologized to her guest for leaving him so long—and for smacking into him. *Lordy. Nothing strange going on here. Enjoy your relaxing vacation.*

No doubt, she looked a mess but didn't dare confirm it by looking in the pier mirror next to the door. She pressed her hands over her skirt then pushed her hair out of her face and plastered a smile on her face. *Shoe leather tastes yummy.* She stepped into the parlor and stared at the empty settee. Odd. Where could Mr. Sinclair be?

Maybe he had given up on her. A familiar squeak from the seventh step on the staircase came from behind her. She slowly turned to the sound.

The pudgy guy stood on the squeaky step and stared at her. A roll of pasty-white hairy flesh showed between his black hoodie and cargo pants that made her want to wash the sight from her eyes. Evidently,

he'd been upstairs, uninvited. And he was alone—
where was Mrs. Sinclair?

He adjusted his glasses then shifted his weight,
purposefully making the stair moan. What adult
does that? Had she accidentally let in a passing
hitchhiker, a mental patient, or what?

The creeper moved down the hall and stood in
front of the bulletin board filled with guest snap-
shots of supposed ghostly sightings. He leaned in to
about six inches in front of the photos.

Holly marched up to him. "You are not Mr. Sinclair."

He shrugged without looking away from the
photos. "I didn't say I was."

"You can't just knock on the door and then roam
around my house without a reservation."

The reflection of the gasolier flashed on his
glasses as he turned. Behind the lenses, flat mud-
brown eyes floated in a don't-give-a-flying-flip look.
"You said to make myself at home. I took that as the
Southern hospitality I've heard about. Guess that's
just part of the act."

"What act? I thought you were Mr. Sinclair. He has
a reservation. You do not."

He gave a nod back at her publicity board. "Is
there really paranormal activity here?"

*Oh. He's one of those.* "Sir, I appreciate the interest,
but if you don't have a reservation, you'll have to
come back during tour time at ten o'clock in the
morning. We can talk about my ghost then." She
folded her arms across her chest.

He squared his body with hers, uncomfortably

close. His stale tobacco breath loitered in the air between them. "Do you believe in ghosts?" he asked.

"I didn't until I got one," she said. "I'll tell you all about him during a tour anytime but right now—"

"Right," He cocked his head back and drew the word out. "It's all about the money. Always is."

*A real peach of a guy. Mercy.* "Sir, I have guests I need to take care of. It's time for you to leave." She made a flourish of pointing to the door.

He glanced at the door and then back at her. "I have a confirmed reservation. Prepaid in fact." He assumed the close-talker position again.

Holly held her breath.

"Are you refusing to accept my reservation and if so, why?"

She took a step back. Last she'd checked, only Miss Alice and the Sinclairs had reservations to-night. "Of course not, if you have one."

"I booked it via your website today." He pulled out his phone and made a few clicks, then flipped the phone around and held it in front of her face.

She read the email, an automatic confirmation time-stamped 3:45 CST. How had she missed that? Holly blew out a deep breath. Mr. Instant Obnox-ious must have made the reservation about the time Sylvia had called and sent Holly into a panic. She vaguely remembered a second alert tone. *Not once* during this day from Hades had she thought to check that alert. This was no way to run a business, especially one that promised Southern hospitality and relied on reservations from the public.

"My mistake." She showed her teeth in a failed effort to smile at a less desired member of the public she could not refuse service. "Like I told you when I nearly mowed you down, I had a small emergency earlier."

He used his index finger to slide his glasses up the bridge of his nose, then looked down at her. "An emergency that is small is a misnomer."

*What a jerk.* "Okay, well . . . It's been a crazy day. I just missed seeing your reservation. If you'll give me your driver's license, I'll get you registered. You can wait in the parlor."

"I waited in the parlor for seventeen minutes and thirty-seven seconds. Fifteen minutes is considered long enough by polite society. I gave you an extra two minutes and thirty-seven seconds." He pulled a stump of a cigar out of a pocket in his cargo pants. "Unless you want me to smoke in your parlor, I'll be outside. Bring me the key when you get your *act* together."

*"Jerk" doesn't do this dude justice.* "Mr. . . . I don't believe I caught your name." If she'd scrolled down his confirmation email a bit farther, she would have read the personalized autogenerated greeting she sent all her guests.

"Truman Jeremiah Stalwort, III," he said, handing her his driver's license. "Everyone knows me as Tru."

*Tru? Tru the truly obnoxious troll . . . Tru the truth teller.* Holly nearly gagged. "Sylvia told me all about you."

"Correction." He pointed his cigar at Holly. "She told you what she believes about me. She doesn't know me."

"I wasn't expecting you until Wednesday when Sylvia and her crew come in for the shoot."

"It's only fair to arrive first, since she's familiar with your so-called ghost and I'm not. Don't you agree?"

"I agreed to a follow-up shoot that starts Wednesday. Sylvia didn't mention you'd be here early. Did she agree to that?"

He shrugged. "It's in my contract."

"It's not in mine." Holly folded her arms. "All I agreed to is a follow-up shoot." Evidently, Sylvia's "let me be perfectly honest" fell short of mentioning Tru's early arrival. That woman could make the Pope cuss.

"That's not my problem." He stuck the stump of a cigar in his mouth and ambled to the front door. He turned and yanked the cigar out of his mouth. "Can't wait to see your ghost on *Inquiring Minds* tonight."

"He'll be there." And somehow she had to make Tru believe Burl still haunted Holly Grove.

"Sure he will." Tru stretched out his words and nodded with a sardonic smirk. "But will he show without TV magic on Wednesday?" He stuck his stogie in his mouth, then walked out, leaving the door wide open.

A gust of winter wind blasted through the hall. The ghost pics fluttered against their pushpins on the bulletin board and reminded her of Burl's old tricks. Instinctively, she looked around for him. Of course, he wasn't there, but Tru didn't know that.

"Better watch out," she called out to Tru. "You're upsetting my ghost."

Tru turned halfway toward her. "Good one," Tru

said, pointing his cigar butt at her. "Wind gusts up to forty miles per hour. Sixty percent chance of rain. Low forty-four degrees. It's called a weather forecast. A scientific measure. Not the power of suggestion. That's all you've got." He thumbed his chest. "Tru knows."

"You don't know jack about my ghost." She marched to the door and slammed it hard enough to rattle the paintings of all five generations on the wall. Holly slumped against the door. *A good bluff. That's all I've got. "The Ghost in the Grove" will be debunked. Reservations will fall off. Bills will pile up. I'll be forced to sell. And Nelda . . . what would she do?*

Holly shook her head. *I can't let that happen. There will not be a follow-up show even if I have to sabotage it at every turn.*

The lights on Holly's Tahoe bounced across the rutted dirt road. Her butt lifted off the seat with every pothole she hit, but she tolerated the rough ride for speed. *Inquiring Minds* would start in less than thirty minutes. She tightened her grip on the wheel. The Sinclairs had been in the dark at Burl's abandoned runway and failed aviation business for thirty minutes. Folks stuck on tarmacs too long get testy with the airlines and take to Twitter or Facebook to tell the world. That wouldn't look good on a review. She goosed the gas and hit a big hole in the dirt road. The thermos Nelda had given her as she rushed out the door went airborne and clattered on the floorboard. Holly huffed. The recipe Nelda had found in the biscuit tin had said shaken not stirred. That Sazerac was shaken for sure.

As she approached the runway, red lights flickered on the far end. She parked her Tahoe and squinted. The lights didn't look right. Too close together. She blinked.

The tiniest plane she'd ever seen taxied toward her end of the runway. That kind of plane is exactly why some people believe in UFOs. Of course, she didn't believe in UFOs, but she hadn't believed in ghosts until her ex came back as one.

Holly stretched across the seat and retrieved the thermos, then unwrapped the linen napkins from around the two crystal lowball glasses she'd wedged in the console. *Maybe a little liquid hospitality will help Mr. and Mrs. Sinclair forget they'd sat on the runway in the middle of nowhere for half an hour.* She inhaled the soothing aroma as she poured two Sazeracs and wished she'd brought another glass. Jake canceling. Mackie falling through the roof. The electrical problems. The debunker. The show coming up tonight. *What a freakin' day and it's not over yet.*

The plane couldn't have been much bigger than a glider. She'd been to lots of air shows with Burl, back in the day, and had never seen anything like it. Other than the call numbers and its name, *No Regrets*, there wasn't any indication of the make or model.

A bald guy with a perfectly trimmed silver beard climbed out of the plane carrying a leather duffel bag. He stood just staring at Holly for a beat too long. Probably ticked.

"I'm so sorry to keep y'all waiting," she said as she walked toward him.

He finally waved at her and smiled like he meant it—as though she hadn't left him stranded on her back forty in the kind of dark that usually freaks out city folks.

"No problem." He looked toward the stars. "I never see the stars like this in San Francisco."

A fellow stargazer. Maybe the renovations on the widow's walk would be complete before he checked out. He'd love her new telescope.

"Welcome to Holly Grove." Holly lifted both low-ball glasses. "I brought y'all Sazeracs to relax after your flight."

Mr. Sinclair glanced behind him then back at Holly and snapped his fingers. "I forgot to tell you my better half isn't coming until later in the week. Is that a problem?"

"Not at all." Holly eyed the extra cocktail. If she wasn't driving, she wouldn't let that go to waste. "Holly Grove is only a half mile away on the other side of the cane field."

He sipped his Sazerac and didn't make a face. A good sign. He seemed to study her, especially her hair, which was probably frizzed to the max in the night air. Maybe there was a bug in it or something. She smoothed her hand over her hair.

"I used to have curls when I had hair." He chuckled, then took another sip of his drink. "There is nowhere on earth you can get a Sazerac like this except in Louisiana."

"Have you been here before?" She accidentally

took a sip of the extra cocktail. As she swallowed the smooth liquid, her taste buds applauded a perfect mix of chilled bourbon, Peychaud's Bitters, sugar, and lemon zest. The extra shaking may have helped, but this was as close as she'd come to as good as Grandma Rose's Sazeracs.

"I haven't been to Louisiana in over thirty years, but this cocktail left a lasting impression. I've ordered it other places, but it's never lived up to my memory." He swirled the ruby cocktail in his glass. "Until now."

Holly could have just about hugged him, but that may have made the man think she was one egg short of a dozen. Instead she said, "It's a secret recipe that's been in my family for generations." *Thank you, long-gone kinfolk, for saving the recipe and Holly Grove in hard times.*

"Hold on to it." He winked at Holly and hefted his bag over his shoulder. "If it gets out of Louisiana, everyone will be drinking these."

Holly pretended to lock her lips. She liked Mr. Sinclair already. Maybe he'd balance out instantly obnoxious Tru.

"What kind of plane do you have there?" She asked. "I've never seen one like it."

"And you won't. I built it from a kit and customized it." He seemed to swell with pride. "It's part of my retirement bucket list."

"Wow! I'm impressed. My ex was a pilot, but I don't think he could have ever built a plane." Or even a picnic table. Holly ambled toward her Tahoe. "What else is on your bucket list?"

"This, for one thing. I'm flying cross-country and stopping at interesting places a week at a time as a reward for building the plane."

"I'm flattered you decided to make one of your stops here at Holly Grove. How did you find out about us?"

"Um, a friend has an interest in *Inquiring Minds*. He suggested we time our trip to watch the 'Ghost in the Grove' episode on location."

"Really?" Holly opened the back of her Tahoe. That *on location* jargon sounded like someone in the business. Mr. Sinclair may be nice, but he may be a producer looking out for his investment, too. At the very least, he's got a friend *invested* in the show. First Tru and now this guy.

*Lordy. Wait. "Interest" could mean an interest in the supernatural. Maybe I'm just being too suspicious, but maybe not. I'll have to keep an eye on Mr. Sinclair.*

# CHAPTER SIX

A blinding light flashed. Startled, Holly blinked and steadied herself by holding on to the banister on the stairs.

"Tarnation! You closed your eyes," Sam said after his paparazzi-style ambush for the umpteenth time since he'd arrived to document the TV premiere of Holly Grove B&B for the *Delta Ridge Gazette*. "Don't move."

"I don't have time to stand still, Sam." And she'd only invited him at Jake's request, and Jake wasn't even coming now. *What's fair about that?* "Don't you think you have enough pre-show photos?" The weekly newspaper only printed about a dozen pages.

"Nope." Sam aimed his new 35mm camera at her again. His bushy gray brows hung over the camera like twin caterpillars. "This new digital camera lets me take all I want for cheap."

*Cheap.* Exactly why Sam was the richest man in Delta Ridge and could keep a weekly rag in the black in a blink-and-you'll-miss-it town. "Well you're going to have to catch me in motion." Holly crossed the hall to the swinging kitchen door. She noticed Nelda's handwriting on a note taped to the door. *Private.*

"Keeping the riffraff out?" Sam asked.

Holly pushed through the door and held it for Sam.

"Gumbo's nearly ready," Nelda said as she stirred the pot. "Fifteen minutes 'til showtime."

Rhett lay curled up snoozing under the planter's table as Miss Alice and the Deltas put away the cards from an impromptu hand of bridge.

Sam meandered to the ladies and started snapping photos.

Holly crossed the kitchen to Nelda, then leaned in close and whispered, "What's with the note on the door?"

"That Tru's been up in my kitchen askin' questions, and I 'bout had enough." Nelda hadn't made an attempt to whisper. The Deltas stopped. A whisper always raised their gossip antennas to high alert. Just what Holly didn't need right now.

Sam snapped a blast of photos of their concentrated stares.

Holly turned her back on them and raised a finger to her lips at Nelda. "Shh."

"Don't shush me. They know all about him." She rapped her wooden spoon on the side of the pot. "Debunk my big toe."

Holly's stomach swirled in a downward spiral. That was the last thing the gossip cartel of Delta Ridge needed to know. As if faking a ghost wasn't enough of a challenge, she'd now have to fight the gossip mill again. "You told them he's a debunker?"

"Sure did. Told 'em about that TV challenge too. They need to know he's out to ruin Holly Grove."

"And that's not good for our town tourism," Miss Alice said. She stood and held her chin high. "Holly Grove is the only attraction in a thirty-mile radius that brings in buses of tourists during the season to visit downtown. It's my civic duty to make sure this establishment is successful."

"It wouldn't be the same if we had to play bridge at the VFW hall." Miss Martha Jane piped up, wringing her hands.

Penny shifted her plump bottom on the planter's bench. "We wouldn't have Nelda's bread pudding there for sure."

"Besides, he can't debunk your ghost. He haunted our bridge game." Miss Martha Jane fit the deck and scorecards into a floral box. "We'll tell him so."

"My mum used to say that the older one gets the less of a veil between the living and the dead. I sense the presence of the dead more and more," Miss Corrine said. Her British accent made everything she said seem as though it came straight from the BBC fact-checked, even if it wasn't. "And I sense it at Holly Grove. He's blind to the spirit, that's all."

They all nodded in unison.

Holly bit her bottom lip to hide a little tremble. The Deltas were mostly too nosy, too bossy, and too chatty, but today they felt like second mamas to her. She wanted to tell them the truth but couldn't trust those mouths of the South with her secret. "I love y'all, but as much as I wish that debunker wasn't here, he is."

"That don't mean he's got to watch the show in my kitchen," Nelda said, thumbing her chest.

Miss Alice grumbled. "He's a troublemaker."

"But, ladies," Miss Martha Jane wrung her hands. "It wouldn't be proper to have a party and exclude one person in the same house."

"He can't watch it anywhere but here because there's no guest Internet and the only cable connection is right there." Holly pointed to the old big-box TV in the corner of the room. "He needs to see proof of the haunting in case Burl doesn't show up."

"But why wouldn't he show up?" Miss Corrine asked.

*Crapola. Did I say that out loud?* Holly shrugged. "Burl wasn't exactly dependable in real life . . ."

Nelda rolled her eyes. "Ain't that the truth."

"The best thing we can do is let Tru watch the show tonight and see the truth," Holly said. "We're just going to have to put up with him until this is over."

"We'll kill him with kindness," Miss Martha Jane said. "Isn't that right, Alice?"

"You kill him with kindness." Miss Alice settled back onto the planter's bench. "I don't suffer fools well. I don't have the time or the energy to engage with the likes of him."

A knock came from the door and Mr. Sinclair poked in his head. No need to tell the ladies he may be on the other side too. Maybe he wasn't.

"Sorry. I saw the notice on the door, but I'm supposed to be in the kitchen at seven for dinner. Am I in the right place?"

"Oh, Mr. Sinclair." Holly waved him in. "We usually

have dinner in the dining room, but this is the only room with a cable connection to watch *Inquiring Minds*." She introduced him to the Deltas.

"Call me Thomas," Mr. Sinclair said as a bright light flashed.

"And that's Sam," Holly said. "He owns the *Delta Ridge Gazette* and is doing a feature story on Holly Grove's TV debut tonight."

Sam whipped out his pocket notebook and asked Thomas for his full name and home city. "You never know if one of my stories may be picked up by the AP."

It had happened once when ICE intercepted a huge drug shipment on the river, practically in her backyard, and he got there first. He also kept Holly Grove in the best possible light in the article. She needed to remember that, since he was being so irritating with his paparazzi camera action.

"Thomas from San Francisco will do," he said. "It smells wonderful in here. Is that gumbo cooking?"

*Hmm. What an odd response . . .* His name on his driver's license was William Thomas Sinclair. Why would he not want his last name in the paper?

"That's award-winning gumbo." Holly pointed to Nelda's Iron Skillet Awards hanging on the wall.

"Impressive." Thomas eyed the collection. "I can hardly wait to taste it."

"That's right," Nelda said, without turning around. Steam curled over a pot as she lifted the lid on the rice. "I'm just about to serve it up, too."

Holly escorted Thomas over to Nelda. "And this

is Nelda Varnado, the best cook in St. Agnes Parish and maybe the South."

Nelda wiped her hands on a white dishtowel, then turned with her hand extended for a handshake. Her usually animated face turned blank. She tilted her head to the side as though studying him. "What'd you say your name was?"

He dropped his gaze to the floor and said his name again, then glanced at Holly.

Nelda's expression lifted as she shook his hand. "Nice to meet ya. My hearin' ain't what it used to be."

Except when she wanted to hear something she shouldn't. Holly pointed to the planter's table. "You have a seat over there next to Miss Alice. Nelda and I will bring the gumbo bowls over in just a second."

As soon as he was out of earshot, Holly whispered to Nelda, "When did your hearing go bad?"

Nelda wrapped a white cotton napkin around a warm loaf of French bread and handed it to Holly. Then she held her hand up to her ear and grinned. "Eh?"

"Really. Why did you stare the guy down?"

"That man's name went in one ear and out the other and I couldn't find it on his face. He don't look like no Thomas to me." Nelda lifted a shoulder. "That Tru's got my skirts in a jumble. I'm tellin' ya, that little turd is on a mission. What we gonna do about him?"

"Kill him with kindness?" Holly sighed. What choice did she have? She couldn't kick him out or she'd violate her contract.

Nelda huffed. "Good luck with that."

\* \* \*

A few minutes later, Tru pushed through the swinging kitchen door. He gave a nod to the note on the door, then slid his glasses up on his nose and eyed Holly. "Private *Inquiring Suckers* party?"

*No, he didn't just say that.*

Nelda groaned and the Deltas exchanged glances around the planter's table.

Holly balled her napkin in her fist. "Excuse me?"

"And you want me to kill him with kindness?" Nelda whispered, leaning in to Holly.

He looked around at the half-eaten bowls of gumbo as he pushed through the swinging door. "I see you didn't wait for me" The doors flapped behind him. Tru sauntered to Nelda's gumbo pot and served himself. "That's okay. I'm a fast eater. I've been smelling this for a while. I wondered when you'd call me to dinner."

Holly scooted off her end of the bench at the planter's table and stood. "I uh—

"Forgot, right Holly?" Tru asked. "Like you forgot to tell me there is no Internet access in the rooms."

She dug her nails into her palms. *I just might forget to replace his toilet paper roll, too.*

"Getting away from the modern world is part of the charm of our B&B," Holly said in the most pleasant voice she could muster. "Internet isn't advertised or expected."

He shuffled to the table and squeezed in next to Miss Alice at the other end of the table. "Is one bar of service on my phone part of the charm too?"

"No. That's part of country life." Holly forced a

smile and rested her palms on the planter's table. She leaned in toward Tru, who sat across from her. "The nearest tower is miles away. My guests come here to escape the twenty-first century."

Between bites of gumbo, Tru turned his attention to the TV, then shook his head. "Even Luddites like this bunch know TVs aren't period accurate for this place."

"Young man." Miss Alice peered over her readers at Tru. "Anyone who has experienced everything from the invention of air-conditioning to the Internet and embraced it all is no Luddite."

"Fair enough." He scrubbed the monogrammed linen napkin over his mouth and dropped the soiled napkin on the table.

*The man must have been raised in a barn, as Grandma Rose used to say.*

"But there's a reason you are all right here." Tru stabbed at the table with his index finger. "Right now, and a reason I wasn't invited. Could it be that your hostess doesn't want me to see how fake your ghost really is?"

But my ghost wasn't fake. Until recently. A queasiness settled low in Holly's stomach. She wiped her clammy palms on her skirt, then picked up her half-eaten bowl of gumbo. "In just a few minutes, *Inquiring Minds* is going to make Holly Grove and our ghost famous."

And yeah, she'd faked confidence. She'd fake a ghost too if necessary. The Deltas backed her up with nods and stern looks for Tru. Holly joined the Deltas' stare down of Mr. Obnoxious.

He adjusted his glasses and smirked. "Excellent!

That'll make me look even better when I expose a famous fraud."

Holly slammed her gumbo bowl on the table. "This is a private area in my home. I invite who I want to and you are *not* welcome." *Way to kill him with kindness, Holly.*

"Yeah." He glanced around the table. "And we all know why."

*Yeah. You're obnoxious and want to ruin me.* "You weren't invited to the preparty because you don't believe. We do, and we don't want you here ruining this big night for us."

"Tell you what." Tru tore off a hunk of French bread and pointed it at Holly like a caveman. "If you'll let me stay for your little party, I won't say a word during the show." He cocked his head to the side. "Fair enough?"

"Not one word." Holly curled all but her index finger into her fist then jabbed that finger at Tru. If her mother hadn't raised a lady, another finger would have expressed her feelings better. "Are we clear?"

Tru held his right hand up in a Boy Scout pledge, but she doubted he'd ever been a scout.

"Now that we've got that settled." Nelda's chair scraped the cypress floor as she pushed back from the table. "I've got y'all some of my famous bread puddin' with bourbon sauce comin' right up."

Bless Nelda for changing the subject before Holly said or did anything she'd regret.

"Gonna raincheck on that, Nelda. I'm thinking about a liquid dessert." Sam eyed Miss Martha Jane's full Sazerac. He pulled out the napkin tucked under his collar. "Are you going to drink that?"

"Oh." Miss Martha Jane's hand fluttered to her chest. "I had a sip or two. It's quite good, but, but it doesn't mix well with my medications. I'm the designated driver anyway."

"You mind?" Sam asked, reaching for the silver julep cup.

Miss Martha Jane's eyes widened as Sam grabbed her julep.

"Well, I never," Miss Alice said.

"Waste not, want not." Sam lifted his glass to Miss Alice. "Benjamin Franklin."

Miss Alice straightened and lifted her chin. "Benjamin Franklin was a lush."

Sam winked at Miss Alice. "He was a ladies' man, too."

If Holly didn't know better, she would have sworn Miss Alice blushed.

Tru raised his hand like a schoolkid.

Holly sighed. "What?"

"May I speak?" Tru folded his hands in front of himself and struck what she supposed he thought was an angelic pose.

Holly shoved a hand on her hip. "Only if it has nothing to do with my ghost."

"Nope. Since you forgot to invite me to happy hour too, I'll have a double shot in my Sazerac."

Nelda snickered.

Tru lifted both hands, palms up. "What?"

"A Sazerac is precise." Holly said on her way to the sink with her gumbo bowl. "There is no double shot in a Sazerac."

"Then I'll have two. I'm going to need sedation to keep my mouth shut during the crap show that's coming up."

Holly gave Tru a stern look.

"What now?" His eyes widened behind his Clark Kent glasses as though he'd been falsely accused. "The show hasn't started yet."

"Not one word when it does or you're out of here."

He held his hand up in a Boy Scout pledge again.

That was the last thing he'd said during the whole meal. Of course, he was busy eating three bowls of gumbo and two pieces of French bread, and drinking his Sazeracs.

"I never forget a face." Miss Alice said to Thomas. "Where did you say you were from?"

"San Francisco," Holly answered for Thomas since he had just taken a big bite of Nelda's gumbo and to spare him a small part of the Deep South interrogation she knew was coming from Miss Alice.

Thomas nodded and wiped the corner of his mouth with his napkin, then placed it in his lap like any civilized man would.

"I know that." Miss Alice looked at Holly like she had grits for brains. She used the sugar tongs to extract a cube of sugar from the blue willow sugar bowl.

Those tongs had gotten Holly in quite a bit of trouble when she was about five. She'd borrowed the tongs to do an operation on her dog. A tickectomy. Luckily, no animals or ticks were injured because her mother busted her before she could complete the operation. Of course, she'd never been able to look at the tongs the same way since.

Miss Alice stirred the sugar into her dark roast coffee, then turned her attention back to Thomas. "I mean where were you born?"

"Mississippi," he said, staring down into his Sazerac as he swirled it around in the crystal lowball glass.

"I knew I caught a bit of a Southern accent." Miss Alice nodded, then sipped her coffee.

Holly had noticed a hint of accent that could have been anywhere in the South, but she hadn't suspected from the state right next door.

Miss Alice sat a little straighter. "What part?"

"The Delta," he said.

Miss Alice's face lit up. "That's it. You look familiar because we could be related. I've got kinfolk all over the Delta from way back. According to my genealogy research, I'm related to several prominent Natchez families."

"I was born there. I didn't say I was from Natchez," he said then checked his stainless steel Rolex that was similar to the one had Burl lost in a bet. "It's almost time for the show to start."

"Oh, one of the little towns nearby, of course." Miss Alice scooted to the edge of her seat. "Natchez was the hub of the Mississippi back in the steamboat days."

"Sinclair." Miss Alice leaned back, seemingly in deep thought. "I don't remember any Sinclairs in my research. What was your mama's maiden name?"

*There she goes with who's your mama.* "Miss Alice, would you like more bread pudding?"

She waved Holly off.

"I'm not sure." Thomas shrugged and fingered his glass.

"It's on your birth certificate," Miss Alice said. "Or you could ask your parents."

"I'll have to look up my birth certificate when I get back to California, because I can't ask my parents unless they come haunt Holly Grove."

"Oh, I'm sorry to hear that," Miss Alice said.

"No need. It's been over thirty years since—

"It's important to know where you come from."

"Miss Alice, everyone isn't as into genealogy as you are," Holly said.

"I'm sure your relatives are fine people, but I wouldn't know them and they wouldn't know me." Thomas's tone was flat and matter-of-fact. "I left over thirty years ago." He stood and collected his Sazerac. "Now if you'll excuse me, I need a refresher before the show starts."

He may as well have said "this subject is closed." Granted, Miss Alice had no boundaries when dissecting someone's family to figure out who they were. Holly didn't blame him for getting annoyed. But she had to admit, there was something not right about a man born in the South not knowing his mama's family name.

"Holly, would you mind showing me how to make this delightful cocktail?" He shook his empty glass. His lips lifted in a stiff smile. "I can't buy these in California."

"Sure." Holly stood as Thomas ambled to the kitchen counter where she'd mixed the cocktails earlier.

Miss Alice grabbed her arm and whispered, "I can't put my finger on it, but I know his people."

Maybe she did and maybe she didn't, but there was something in that family tree he was hiding, but what? And why?

Holly's heartbeat ticked up a notch as the TV screen filled with a pan of the oaks stretching over Holly Grove at dusk. The somber background music grew louder as the camera zoomed in on the front door. It swung open with an eerie groan as though it opened by itself.

Chills lifted the hair on Holly's arms. The image was way scarier than she'd ever seen Holly Grove. The time of day? Filters? The music? It all worked. She cut a quick look at Tru. He scarfed down another spoonful of gumbo and dribbled it down his T-shirt. *So much for a reaction there. At least he's keeping his silence.*

The music softened and Sylvia's pitch-perfect voice sounded from the TV. "Haunted, some say. But *Inquiring Minds* doesn't report hearsay. Tonight, *Inquiring Minds* takes you to a nineteenth-century B&B on the banks of the Mississippi River in the Deep South to witness," she took a theatrical pause, "The Ghost in the Grove."

The program cut to a commercial. Holly exhaled and glanced around the table. Miss Alice sat on the edge of her chair. Miss Martha Jane's hand covered her mouth. Tru nursed his Sazerac. Thomas's mouth hung open.

A bright light flashed. "A picture is worth a thousand words," Sam said, lowering his camera.

"Well then, this show is going to be epic," Thomas said.

"And just think. Millions of people are watching this." Sam checked his shot on his camera screen. "Holly Grove is going to be so famous we'll have to make reservations months in advance just to visit."

Holly giggled. "I hope so."

"Now that's job security," Nelda said from the kitchen.

"What are you doing back there?" Holly asked. "I'll clean up later."

"Humph," Nelda said. "I know that ghost can't reach through the TV, but ain't no need bein' close enough for him to think he might."

"Do you think your ghost will show up for his debut?" Thomas asked.

Tru coughed.

Holly sent him a stern look. "You never know when or if a ghost will show up, but you'll get to see his handiwork on the show tonight."

"You got that right," Nelda said.

Holly joined Nelda at the back of the kitchen, partly to keep her company and partly so no one would see her reactions if the show ended up a flop.

The show resumed with the séance in Holly Grove's candlelit dining room and the medium calling the spirit of Burl Davis to make himself known. A few of the candles sputtered out. Everyone around the table eyed each other. Then Angel, the medium, announced his presence and invited him to speak through her. Instead, Burl's voice came from Sylvia's mouth, calling out to Holly.

Gasps came from everyone around the table except Tru.

*Guess it's not working for the skeptic. Lordy.* If the show with a real ghost hadn't made him a believer, how on earth was Holly going to do it without a ghost? But she couldn't let that thought ruin tonight. She stood a little taller. Tonight, Holly Grove was a star.

Holly turned her attention back to the show. Burl continued to speak through Sylvia but refused to say what his unfinished business was. Finally, Sylvia slumped against her chair and the medium told everyone the spirit had left the premises.

The theme music played as the show resumed with interviews of the Deltas, Holly, Nelda, and the teenager, Matt, about his viral video of his encounter with the ghost. During the next commercial, everyone chatted about their fifteen minutes of fame and congratulated Holly on the show. Her cheeks hurt from smiling so much. She could have never bought the kind of publicity she'd get from tonight's episode of *Inquiring Minds*. All she had to do was keep the legend of the ghost alive to secure her and Holly Grove's future.

The show ended with a wide view of Sylvia strolling across the front porch. "There is no doubt in my mind the Ghost in the Grove is real," she said, as the camera zoomed in for a close-up. She lifted a perfectly plucked brow. "And now there is no doubt in yours."

Everyone stood and clapped, except Tru. But Holly didn't care.

"Y'all, this is the best thing ever." Holly swirled in

a circle as rapid-fire flashes from Sam's camera lit the room like a disco dance floor. She stopped and clasped her hands together over her chest. "Do you know what this means for Holly Grove? For all of us?"

"We're going to be on the map as more than a dot now," Sam said. "And I'm going to put all of it in the *Gazette.*"

The Deltas, Sam, and Nelda swarmed her with hugs and congratulations.

Holly caught a glimpse of Tru sulking at the table. He had to be thinking he could never debunk "The Ghost in the Grove." He probably hadn't said a word during the show because he knew he couldn't debunk any of it. Holly almost felt sorry for him. Almost. "Sazeracs for everyone!"

Holly grabbed two shakers of the premixed cocktail from the refrigerator and added ice. She shook the mixture, then poured it in crystal lowball glasses for her guests. After everyone had their Sazerac, she raised her glass. "To the Ghost in the Grove. May he haunt forever."

"That was quite a show," Thomas said, all smiles. "The only thing better would be to witness the ghost firsthand."

Holly's high crashed down. No one would ever witness the ghost of her not-so-dearly-departed again. But she couldn't worry about that. Millions saw the show. The seed had been planted and now when tourists came to visit that little seed would grow in their minds. Every shadow and sound would confirm what they wished to see. Holly Grove would always be haunted, thanks to *Inquiring Minds*.

A loud, slow clap echoed off the beaded panel ceiling and cypress floors. Tru stood and walked her way with cocky swagger. "Bravo. Bravo. Bravo."

*Uh-oh.* Holly stood tall and faced him. There was no way he could debunk what they'd all seen.

"Fiction at its best." Tru clinked his glass to Holly's.

She curled her fingers in a death grip around the crystal lowball glass. "Fact."

Tru raised his glass and took a sip. "I could pick apart that staged haunting in five minutes, easy."

"Excuse me," Holly said. "I was there. There was absolutely nothing staged in that show."

Tru stepped into her space. "Ghosts *do not* exist."

"Well then," Holly lifted her chin a fraction but didn't give an inch of ground. "You're going to have to prove it."

"All in due time." Tru stood so close she could smell the bourbon on his breath. "People like you profit off the gullible."

Holly swallowed hard. She was saving her home and business. Helping to revive a dying town. She wasn't taking advantage of people. Was she?

"You may be able to sucker these old geezers and the brainless who watch that D-rated television show into believing your place is haunted, but anyone with half a brain would see right through your ruse."

"Who you sayin' is brainless?" Nelda asked, coming to Holly's side.

"Don't take offense." Tru looked down on Nelda like she was a bug. "It's not your fault you're suckered in by someone who profits from the unfortunate or the desperate."

Nelda's nostrils flared like a bull ready to charge.

"Don't pay any attention to him," Holly said, stepping in front of Nelda to face Tru.

"That's right." Tru pushed his glasses up on his nose. "You don't want them to know the truth because you'll lose your gravy train."

Nelda did know, but she'd stuck up for Holly anyway and she loved her for it. The Deltas would always be mouths of the South, and Sam would print anything to sell papers. As much as she'd like to tell them the truth, she couldn't. She needed them to believe. Her ugly secret churned in her gut.

Tru pointed a finger in Holly's face. "You use people."

"I do not."

"You use people like her." He pointed to Nelda, then the rest of her guests. "And these defenseless old people to back up your lies, don't you?"

Holly shook her head. She wasn't using them. Was she? Her chest heated.

"All for money because you know no one comes back from the dead. You know it and you use the promise of something beyond the grave to make people believe life doesn't end. Don't you?"

"No!" Holly screamed. "Burl did come back from the dead. He did. I swear he did."

"Then where is your ghost right now, huh?" Tru strutted in a circle and eyed the beaded board ceiling, the walls, and the cypress floors. He stopped inches in front of her face and glared down at her. "You've got the power. Call him up. Prove me wrong."

With each word his voice grew louder, drowning out the lie she had to defend. Holly blinked and stumbled backward. "You don't understand. It doesn't work like that." She rubbed her hand across her collarbone where she knew red blotches congregated every time she feared she'd get caught in a lie.

"No it doesn't, because it can't." Tru glared at her as though she was a lowlife criminal.

Thomas put his hand on Tru's shoulder. "It's only a show, man. Calm down."

Tru shook Thomas's hand from his shoulder and got in Holly's face.

"It works by you suckering people into believing you." Tru's eyes narrowed into angry slits and his spittle peppered her face. "And you, Holly Davis, are a fake and a liar and—"

A sharp slap sounded, and her hand stung before her mind caught up with her reflexes. Tru's glasses skidded across the cypress floor and landed at Sam's feet.

Tru stood stunned, staring at her and holding his red face.

"Get out!" Holly screamed.

"My glasses." Tru frantically looked around the room. "Where are my glasses?"

"Right here." Sam bent over to pick up the glasses, and his drink spilled all over them.

Tru snatched his glasses from Sam and frantically dried them on his T-shirt. He looked back at Holly. "Look what you've done! Are you nuts?"

"Yeah." Maybe she was, but she couldn't stand to hear one more word from him. Had his words hit too close to home? She widened her stance and pointed to the door. "Leave before I call the sheriff."

Tru put his glasses back on and glared at Holly. "Yeah, why don't you do that so I can press charges for assault."

"You deserved it and worse," Holly said. "Now leave."

Tru stood like a linebacker in the middle of her kitchen. "Tell the cop."

"Look." Thomas stepped between them. "I think you are both overreacting a bit here. Can't you work something out without calling the police?"

"Uh-huh," Nelda said. "You know we had a little trouble with your last run-in with the police?"

Holly folded her arms. "I want him out of here."

"Fine." Tru mocked her crossed arms. "As soon as the cops come."

"I'll get the sheriff to evict you." Holly marched toward Tru and wagged her finger at him. "Read the fine print on your reservation."

Thomas held them apart. "How about we don't call the police and Tru here goes to his room to cool off?"

Tru gave a smart-aleck grin. "Read the fine print on the *Inquiring Minds* contract. I hear you have to honor the option clause. You can't kick me out."

# CHAPTER SEVEN

The nerve of that guy—calling her a liar to her face. Holly fumed as she passed Tru's room the next morning. She stuffed the dirty sheets from Thomas's room into a basket then tugged her "Domestic Diva" T-shirt back into place with gusto.

*Liar? Lordy.* Technically speaking, she wasn't lying. She'd *had* a ghost. She just hadn't told the whole truth, and she'd have to live with that. She wasn't sure she could live with Tru through shooting the follow-up *Inquiring Minds* episode. If she couldn't kick him out, how could she make him want to leave?

Nelda thumbed back to the Audubon suite at the other end of the hall. "You want me to help you clean up his royal-pain-in-the-rumpus's room?"

Holly would rather take a beating than clean up after him, but she had to. Or did she? Maybe a little reverse Southern hospitality. "Mr. Royal-Pain-in-the-Rumpus doesn't deserve our Southern hospitality."

"I can't say I blame ya." Nelda ambled toward Tru's room. "But he's payin' for a room."

"He won't get clean sheets or so much as a washcloth out of me, not that a slob like him would care." Holly picked up the laundry basket and her cleaning caddy. "He's not even getting toilet paper." Holly thumbed her chest. "I deserve some respect in my own home and I'm going to get it."

"Humph." Nelda leveled an eye at Holly. "What if ya don't?"

"No cleaning service is just a start." Holly cocked her head to the side and gave a sly grin. How could she jack up his room? "Remember when we had plumbing trouble a while back?"

"Which time?" Nelda scrunched up her brows. "The time the plumber found a pair of panties stoppin' up the toilet in the Longfellow suite or the time the water pressure was more like a dribble in the Jackson suite, or—"

"All of them." Holly gave a wicked grin. "I see some serious problems ahead for Tru's level of comfort in his suite here at Holly Grove. Of course, I'll apologize profusely and offer the only room I have left."

Nelda shoved a hand on her generous hip. "You gonna put him out in the woods in Abe's cabin?"

"Or he can stay at the hotel about thirty minutes down the road." Holly shrugged. "The farther away the better."

"Can't say I blame ya."

"Who would? Can you believe anyone could be so rude?"

The Longfellow suite door swung open and Tru stepped into the hallway. He didn't even give them a sideways glance as he put a DO NOT DISTURB sign on his door. "I hope you two can read. I expect privacy for my entire stay." He flicked the sign.

As he walked away from them, the sign dangled back and forth on the doorknob.

*So much for my bright idea to make him miserable by not cleaning his room or stopping up his toilet. Lame idea anyway, but I'm getting desperate.*

"Ya think he heard us?" Nelda whispered as Tru descended the stairs.

Holly caught her lip between her teeth. "So what? He's getting what he wants." Holly winked at Nelda. "And deserves. No clean sheets, towels, or anything else."

"Ha! That man can't hold on long without toilet paper 'cause he's full of it." Nelda slapped her thigh.

Holly chuckled. "Let's freshen up the attic rooms. The rest of *Inquiring Minds* will be checking in before we know it"

"Yeah. That musty old house smell gets in there if no one stays there." Nelda turned toward the attic stairs at the opposite end of the hall and stopped short. "Did you decide to move the mystery lady again?"

Holly turned and followed Nelda's gaze to the mystery portrait leaning against the wall. "How did that happen?"

"Don't you tell me you didn't do that or you gonna give me the heebie-jeebies."

"I didn't move it."

"You've got my skin crawlin' now." Nelda did a little shimmy. "That thing was crooked yesterday when I was dustin'. I straightened it out, too." Nelda flattened her brow and shook her head. "I'm tellin' you something ain't right around here."

*Lordy.* All Holly needed was for Nelda to get spooked and leave with a house full of guests coming and the whole debunking thing going on. "Don't get your panties in a knot. The wire strung across the frame probably gave way. It may have been on there a hundred years or more." Holly marched to the painting and inspected the back of the frame.

Nelda looked over Holly's shoulder. "Ain't broke, is it?"

"No," Holly said, puzzled.

"It sure as shootin' didn't jump off that wall on its own." Nelda glanced over her shoulder as if to check to see if anyone was there. "If it ain't Burl, God rest his soul, maybe we got another ghost. You'd tell me if we did, wouldn't you?"

"If we did, I'd see him just like I saw Burl." *Wouldn't I?* Could there be another spirit roaming around Holly Grove and her not know it? Surely not. "I bet all that banging Mackie's been doing on the widow's walk jarred the portrait crooked and then off the hanger. That's the only logical explanation."

"Ain't nothin' logical 'bout ghosts."

"A ghost didn't do that. Believe me, if ever I wanted to have a ghost, it's now, so he could shut up that royal-pain-in-the-rumpus."

Nelda grinned. "You got that right."

"Wait just a pea-pickin' minute." Holly paced to Tru's door. "You just gave me a great idea."

Holly fished out her keys from her pocket and stood in front of Tru's door.

"Tru was right." Nelda pointed at the sign. "You

can't read. Girl, trouble is your middle name and you're askin' for it."

"No. Tru's asking for it, and I'm going to give it to him."

"What you gonna do in there?" Nelda asked, leaning over Holly's shoulder. "Stop up his toilet?"

Holly glanced back at Nelda. "You gave me a better idea."

"Yeah." Nelda's eyes widened. "What was it?"

"I need to set the mood for ghosting." Holly held her palm out for Nelda. "Give me a hairpin."

Nelda pulled a black hairpin out of her hair. "I don't even want to know what you're gonna do with that, and I don't want it back."

"I'm going to leave him a message or two from our ghost." Holly inserted the key in the lock.

"That ghost we don't have, right?"

Holly unlocked the door. "Yep."

"You gonna make that trouble on your own." Nelda balked at the doorway. "Nobody's gonna accuse me of trespassin'."

"Fine." Holly huffed. "You go stand at the stairs and tell me if he's coming."

Nelda cocked an eye at Holly. "You want me to be an accessory to trespassin'?"

"I'm not trespassing. This is my house." Holly swung the door open.

Nelda whistled.

The bedsheets were tangled on the floor. Wadded-up wet towels filled a corner in the room. The duffel bag looked like it had exploded. Dingy clothing lay all over the floor along with candy wrappers, chip bags, soda cans, and gum wrappers. And where had he gotten pizza?

"There's messy and there's pigsty messy." Nelda shook her head. "No wonder he didn't want us in his room. He ought to be ashamed."

"If he is, that means he probably didn't hear us talking about stopping up his toilet."

Nelda took her cleaning caddy and pretended to dust the stair rail. She gave Holly an all-clear nod.

Holly rushed into the bathroom and turned on the hot water, full blast, then closed the door. While that ran, she dashed back to the bedroom and opened the armoire. She clamped the hairpin over the hinge and closed the door. It swung back open. *Yes! It worked.* She pumped her fist.

What else could she do? A draft from the floor-to-ceiling windows dusted her shoulders. If she opened the top of the double-hung window, he may not notice, but it'd get mighty cold in there after midnight when the temperatures dropped to the low forties. Holly flung open the lace drapes, then tugged on the top frame until a six-inch gap let the air in near the top of the twelve-foot ceiling. She flipped the thermostat to OFF. *Oh, yeah. He'll wake up in a frosty room and everyone knows it gets cold in the presence of the dead. Or under the right circumstances.* She dusted her hands together.

Holly dashed back to the bathroom. A fog coated the small medicine cabinet mirror. Perfect. She turned off the water. With one finger, she scrawled a message on the mirror. *Go home or else.*

She stood back and admired her handiwork. Next

time Tru shaved and fogged up the mirror, her ghostly message would appear again. One way or another, she would make him believe. She had to.

A knock came from the door.

Holly jumped. The knock was too far away to be at the bathroom door. She eased the bathroom door open.

Another knock came from the hallway door. "Yoo-hoo," Miss Alice's voice came from behind the door. "Tru. Are you in there?"

*Oh, crapola. Why didn't Nelda warn me? Don't panic. The door is locked. She can't get in. But what if Tru comes back while she's standing at the door?* Holly's heart thumped so hard she could barely hear anything else.

*I've got to hide.* She scanned the room. *Under the bed? The armoire? Behind the drapes? The windows!*

She tiptoed to the floor-to-ceiling windows and eased one open, then stepped through. *When I get my hands on Nelda, I'm going to strangle her.*

Holly made her way to the riverside of the balcony and opened her bedroom window, then stepped through and into her bedroom. As she passed her dresser, she caught her reflection in the mirror. Her hair had taken a walk on the wild side. *Mercy.* What could she expect after she'd had the bejesus scared out of her? Holly smoothed her hair as she crossed her bedroom. She took a deep breath and opened the hallway door.

"Miss Alice," she said. "Whatever brings you up here?"

The old gal wheeled around like she was thirty years younger. "I have business with Tru."

"What kind of business?"

Miss Alice peered over her glasses. "That is between Tru and me."

"Why didn't you warn me Miss Alice was coming?" Holly asked Nelda as soon as they entered the attic bedroom Holly had named the Mississippi suite.

"First, how was I supposed to know Miss Alice was gonna knock on Tru's door?" Nelda caught her breath. "Second, ain't nobody gonna stop Miss Alice from goin' where she wants to go."

Holly pushed the heavy drapes on the dormer window open. Sunlight slashed across the antique rug and dust particles danced in the beam of light. She fanned the dust. "It does smell stuffy in here."

"Always does." Nelda opened the drapes on the other dormer. "What'd she want with Tru anyway?"

"She wouldn't say." Holly ran a dustcloth over the side table next to the canopy bed. "The only kind of business Miss Alice could have with Tru is probably not good. She either wanted to get some sort of scoop from him or give him some. Gossip is Miss Alice's commodity."

"You got that right." Nelda shoved open the dormer window. "You think she wanted to set him straight about Burl being a real ghost after Tru made such a fool of himself?"

Holly shrugged. "I think she would have done that last night if she wanted to. It's never good when she starts nosing around."

"Speakin' of nose." Nelda wrinkled her nose up "I smell somethin' burnin'."

Holly sniffed the air and followed the scent to the dormer window. "That's cigar smoke. Only one person here smokes cigars, and he's not supposed to smoke anywhere except the back balcony."

"You think Tru's smokin' in his room?" Nelda asked.

"I don't know, but I'm going to find out." Holly stepped out into the hall and down the stairs to the second floor. She beat on Tru's door.

No answer. Holly sniffed the air, but didn't smell cigar smoke like she had at the attic level. She marched up the steep stairs to the widow's walk, then shoved the door open.

Tru stood surrounded in a fog of cigar smoke.

She slammed the door behind her.

He pivoted enough to see her, then blew out a smoke ring. "Keep your distance, unless you want me to get a restraining order on you."

*Restraining order my foot.* "You can't get a restraining order on me in my own home. If you don't like it here, leave."

"Oh, I like it fine." He sucked on his cigar. "It's you that has a problem."

"The only problem I have right now is you breaking the rules."

"What rules?"

"Smoking is only allowed in the designated area."

"You expect me to walk all the way down to the back of the house every time I want a puff?" He made a flourish with his hand at the view of the Mississippi River. "When this is right here?"

"This area is under construction."

Tru shrugged. "Doesn't take away from the view

or the convenience. I get a better signal on my phone up here, too."

"It's closed to guests."

Tru surveyed the widow's walk. "I don't see any construction. No signs. No tape to rope off the *said* construction area. Sounds like you just don't want *me* up here."

"Look, no one is supposed to be up here. The inspector said I had to raise the railing before guests could come up here." She pointed to the hole in the deck. "My carpenter fell through a rotten spot."

Tru glanced at the wrought-iron railing. "Anyone ever fall off before?"

"Not that I know of."

"So what's the problem?" Tru puffed his cigar and the smoke drifted over the rooftop. "Any idiot would know not to lean over the railing or step in a hole."

"It doesn't matter. This is my house and my rules."

"I could open a window and blow the smoke out."

Holly folded her arms over her chest. "Read the fine print on your reservation. There's a three-hundred-dollar fine for smoking in the rooms."

"Or a free space right here."

"You know what? I hope I catch you again. I'll evict you and you can stay at the No Tell Motel thirty miles down the road until Sylvia gets here for the shoot."

He thumped his cigar ash on the deck. "I don't think so."

"Try me."

"Sylvia is here." He pointed behind Holly.

She looked over her shoulder at a red convertible speeding down her driveway. "She's not supposed to be here until tonight. What makes you think that's her?"

"Google alert." He took another puff of his cigar. "She posted on Twitter that she was on a red-eye to New Orleans to revisit 'The Ghost in the Grove.'"

"You really are a troll."

He shook his head. "I'm a truth finder."

# CHAPTER EIGHT

Sylvia Martin exited the red convertible rental car with the grace of a Hollywood starlet. Sylvia's blond Bergdorf locks brushed her shoulders as her never-ending legs lifted her on killer heels to a nearly six-foot height. The blue designer dress probably matched her eyes. Just her looks made it hard for Holly to like Sylvia, but it was more than that. Sylvia didn't seem to care about anyone except herself. No secret there. But that was also her greatest weakness, and Holly intended to use that to get what she wanted.

Holly eased down the front porch steps to meet Sylvia at her car for a private chat. Somehow, Holly had to convince the TV host to either cancel the show or enlist her in helping fake a ghost without telling her Burl's spirit had left the building, for good.

"I'm glad you came a little early, too." Holly wasn't, but she needed to say something nice besides "great shoes."

"What do you mean 'too'?" Sylvia slid a high-dollar clutch bag under her arm.

"Tru checked in last night to watch the show."

"What?" Sylvia snatched off her oversized designer sunglasses and looked toward Holly Grove. "Where is that little troll?"

"My sentiments exactly." Holly cast a pointed look at the widow's walk at the top of Holly Grove. "Up there."

Tru waved as he sucked on his cigar.

Holly was tempted to wave back with her fist. "He's not supposed to be up there, much less smoking."

"I hope the little troll falls off." Sylvia leaned against the car and popped the trunk with her key fob. "He thought he could get a jump on me and you didn't even tell me he came in early."

"I thought you knew." Holly flopped her arms at her side. "He told me coming early was in his contract."

Sylvia cocked her head to the side and arched one eyebrow. "He lied."

A ticked off stream of heat rushed up Holly's back.

"And you believed him." Sylvia gave a grand eye roll. "I hope you haven't told him anything about your ghost. Has he been snooping around?"

"No and yes," Holly said. "He had to be snooping to even find his way to the widow's walk. That door is always closed and not marked."

"Don't tell him anything." Sylvia walked around to the trunk of her car. "My bags are in there. Thank

God, I'm not staying in that shack you called Abe's cabin this time."

Holly took a fortifying breath. No matter what Sylvia said, Holly needed to suck it up. She needed to be on Sylvia's good side if she had one.

"You're in one of my best suites this time." Holly grabbed one of the five bags in her trunk. *Lordy, she must pay a fortune in extra baggage fees.*

Sylvia inspected her perfectly manicured nails. "Don't you have a bellman, or is that hunky Jake still around?"

Obviously, she believed her bags magically appeared in her room on her last visit. "Most people carry their own luggage."

Sylvia shoved off her perch against the car. "You don't expect me to—

Holly forced a grin through gritted teeth. "I wouldn't want you to break a nail before the show."

A shadow of a smile crossed Sylvia's powdered face.

"Speaking of the show," Holly added casually, "I need to talk with you about that while we're alone."

"Look." Sylvia sashayed to Holly at the trunk. "I know you're not happy about this, but it's going to be fabulous. Your reservations will go through the roof."

"Last night's show did that! And I'm thankful." Holly pinched her brows together and tilted her head in her best impression of concern. "I'd hate for your ratings to go down if Burl is a no-show."

Sylvia folded her arms and tapped her designer-clad foot. "Don't tell me you haven't kissed and made up with your ex? I mean ghost."

Holly cringed. "That's what I need to talk to you about."

"Please don't tell me you're still not speaking."

"We're not speaking. That's why you really need to call this off. It could be a disaster for your career and my business. It's not too—"

"I am not canceling." Sylvia drilled Holly with a laser stare. "I can't."

"Sure you can. Just call it off. Say you're sick. Whatever it takes."

"I will not let a lovers' spat ruin this. You have no idea how much buzz this shoot is getting." She pointed her red-hot laser focus up at Tru. "And I'm taking down that little troll."

"I'm with you on that, but what if Burl doesn't show? The troll wins."

Sylvia looked down at Holly as though she were handing down gospel. "I know how to handle men. Whatever it is you're fighting about with your ghosts, just tell him it's all your fault even if it isn't. Lie. Tell him you'll never do it again. If he did something, suck it up, buttercup. Tell him you forgive him even if he didn't ask. Just end it, so we can get on with this."

"But I've tried everything." Even if she had, he wasn't coming back.

Sylvia folded her arms and eyed Holly. "And he's still not speaking to you?"

*Not this side of Heaven.* "Evidently he holds a grudge. I guess he figures he has all eternity to be mad at me. What's weeks, months, or years to him?"

"I don't care how you do it, but you've got to get some action out of him or else."

"Or else what?" Holly shrugged. "What can I do to a dead guy?"

"You better think of something." Sylvia slipped her sunglasses back on. "Because the show must go on."

"Then we have a problem," Holly said.

"No. You have a problem."

A low buzz sounded from inside Sylvia's Prada purse. She dug out a phone and checked the screen. "I've got to take this."

"But—"

Sylvia turned her back and walked down the driveway. *Okay, she's not going to cancel, and Burl can't make this command performance.*

Holly could make out bits of Sylvia's conversation as she walked away.

"Yeah," she said into the phone. "He's here and clueless, I'm sure. You take care of the money end. You just get me what I need before the shoot."

The rest of the conversation faded as Sylvia disappeared behind a two-hundred-year-old oak tree.

Interesting. There were a lot of adjectives Holly could use to describe Tru . . . rude, messy, stinky, pushy . . . but clueless? And what did Sylvia need?

Sylvia stepped from behind the ancient oak and dropped her phone in her purse. "Okay. What are you going to do if Burl doesn't show?"

"Me?" Holly pointed to her chest. "You were going to fake it?"

"And risk my journalistic reputation?"

Holly blinked. "But you said you'd . . ." And since when was a paranormal investigation show journalism?

"I said I would act if I had to." Sylvia gave a wry grin. "It's up to you to set it up."

*Oh, crapola.*

"Need a hand with that?"

Holly whirled around to find Thomas standing behind her, staring into Sylvia's loaded trunk. So much for finishing her private chat with Sylvia. "That would be great. Thanks."

It seemed like he showed up every time she needed help. Coincidence, or was he watching her as much as she felt watched?

Footsteps crunching through gravel sounded behind Holly.

Sylvia held her arms out for balance. "This stuff is a hazard in heels. Have you ever heard of pavement?"

"It's better than the mud pie of a dirt driveway I had until recently," Holly said. *Thank you, Burl, for making Holly Grove profitable.*

When Sylvia looked at Thomas, her eyes lit up like stage lights. "I don't believe we've met in person." Sylvia extended a slender hand. "Sylvia Martin. *Inquiring Minds.*"

Holly blinked. *In person?*

"I recognize you from the show." Thomas shook her hand. "Although you're more beautiful in person."

She all but batted her lash extensions. "Thank you . . ."

Holly stood there with her mouth open. "You know Thomas?"

"Of course, I know *the* Thomas Sinclair of T&C Sinclair Producers of San Francisco."

Something about the fan girl act didn't ring true to Holly.

He smiled. "Just Thomas."

"Don't be modest," she practically cooed. "You've been a producer of some of the most successful cable shows." Her well-manicured fingers fluttered to her chest. "Including mine."

"You're with *Inquiring Minds*?" Holly asked Thomas. She couldn't hide the incredulous tone in her voice. In spite of Nelda's instant dislike, she'd really liked him.

"Not at all. T&C is my better half's pet project. I really don't consider entertainment in my wheel-house. I balance our portfolio with tech investments. Chris has a knack for picking winners in entertainment. I have little to do with it except writing checks." He shrugged. "And our investment in the show is minor. "

"We all do our part," Sylvia said, wrapping her arm around his. "Let's go inside and chat about the show. Have you heard the buzz?"

"Chris should join me any day now. You two will have lots to talk about." Thomas freed his arm and picked up two suitcases, then turned toward Holly Grove. "Why don't you grab a bag and we'll have you unloaded in no time."

Sylvia eyed the three suitcases left in the trunk and picked the small train case.

Holly still liked him. Could she fault him for wanting to check out the setting for what Sylvia said was their best show of the season?

Holly mentally shook her head. Just because she liked him didn't mean she should trust him.

Tru strolled out on the front porch and eyed Sylvia through his Clark Kent glasses as though he had them set on X-ray vision. "Well, well, well. The star has arrived."

*Diva is more like it.* Holly hefted two suitcases and trudged up the brick stairs behind Sylvia.

"That's right." Sylvia said, as her heels hammered the brick steps to the lower balcony. Never slowing down, her chin tilted higher than any sorority girl in the history of Ole Miss. "All you're trying to do is make a name for yourself and cheating too."

Tru trailed after her. "I don't need to cheat to debunk the fabrication I watched last night."

"Oh, yeah." Sylvia whirled around. "Then why did you lie to Holly about a contract to come a day early to get a jump on me?"

"I came early because I do my homework, unlike a talking head like you."

"You couldn't catch up with me if you came a week early."

*Mercy. Thank goodness he didn't.* Holly stood holding the suitcases between round one of the Tru and Sylvia match. Her head hurt just thinking of them arguing over the next few days. *At least, she's on my side this time.*

"No need." Tru lit up his stump of a cigar and turned his Clark Kent X-ray vision on Holly. "Not one sign of a ghost since I got here."

*And there wouldn't be.* She gulped then dropped the

luggage. It hit the painted cypress planks with a thud. "Maybe you don't have the gift, Tru."

He groaned and pointed his stogie at Sylvia. "The supposed ghost will show up now that the special effects team is here."

*Not this side of Heaven.*

"I don't and did not use special effects." Sylvia seemed to measure her tone, but the tight set of her jaw told Holly it wouldn't last. "You saw the show last night. How could I fake that?"

Tru shrugged. "Women fake things all the time, believe me."

"I'm sure they do." Sylvia paused for effect and lifted an eyebrow. "For you."

Holly stifled a laugh.

"I wouldn't fake this for anyone," Sylvia said.

*Crapola. She can't back out of faking the haunting. I've got to get her away from Tru.*

He blew out a cloud of cigar smoke.

Holly fanned the air, then wrapped her arm around Sylvia's like they were BFFs. "Don't let him get to you. Let's get you settled in your suite . . ."

Sylvia didn't budge. She latched on to Holly's arm and glared at Tru. "Do you know what that smoke smells like?" She asked through gritted teeth.

Tru smirked.

"Death," Sylvia whispered and tightened her hold on Holly's arm.

He eyed his stogie. "So I hear."

"Life as you know it is over. You will fail on my show, and we're going to troll you with that failure all over the World Wide Web until you crawl under a bridge and die."

"We?" Holly croaked out.

Sylvia held on to Holly's arm and nodded as though they were a team.

Tru adjusted his glasses. "Are you two threatening me?"

"We're promising to destroy you," Sylvia said as though she meant it.

"Ladies," He lifted his hand, palms up. "All I do is tell the truth. I've got nothing to lose. You on the other hand have a nice cushy j-o-b to lose or a business to dry up after I debunk 'The Ghost in the Grove.'" He thumped the stump of a cigar into the azaleas Grandmother Rose had planted when she was a young bride. "I'm willing to gamble. Are you?"

# CHAPTER NINE

Holly plastered a sign on the door to the widow's walk. She stood back and inspected her work. The computer-generated black and yellow caution border around the sign made it look official: DANGER. DO NOT ENTER. UNDER CONSTRUCTION.

Tru couldn't say he wasn't warned in writing and in person. If she caught him up there one more time, she'd have every reason to tear up his reservation and boot him to the curb. She dusted her hands of that chore, but she wasn't finished.

She needed help dragging a four-by-eight-foot sheet of plywood up the stairs to cover the hole Mackie had left in the decking. Miss Alice was too old to help. She wouldn't think of asking Tru, even if it was for his protection. She couldn't expect guests to do chores, which knocked out Thomas and Sylvia. That left Nelda, and she wasn't going to be excited about it.

Holly bounded down the stairs to the kitchen. The scent of comfort trailed up the stairwell. Nelda's homemade dumplings. She sucked in the rich aroma.

At least she could eat guilt free after all the flights of stairs she'd clocked today. The door flapped behind her as she entered the kitchen.

"I told you to get out of my kitchen," Nelda said, as she stirred a pot on the stove.

Holly stopped short and looked around.

Rhett perked up from his place in the sun and trotted to her side.

The bench sat askew at the planter's table. A cup of coffee and a half-worked crossword puzzle littered the table. Holly scooped Rhett up and rubbed his head, and studied Nelda. "Who peed in your soup?"

Nelda whirled around, brows pinched. "I thought you was somebody else." She waved her wooden spoon at Holly. "We need to put that PRIVATE sign back up on the door."

"Has Tru been bugging you again?"

Nelda turned and stirred again. "He bugs everybody."

"I know! He's ticked off everyone here. We need a truce at least until the shoot."

"Truce? Those folks fight worse than politicians." Nelda wiped her hands on a dish towel. "I just hope Miss Alice is the only one packin' or someone is gonna get killed."

"I don't think anyone is ready for literal murder. They're all talk." She sidled up to Nelda. "But we do have that big hole in the floor of the widow's walk that could be dangerous. I caught Tru up there smoking his cigar this morning."

"Good. Maybe he'll fall through and hurt his back like Mackie."

"And sue me. Unlike Mackie."

"Yeah." Nelda nodded. "You right 'bout that."

"So I need to fix the hole, but I need your help."

"Ain't no carpentry on my résumé."

"I'll do the carpentry. It's just nailing a piece of plywood over the hole. I need you to help me carry it upstairs."

"Do you know how many sets of stairs to the top of this house?" Nelda's eyes widened as she counted on her fingers. "One, two, three, four."

"We don't have to do it all at once. Just help me get it to the second floor. Then you can rest a while and we'll take it up another flight," Holly pleaded. "Please."

"Humph." Nelda shook her head. "Since Mackie's laid up, you ain't got nobody else to help you, do you?"

Holly sighed. "Just you. He said he needs a day to rest his back."

"I know you say you don't want a man," Nelda snatched off her apron, "but I say you need one and I'm thinkin' of one in particular."

"The one that bailed at the last minute?" She didn't need Jake, not that it mattered. He'd made his feelings clear. "I don't need a man, I need muscle."

"So, you're askin' me?" Nelda glanced down at her full figure.

"Please?"

"You might as well ask puddin' to be steak," Nelda shook her head and yanked off her apron. "This could take all day."

Holly hugged Nelda. "I'd be sunk without you."

A few minutes later, Holly and Nelda struggled

to carry the plywood up the main staircase in the entrance hall. "Who knew a piece of plywood could weigh so much?" Holly asked.

"I coulda told you it was too heavy." Nelda said. "This may take days."

Holly grunted to lift her end over the banister and then the load lightened. She looked behind her and Thomas had added his strength to her heft.

"Where are you going with this?" he asked.

Holly glanced upward. "All the way up to the widow's walk."

"You get on Nelda's end and I'll take this end." Thomas lifted the plywood high enough for Holly to pass under to join Nelda higher on the staircase.

"We've got this." Nelda's face seemed to be swollen in a pout.

"But Nelda . . . muscle."

"Humph. Since when can't we do anything we want to?"

Holly leaned in to Nelda and whispered, "Don't you always tell me not to look a gift horse in the mouth?"

"You and your gift horse tote this piece of wood up four stories. I've got supper to cook. Anyway, I got a good back and I want to keep it that way," Nelda said, not bothering to whisper.

Nelda huffed off, leaving Holly with her end of the lifting.

Heat rose in Holly's cheeks. What was it about Thomas that ticked off Nelda?

"It seems like Nelda and I got off on the wrong foot," Thomas said.

"I'll say." Holly glanced back at the kitchen door as it flapped shut. "That's really not like her."

"It could have been because I wanted decaffeinated coffee this morning and she had to brew a pot."

"She has been in a mood lately. I'm going to have to talk to her about that and see what's going on."

When Holly and Thomas reached the widow's walk they were both winded and sat down on the painted planks to take a break.

"I really don't think Nelda and I could have done that without taking a big break between floors. You seem to have good timing about helping out around here."

Thomas grinned. "Chris says I've got *as needed* ESP."

"You do." Holly got up and dusted off her rear end. "Thanks again."

He pointed to the jagged hole in the decking. "How did that get there anyway?"

"Mackie fell through a rotten spot in the decking. He hurt his back, but it could have been so much worse. He's hardheaded too. He won't go to the doctor." She opened up a toolbox and removed a pair of leather gloves. "If I know him, he'll be back tomorrow to finish the job, even if he's gimpy."

"Is he someone who cares about you?" Thomas raised his brows. "A boyfriend?"

"Lordy, no." She cocked her head to the side. Was the old guy hitting on her? Surely not. "He's probably sixty-five years old." Holly covered her mouth. "Not that that's old, but he's old enough to be my father."

Thomas's face contorted in confusion. He held his

hands up like stop signs. "I wasn't asking because . . . I mean I wasn't flirting . . . Uh, I hope . . ."

"I didn't take it that way." *The little lie may make him feel better.* Really, she didn't get the vibe he was hitting on her, but something was off. *And ew, Mackie is Jake's dad.* Jake, the old flame that wouldn't die, dang it. Her cheeks heated. "He's my old boyfriend's dad. I've known him almost forever."

That must be why the question set off her creep alert. She shivered inside. Who wants someone to ask if your crush's dad is your boyfriend?

"So you're close?" Thomas asked as if he cared.

"To be honest, I try to take care of Mackie. Everyone in town does. He's had a tough life, and he doesn't have any family here."

"What about his son?"

Holly shrugged. "Out of town." Out of her heart? Obviously not. "Anyway, I wanted to open the widow's walk to guests, but the railing is too low for code." She glanced at the ornate wrought-iron railing. Even though it had a bit of rust, it was still strong. Just like the rest of Holly Grove.

He frowned. "You aren't replacing it, are you?"

"Mercy, no. It's too beautiful to replace." The wind kicked up and blew her hair in her eyes. She did her best to push her hair back wearing oversized gloves. Puffy clouds raced across a bluebird sky that skimmed the tree line along the Mississippi. "I want everyone who comes to Holly Grove to see this view."

"I wouldn't have known it was here if I hadn't stepped in to help." He rubbed his hand over his bald head and smiled. "This *is* spectacular."

"You should see it at night." She pointed to a box

covered in a tarp. "I even bought a telescope for stargazing."

"Was your handyman supposed to install that too?"

"Unfortunately." Holly sighed. "He'll get it done, but it may be a while. In the meantime, I better get to nailing down that plywood." She dug a hammer and a sack of nails out of the toolbox. "Don't forget dinner's at seven. Nelda made chicken and dumplings."

And she hoped dinner wouldn't be a brawl tonight. She kneeled beside the plywood and held a three-inch nail in the ready position for hammering. With a quick whack of the hammer she bent the nail, and the hammer bounced off the nail and smacked the edge of her thumb. Pain shot all the way up to her wrist. "Sh . . . oot!"

"You okay?" Thomas took a few steps toward her and put his hand on her shoulder.

"Yeah," she said, holding her throbbing thumb. "I must not have held my mouth right."

"Huh?"

Holly glanced over her shoulder at him. "Grandma Rose always said you have to hold your mouth just right to drive a nail."

He chuckled. "Never heard that one."

Holly positioned another nail and hammered it in halfway before she bent it flat. "Well, it doesn't have to be perfect."

"Um, do you need a hand with that?" Thomas asked as Holly pounded on another nail.

"Thanks, but you've done enough," she said, but

he was already kneeling beside her. "Seriously, you're a guest. You're here to relax, not work."

"Can I tell you a secret?" He took the hammer from her.

Holly settled on her haunches.

"I've never been good at vacations. In fact, this is the first real vacation I've ever had."

"Really?"

"Yep. You know what I usually do with my time off?" He didn't wait for her to guess. "Chris and I renovate old houses and flip them. We've done about a dozen. So, you see, if you'd let me help you fix up your widow's walk, you'd make this a perfect vacation."

Holly sat there gobsmacked. Gift horse, indeed. With as much as she had going wrong, maybe she deserved a good turn of luck. Still, it didn't feel right.

"I can't." She shook her head. "I can't have a paying guest working. Besides, Mackie needs the money."

"If Mackie is able to work, I'll help him with the lifting. If not, this project would help me to *relax*. Chris calls it my carpentry therapy. I bet there's plenty of work for a handyman anytime to maintain a place this old."

"Tell me about it." If she could afford it, and maybe she could with all the ghost publicity from the show. Her stomach dipped a bit. If Tru doesn't debunk the "The Ghost in the Grove" and make her look like a big scammer.

Thomas sighed and stared down at her bent nails. "I'd like to do this for you."

"Why?" She studied his face. "You don't even know me."

"I had a daughter," he said, never looking up at her. "But . . . She'd . . . uh . . . she'd be about your age if . . ." He looked at Holly for a nanosecond before focusing on the mutilated nails again.

The pain in his eyes hit her in a freeze-frame. Something terrible must have happened to her. Holly swallowed hard. Maybe he was unusually nice to her because she reminded him of his daughter. "I'm so sorry," she said.

"Don't be," he said. "It was a long time ago." It was as though a switch had turned off the flash of pain she'd seen in his eyes just a moment ago. "I'd like to think it'd be good karma to help you."

She softened to the idea. Maybe it would be good karma for her too. "How about we trade room and board for the carpentry?"

He shook his head. "How about you give me credit for my next stay?"

"Deal." Holly handed him her hammer. "On one condition."

"What's that?"

"You only work when I can help you. I don't want anyone else having an accident up here."


"I didn't think I'd ever get back to this beautiful place again," Liz said as she climbed out of the rented panel van. She flipped a rubber band off her wrist and tied her auburn hair in a ponytail. "I don't miss this humidity, though."

"This is nothing. Come back in July." Holly hugged

Liz, the *Inquiring Minds* producer and her friend. "I'm glad to see you again, but I wish you were just coming for a visit. By the way, you'll have running water and indoor plumbing this time. I'm putting you in the carriage house next to Miss Alice."

Bob the cameraman went around the back of the van and started unloading equipment onto a cart without so much as a *howdy-do* or *kiss my grits*. She wasn't sure she'd ever heard him say a word to anyone except Liz or Sylvia.

"Hi, Bob," Holly said with a wave.

He gave her a good ol' boy nod as he tossed bags on a cart.

"Where's Jake?" Liz looped her thumbs in the side pockets of her cargo pants and glanced around.

"Still in Guatemala." Holly shrugged. "Anywhere but here, evidently."

"No way. I thought you two were," she lifted a pale eyebrow, "you know."

"I thought so too, but you know the old saying. It takes two." And she obviously wasn't going to be the one to break the curse on the women in her family with men. At this rate, there wouldn't be a sixth generation to have bad luck with the opposite sex.

"I heard you weren't too thrilled about doing the follow-up show."

"To say the least."

"You aren't the only one. Angel wasn't too pleased about leading another séance. I had to do a little arm twisting."

"Let me guess." Holly tapped her temple as though she was thinking. "The option clause."

Liz winced. "Sorry about that. We have never

enforced it before. Never had a follow-up show either."

"I'm a wreck about doing this." Holly grabbed Liz's arm and pulled her to the side. "The show last night was amazing. I've got reservations out the wazoo, which is great, but if this show bombs I lose it all." Holly looked back at her beloved Holly Grove and then clamped down on Liz's arm. "Everyone will think the first show was smoke and mirrors."

"I can testify that it wasn't. Sylvia told me your ghost of an ex is not cooperating."

"Burl isn't speaking to me. I can't even see him." *And won't for good reason.* A twinge of guilt pricked Holly for lying to someone as sweet as Liz. "It's going to be a disaster. You're the producer and I know you want a good show. Can you try to talk some sense into Sylvia? Get her to cancel? Reschedule?"

Liz shook her head. "She's convinced this show is the leverage she needs for her contract negotiations, which are coming up soon. On top of that, she's lapping up all the buzz about the challenge like a feral cat. Her picture is going to be in some celebrity magazine with an article about her paranormal experience."

"But what if there's not another paranormal experience?"

"She believes since Burl possessed her." Liz drew quotation marks in the air. "They have a connection and he's going to show up for her." Liz rolled her eyes. "She's that special."

"What an ego."

"Tell me about it. I've been working for her for

three seasons. It doesn't matter what I say, she won't change her mind."

"Why don't you get a new job?"

"It's complicated."

Bob rolled the luggage cart around the van. His wore biker clothes and had symbols tattooed on each knuckle. He just stood there staring at Liz.

She cut her eyes at Bob. "Maybe he could talk her into backing out."

*Huh? Bob talk?*

"What did you mean when you said Bob may be able to talk Sylvia out of the shoot?" Holly asked after Bob left to unload the equipment in the house.

"I was giving him a hard time," Liz said as they walked to her suite in the carriage house. "He rarely talks at all, but if Sylvia says jump, he's midair. I swear I think he has a crush on her." Liz groaned. "Can you believe it?"

Reflecting back on their last visit, it seemed Liz spent a lot of time with Bob, standing close, whispering . . . Holly stopped. "Liz, do you have a thing for Bob?"

"Of course not. I just think it's funny."

Or did she? "It's always the quiet ones that are hard to figure out, huh?"

Liz kicked a pebble on the path with her Birkenstock. "All men."

"I hear ya, but I was hoping he really did have an in with Sylvia. I don't know what I'm going to do if my ghost stands us all up."

"Look, you've got until tomorrow night to get

him to come out. Why don't you encourage Sylvia to help you? If you can't raise him," Liz giggled, "maybe Sylvia can."

"You're brilliant!" Holly squeezed Liz's shoulders. "That's it. If Sylvia can't get the ghost to show up, she'll have to cancel to save face."

"All you have to do is convince her to do a trial run."

*How hard could that be?*

# CHAPTER TEN

"Have you heard from that medium?" Sylvia spun on a stiletto to face Liz as they entered the candlelit dining room. "What's her name?"

"No, but she confirmed and received payment," Liz said as she padded across the hardwood floor in her flats that looked worthy of a mountain hike.

"Her name is Angel Dupree." And Holly needed to intercept her before she came into the house. That's why she'd called Angel and left a message to call when she was close so they could meet her outside. Angel would know immediately that Burl was gone, and that had to be handled delicately. Then maybe Holly could get her to convince Sylvia that Burl wasn't going to show up and not tell her he was never going to show up.

Nelda placed an oval pan loaded with buttery chicken and dumplings into a sterling silver chafing dish. Steam curled over the dumplings and filled the room with deliciousness.

Sylvia peeked at the dumplings, then wrinkled up her perfect nose. "That looks disgusting."

Of course it did to her. That's why she probably wore a size two and had no stress buying swimsuits.

"Humph." Nelda wadded up a potholder in each hand. "I bet you never even ate a bite of chicken and dumplin's, and I know you ain't had the best 'cause you're lookin' at 'em."

Liz shook her head. "I don't care what it looks like. Anything that smells that good has to be awesome."

"You got that right." Nelda said. "Just wait until you taste my dumplin's.

"That's why you can't lose any weight, Liz." Sylvia screwed her nose up like she'd smelled something rotten. "Paste, animal protein, and fat."

Nelda stirred the dumplings and rapped the spoon on the side of the dish. "Maybe if Miss Sylvia Martin ate a little fat it'd fill her cheeks out and make her look younger on TV."

A snicker that quickly turned into a cough erupted from Liz.

"Well," Sylvia folded her arms over her chest and patted the floor with her red stiletto as she stared down Nelda.

Ignoring Sylvia, Nelda wiped a little dribble off the side of the chafing dish before ambling back toward the kitchen.

Sylvia picked up a Sazerac from the side table. "Your cook would live a lot longer with a lot less fat on her hips."

Nelda stopped.

Sylvia froze with her glass halfway to her lips and expressionless, which could be due to the Botox.

Nelda's shoulders rose and fell as she stood there for a beat, then shook her generous rump. "You're just jealous." She pushed through the side door to the kitchen, and the door slammed against the wall.

*Go, Nelda.*

Sylvia still stood holding her glass as if it was frozen halfway to her lips. "Did she just—

"She rocked it too." Liz fell out laughing.

Sylvia shut her up with a dead-cold stare.

"Ah-hum." Liz rubbed her hand across her mouth. "Not everyone has the willpower you do."

Sylvia huffed and turned to Holly. "Did you and your cook remember I'm a vegan?"

"Yes, and you requested vegetarian meals on your reservation." Holly waved her hand—Vanna White of *Wheel of Fortune* style—across the loaded sideboard. "Nelda made you a vegetable buffet. Black-eyed peas, collard greens, cornbread, and sweet potato pie." All cooked with bacon fat except the sweet potato pie, which Nelda used a slab of butter for. Maybe all of it would stick on her skinny little heinie. "We aim to please."

"I've never eaten any of that." She practically sneered at the food.

"Oh, come on," Liz said as she served herself from the buffet. "Live a little."

Holly grinned all the way to the kitchen.

Nelda met her at the door with a pitcher of iced tea. "Here. You better pour their tea. I don't trust what I might say to Miss Smart Mouth."

"Sylvia deserved it." Holly took the pitcher of tea. "And I loved it."

"She was right though. This thing sure is a killer." Nelda slapped her backside and cackled. "A man killer."

"Nelda," Holly said, faking shock before she pushed through the kitchen door.

Thomas stood with Sylvia and Miss Alice in the corner of the dining room sipping Sazeracs. Liz and Bob sat side by side at the table. Liz was doing the talking as usual, but Bob seemed to hang on her every word. Tru hadn't shown up yet, but she doubted he'd miss a meal. Holly sat the iced-tea pitcher on the sideboard and then fished her phone out of her pocket. No missed calls. Angel should call her any minute.

Holly filled the tea glasses and lingered beside Liz and Bob as the others served their plates at the buffet.

"You know she'll take advantage of you, right?" Liz asked Bob. He barely lifted a shoulder to blow off her question before shoveling in another forkful of chicken and dumplings.

*Who? A girlfriend? Sylvia?*

"She owes you," Liz said, leaning closer to Bob. "Not the other way around."

When he didn't respond, Liz stood and carried her crystal lowball glass to the side table where Holly had placed two shakers filled with Sazeracs in an ice bucket.

Holly sauntered to cocktail central. "Let me help you with that." She grabbed a silver shaker from the ice bucket and gave it a good shake, then poured a Sazerac for Liz. "How's Bob?"

"Maybe I expect too much." She cast a glance laced

with longing and disgust his way. "Ever since Sylvia started paying attention to him, it's like I'm invisible sometimes. I thought we were friends."

Holly put the shaker back in the ice bucket. "Do they have a thing going or something?"

"No. He's beneath her." Liz took a sip of her Sazerac. "He can dream though."

"Can't we all."

Tru strolled into the dining room and headed straight for the buffet. He'd piled his plate so high the cornbread looked like a tombstone on top.

"Want to bet on how long it takes before he ticks someone off?" Liz asked.

Holly gave Liz a wary eye.

A draft drifted into the dining room and the flames on the candelabra bent with the breeze. Then the front door slammed. The chatter in the room stopped.

# CHAPTER ELEVEN

Angel Dupree's flowing black dress seemed to have a motion all its own as the medium practically floated into the silence of the dining room. She paused, then tilted her face upward and lifted her arms. Eyes closed, her long black lashes rested on her porcelain skin as she took a deep breath.

It was as though Holly and everyone else in the room held their breath.

"I sense a presence in this house," Angel said in a voice just above a whisper without opening her eyes.

*She does?* Holly swallowed hard and searched the room for Burl's ghost. Nothing. What was Angel doing? Faking it?

The metallic scrape of a fork broke the silence.

Tru licked the last of his sweet potato pie off his fork, then shoved the blue willow dessert plate away.

Angel's crystal blue eyes fluttered open.

Tru held his hands up as though innocent. "I didn't say a word."

He didn't have to. He'd broken the spell.

"Shh," Miss Alice said. "She can't connect on the spirit world with your distractions."

Holly pushed her chair back from the table. "I believe everyone knows Angel Dupree except Tru. She's the world-renowned medium from New Orleans who conducted the séance we all watched on *Inquiring Minds* last night."

Angel dipped in a bow.

Without giving her a chance to speak, Holly rushed to Angel's side and locked arms with her. "Now if you'll excuse us, I've got to check Angel in. We'll be right back."

"You can do that later," Sylvia said as she stood. "I think she felt something."

"I—"

"Don't you want to get that on camera, Sylvia?" Liz asked.

"Bob, you set up while she's checking in," Sylvia ordered, then shot Tru a faux smile.

Tru pushed his glasses up on his nose. "By all means."

Holly shot a pained look at Liz. She'd wanted a trial run with just Sylvia, not the debunker. "Correct me if I'm wrong, but my option is for one shoot, not days of shooting."

"That's right," Liz said, stammering a bit. "Besides, it'd take a while to get the cameras set up."

Tru grunted. "You mean rig the show, don't you?"

"Absolutely nothing was rigged on that show." If looks could kill, Sylvia's dagger of a stare would have been fatal to Tru. "I can't wait to prove you wrong."

"Why wait?" Tru leaned back in Holly's antique

Queen Anne dining chair. *Mercy. He must not have gotten any raising at all.*

"Because we've already scheduled it for tomorrow," Holly said. She needed time to prepare. To talk to Angel. To make sure Sylvia could do her part.

"Shoot the whole thing tonight." Tru let the chair drop back onto all four legs. "You don't need much time to set up since you're not rigging anything, right?"

"We can't," Holly blurted out. "Sam's not here. I promised him he could document the shoot for the *Gazette,* and I'd never go back on my word." She made a sad face. "Guess we'll have to wait until tomorrow after all."

"And let that young man accuse you of rigging the haunting? I think not." Miss Alice pulled her cell phone out of the suitcase that she called a purse, then punched a few numbers on her phone.

"Sam can't just drop everything and come right now." Holly wasn't ready. This was going to be an epic disaster.

"Never put off until tomorrow what you can do today," Miss Alice said, peering over her glasses at Holly. "Benjamin Franklin. Sam's second-favorite Franklin motto."

The old miser had quoted the first so much it was burned into Holly's brain: *A penny saved is a penny earned.*

Miss Alice covered one ear and pressed the phone to the other ear, then yelled into the phone, "Sam, get out to Holly Grove quick to get the scoop. Holly's making the news again."

"*Again,* Miss Alice?" Holly groaned. "Really?"

Miss Alice took her glasses off and let them dangle by the chain around her neck. "That was explanation enough to get him here if he heard it. The man is close to deaf."

"I'm ready for a séance." Tru rubbed his hands together and zeroed in on Holly. "Are you?"

"I'm ready," Sylvia answered. She nodded at Bob. "Why are you still sitting there? Get set up to shoot ASAP."

"No-o-o!" The word echoed in Holly's head. *If I had a chance to get Sylvia to do a trial run to call up Burl, she wouldn't be so ready to do this.*

"Why not?" Sylvia's high-dollar heels clicked as she crossed the room to Holly then stopped in front of her. She parked her hands on her hips and tossed a nod at Tru. "I want to shut this guy down. Don't you?"

"I-I." Holly grabbed the hem of her blouse. "Need to change clothes. I need more makeup."

"Oh . . ." Sylva's mouth hung open for a moment. She ran a manicured fingertip across her jawline. "Right. I'll need thirty for stage makeup."

Holly motioned toward the table. "And the dining room has to be cleared and . . . and . . ." She sidled up to the medium. "Angel is probably hungry."

"Frankly, I've lost my appetite," Angel said. "Why don't we get this over with? I'm not liking the vibes here. I'd prefer not to stay the night if it's not necessary."

"Y'all, I agreed to Wednesday night. Not now!" *What is this, a conspiracy? Jeez.*

"You'll never be ready because you don't have a ghost." Tru stood in the middle of the room and turned in a circle as he addressed everyone like a politician reading across three teleprompters. "They. Do not. Exist."

"I'm ready to prove it right now!" Sylvia shouted, and it got louder from there until everyone started shouting at once.

"Who wants coffee?" Nelda stood holding a silver coffee service and using her killer backside to hold the kitchen door open. "Never mind who wants coffee. You all need coffee to sober up. It sounds like a brawl in here."

"Y'all fight it out. I'm not having the séance to-night." Holly glared at Sylvia. "I signed a contract. You booked a follow-up shoot. It's tomorrow. End of story."

"Not quite," Tru said.

Holly ignored him and took Angel by the arm. "I've got to talk to you," she whispered as she towed her toward the entrance hall.

"Wait." Tru came from behind them and blocked their path.

So much for a private word with Angel.

The electrified gasolier glowed from the foyer behind him. One of the lightbulbs flickered on and off, then glowed steady. Another loose bulb?

Slipping from Holly's grasp, Angel walked to Tru as though she were in a trance. She traced around his head and stopped with her hands folded prayer style in front of his heart but never touched him

Tru straightened. "What?"

"Nothing," she said the trance broken.

"What's going on?"

Holly jumped at the voice behind her, then whirled around to Miss Alice. She held a china cup filled with black coffee and a spoon balanced on the saucer that didn't so much as clink once. *I swear. That woman needs a bell. Those orthopedic shoes could be used for covert operations.*

"I don't believe we were finished with our conversation," Sylvia said as her heels clicked across the cypress planks.

"No, we haven't." Tru took a few backward steps into the dining room from the entry hall and motioned for everyone to join him.

No one moved.

"Gather round, folks. I've got a story to tell you," he said like a carnival barker. "A ghost story."

*He's up to something. I just know it.* "I thought you didn't believe in ghosts." Holly said.

"Ah, then you'll have to listen to my story to find out." He waved them into the dining room with a flourish. They joined Liz, Bob, and Nelda, who still hung around the table.

Sylvia rolled her eyes and propped her elbows on Bob's chair.

"Get on with it then," Miss Alice said as she placed her coffee cup on the dining room table and parked herself in a chair.

Holly walked to the back of the room and stood near the sideboard and close to the kitchen door for a quick escape.

"Coffee may help," Angel whispered, as she

picked up the silver coffee server and poured dark roast into a china cup. The tiniest tremor rocked Angel's coffee as she picked up her cup and stared at Tru across the room. That seemed odd for someone who practically chanted when she spoke.

Tru took center stage in the dining room. "Let me ask you all a question. Since you spent the night in this *said* haunted house, did you have any paranormal experiences last night?" He stroked his chin. "Today?"

They exchanged glances.

He held his hand to his ear. "Anybody? Anybody? Bueller?"

No one said anything.

"Was your room exceptionally cold?" he asked.

A few heads shook.

"No." He widened his eyes faking shock. "Last night, I went to sleep in a snug warm room. Sometime after midnight, I woke up in a very cold room. You've heard the temperature drops when a ghost is around, right? Do you think a ghost visited my room last night?"

"I sure hope not." Nelda fanned herself.

No doubt he'd gotten cold in the night from the window Holly had left open. She hoped he caught pneumonia too. The sooner the better.

Tru eyed Holly.

Heat crept up her shoulders and wrapped around her neck.

"Did doors that you closed pop open?" Tru asked.

He couldn't possibly know she'd placed the bobby pin in the armoire hinge, could he? She dared not run her fingers under her collar to relieve the heat brewing beneath her sweater.

He raised a finger. "Or did you find a message written in the fog on your mirror after you showered?"

Nelda gasped.

"No?" He paced in a circle. "Just me?"

"Maybe you don't believe me." He shrugged, then adjusted his glasses. "I wouldn't blame you. I'd want proof."

"Guess what?" He pulled out his cell phone. "I've got proof right here."

He stopped in front of Holly. "Look at this message your ghost left for me."

A snapshot of the message she'd written in the mirror covered his phone screen.

"Why don't you read the message since you are so intimate with this ghost." He held his phone in front of Holly. "Maybe you can explain what he meant?"

"Go home or else," Holly read. "Seems pretty clear to me."

"Or else." Tru rubbed his chin. "That's the part that bothers me. It sounds like a threat."

"Sounds like my ghost doesn't like you." Holly folded her arms. "What could a ghost do to you anyway?"

"It's not the dead I worry about." Tru played to the audience. "They're, well, *dead*."

"What are you saying?" Sylvia asked.

"Someone." He held her stare then turned back to Holly. "Or more than one person wants me to believe there was a ghost in my room. And they probably have and will do the same thing to fool the public for their own gain if they have the opportunity to rig . . . oh, I don't know, a TV show."

All eyes turned to Holly.

"Or maybe there was a ghost in your room." Holly lifted her chin and stood a little taller, faking it until she made it. "You'll have to prove there wasn't. That's what debunking is, isn't it?"

"He's messing with your head." Sylvia marched to Holly's side. Right now, Holly would take anyone in her corner, even Sylvia.

"I know this woman couldn't have possibly rigged Burl possessing my body." Sylvia patted her chest. "And he did."

"I didn't rig anything. He probably said all that just to make it look like we staged the haunting." The lies rolled from her tongue, but what else could she say? She couldn't let him debunk her ghost.

Tru grinned. "The sooner we have the séance, the sooner we'll know."

Angel had been staring at Tru the entire time as if in a trance. "Your aura."

Tru pinched his brows together. "What about my aura?"

"Nothing. It's just not what I expected to see."

"Oh, I get it. You want me to pay you to find out how to fix my aura so I can be all happy and sappy, right? No thanks."

"It's not that." Angel placed her hand over her heart and shook her head. "I don't want to be right and maybe I'm not. I've never seen this before."

"I'm not buying." Tru walked over to Holly and took her hand. "You don't have a ghost of a chance."

She tried to pull her hand back, but he held tight and kissed it.

Tru slipped something small into her palm. "See you in thirty or else."

Holly unfurled her fingers and stared at the hairpin.

*Or else. Crapola. He knows. He knows I wrote the message in the mirror, punked his armoire, and left his top windows open to let a ghostly chill into his room. How can I fake a ghost for someone like that? He is so going to debunk the haunting at Holly Grove. He truly doesn't believe there is a remote possibility that ghosts exist. Lordy, I don't wish Burl to come back, but I need a ghost.*

"Okay, everyone." Liz clapped her hands. "Change of plans. We're going to have the séance tonight due to popular demand. Meet back here in thirty minutes."

# CHAPTER TWELVE

"What did Tru put in your hand?" Angel asked as she climbed the stairs with Holly.

"Nothing." Holly balled her hand into a fist. "Let me get you settled in your room. We need to talk." Finally.

"He's a tortured soul."

"He's torturing me right now." Holly glanced back at Angel. "Is that what you saw in his . . . what did you call it?"

"Aura." Angel steadied herself on the rail.

"Are you okay?" Holly reached out to help Angel. She nodded and stepped onto the second-floor landing. "It's best he didn't want to know. I'm not sure I could have told him."

"Why?" Holly asked as she led the way to the Jackson suite. "Was it something bad?"

"I've never seen an aura like that." She looked upward as though she were re-creating the image in her mind. "So thin and broken and yet he's not ill, is he?"

"Not that I know of." Holly pulled a key out of her pocket.

Angel pressed her fist to her heart. "Unless his death won't be from an illness."

The key clattered to the hardwood floor. "Death?"

"It's good he doesn't know." Angel picked up the key and handed it to Holly.

Holly swallowed hard. "When? How?

"It could be soon." She stared into the distance as though searching for an answer. "It could be months, but he won't see his next birthday." She glanced at Holly. "How? I couldn't see."

"But are you sure?"

A faint line marked Angel's forehead. "I'm certain he'll die, eventually. We all do."

*Well that's as creepy as it gets.* "How's my aura?"

"Do you really want to know?"

"On second thought, I'll pass." Holly stopped in front of the Jackson suite and slid the key in the lock, then swung the cypress door open. She stood aside for Angel to walk into the suite first, but she wasn't there.

Angel stood in the exact middle of the hall with her palms in the air and her eyes closed. "The spirit I mentioned last time is getting stronger."

"What?" Holly spun around looking for him. "Burl?"

"He's not here. Your dearly departed has moved on to peace."

It's a good thing Angel said that now rather than at the séance. "How do you know that?"

She offered a slight smile. "We had a connection."

*Lordy, does every woman think she had a connection with him?*

"If he were here, I'd sense his presence," Angel said.

"That's what I wanted to talk to you about, privately." She waved Angel toward the Jackson suite, but Angel missed the motion because her eyes were closed. "Psst."

Angel's eyes fluttered open.

Holly waved her in again.

"Oh, I'm sorry." She glided into the room, which was weird. How can a woman never bounce at all when she walks? "I got carried away."

Holly closed the door. "I didn't tell anyone my ghost moved on," she drew quotation marks in the air, "to peace." Except Nelda and Jake, but Angel didn't need to know that. "When Sylvia called to do the follow-up show, I definitely couldn't tell her unless I wanted that story on TV, and I didn't. Holly Grove B&B was dying on the vine until it became haunted and then famous thanks to YouTube, *Inquiring Minds*, and you." Holly paced. "Face it, my B&B in the middle of nowhere would have never been this successful without Burl's haunting. He made Holly Grove so famous, I've got a debunker downstairs. He wants to ruin Holly Grove just because my real ghost moved on."

"And you want me to save you by pretending to connect with Burl?"

Holly cringed. "And yourself. This debunker will ruin your reputation, too. At least, say Burl is unavailable right now. I told Sylvia he's not speaking to me because we're fighting, which would have been true if he hadn't passed on, only it would be *me* not speaking to *him*."

"I know mediums are known as scam artists, but I'm not one. If I exploit this gift for ill, the spirits will not be happy with me. I know too many spirits and not all are benevolent."

"But you realize he's trying to debunk your ability too, right?"

"All I can do is speak the truth for the spirits. And they will protect me."

*I'm so screwed. Unless I have a spirit to protect me.* "What about that presence you mentioned earlier? Could you summon that one?"

Angel sighed. "I don't know. It's very weak. A forgotten soul, but I felt it as soon as I walked into Holly Grove."

"Is this a good ghost or a bad ghost?"

"I don't know, why?"

"If you can conjure up the right kind of ghost, I have a vacancy right now." Holly gave a pleading grin.

"I don't have time for games right now, Holly. I must think." And with that Angel swept into her room and closed the door behind her.


"You're gonna ruin those candles," Nelda said as Holly used a baster to add a few drops of water to the twelve votive candles she'd placed on the dining room table in front of each chair.

"Insurance." And Holly needed all she could get. "Just make sure no one comes through those doors."

Nelda saluted Holly and stood like a sentry in

front of the closed ten-foot-tall pocket doors to the entrance hall.

Holly climbed a wobbly wooden ladder to close off the heating vents. From the top of the ladder she surveyed the room. What else could she do?

"Five minutes until I gotta let 'em in," Nelda said.

The rumble of thunder in the distance promised added ambience. For once, luck had sided with Holly.

She rocked with the sway of the ladder as she backed down it. If she fell, maybe they'd cancel the show. She chuckled to herself. Nope. She could hear Sam now with one of his quotes. *The show must go on.* She folded the ladder and held it in the middle. "This is really a two-man job."

"You've been needing a man for lots of things lately, but you never believe me when I tell you that *you need* a man."

"Remind me to get a lightweight ladder."

"Or a heavyweight man, all muscle like your Jake." Nelda's bright smile glowed as a sliver of moonlight from a gap in the heavy curtains drifted across her face in the dimly lit room.

*My Jake.* "Really, Nelda?" Holly asked as she hauled the ladder out through the side door to the kitchen."

"Just helpin' ya think." Nelda rocked back on her heels.

Holly ignored that and carried the ladder outside, and propped it against the house where it'd been forever, which was probably why it was wobbly. By the time she got back to the dining room, Nelda had opened the door but wouldn't let anyone come in.

For once, she was doing exactly what Holly had told her to do and without any grumbling.

"As soon as everyone gets down here we'll take our seats," Holly said. *And pray somehow it all works out and I get to keep my ghost that's gone.*

"This low-pressure front has my bunion killing me," Miss Alice said as she walked right by Holly and Nelda. "I'm taking early senior citizen seating."

"Speak for yourself." Sam flashed a yellowed old-school press pass. "I'm just going to stand in the back with my camera."

"Wait." Holly took the camera from around his neck. "Remember, no flash photos during the séance."

He pulled a pocket pad and pen from under his jacket. "Then I'll take notes."

She snatched that too. "You're supposed to write a local color story about the experience. You can't experience the séance while you're taking notes."

Sam tapped the wiry gray hair at his temples. "Steel trap, darlin'."

Miss Alice took her place in the middle chair on the window side of the dining room and Sam sat beside her.

Tru stood against the sideboard and cleaned his glasses with a black handkerchief. He wore a sports coat, T-shirt, jeans, and a felt fedora, all black, which made his pale skin stand out. Then again, black was a good color for him compared to his usual dingy du jour.

The thunder came in rolls that seemed to match the churning in Holly's stomach. Everything she cared about could be gone after tonight. She'd be satisfied with a draw. This was so unfair. She'd had a ghost. It wasn't her fault that he'd moved on. She sighed. Actually, it was, in a way. A good way.

Bob and Liz came in red cheeked from the chilly wind. Bob carried canvas bags with the *Inquiring Minds* logo stamped on their sides. They both were in the same clothes they'd had on at dinner but wore suspiciously happy smiles.

"Where have y'all been?" Holly asked.

"Getting some extra equipment out of the van," Liz said, still grinning.

Bob set up behind the camera, but there wasn't a second camera for Liz like there was last time. Hmm. Was that intentional? Could they do as many cool effects with just one camera? Holly walked over to Liz. "Where's the second camera?"

"Damaged." Bob finally spoke.

"Flying is rough on our equipment. Don't worry. We'll get it all." Liz patted Bob's arm. "He's the best in the biz."

"Liz!" Sylvia's voice came from the top of the stairs.

Liz rolled her eyes. "She's helpless."

"Liz!" Sylvia called again as her buff-colored heels clicked with every step down the staircase. She wore an off-the-shoulder black cocktail dress with translucent sequins. Overdressed much?

"I'm coming." Liz shook her head and met Sylvia at the foot of the stairs.

Sylvia pointed to her back. "I need help with my lapel mic and my zipper. Watch out for the sequins."

Thomas jogged down the stairs. He wore a navy cable-knit sweater over a white oxford cloth shirt and wool dress slacks. It seemed everyone had dressed for their fifteen minutes of fame except Bob, and Liz. Of course, they weren't going to be on camera.

"I'm 'bout ready to go," Nelda said. She had Rhett in her arms. "You gonna have to hold him. That storm comin' has him jumpin' at his own shadow."

When Holly took him she could feel his little body shake. *Poor Rhett.* "I don't know what I'm going to do with you."

"It's the static electricity," Miss Alice said. She dug in her purse and pulled out a tissue. "Give him to me."

Holly put Rhett on Miss Alice's lap. A floral scent drifted up from the tissue. Holly recognized that scent from the laundry room. Either Miss Alice's eyesight or her mind was going bad. "Miss Alice, I think you mistook fabric softener sheets for tissues."

"Most certainly not. I can well tell the difference, and I haven't lost my mind yet." Miss Alice rubbed the scented sheet across Rhett's back. "If you rub a dog's fur with a fabric softener sheet, it will cut the static and calm their nerves."

"Worth a try." Nelda shook her head. "I ought not ask, but why do you keep fabric softener in your purse? You don't even have a dog."

"It's versatile and I like to be prepared," Miss Alice said. "I can dust my dash with it. It makes my purse smell good. And if my dress creeps up over my knees because of static electricity, I can rub it over my dress to eliminate the problem."

*What doesn't that woman have in that wonder purse?*

"Humph," Nelda said. "I'm gonna get me a sheet on the way out tonight."

"Aren't you going to join us for the séance?" Miss Alice asked.

"Y'all call the dead all you want. I'm lettin' them lie where they're buried," Nelda said, then poked Holly with her elbow. "She can't pay me enough to stay up in here for that. Soon as I get my kitchen clean, I'm a gone pecan."

"Where is the medium?" Sylvia asked from the doorway.

"The last time I saw her she was putting her suitcase in a car," Tru said from his perch against the sideboard.

Sylvia jerked to attention. "What?"

Liz jumped to her feet as though she'd been caught off guard. "I'll see if she's in her room."

Something had jingled when it fell off her lap and hit the floor. Sam leaned over and picked up whatever it was.

Could Angel have been *thinking* about bailing out without telling anyone? If she did, the séance was off. Holly held her lips tight to keep her smile from showing. Inside she was doing fist pumps. That would be the best luck ever! If it happened.

Holly slipped out the door and through the kitchen to see if Angel's car was still parked with the others.

"Where you racin' to?" Nelda said, up to her elbows in suds as Holly flew though the kitchen to the back porch.

The wind caught the screen door and it flapped against the house. *Please be gone. Please be gone.*

Holly rounded the corner of the house and counted the cars. Sam's truck, Miss Alice's old

Fleetwood, the van for Liz and Bob, Sylvia's red rental, Nelda's Toyota, and her Tahoe. Six. That's it. She's gone! Holly fist pumped. A reprieve.

Holly turned around to go back in and tell everyone the séance was canceled when headlights flashed against the house.

# CHAPTER THIRTEEN

Holly could only hope Angel was gone for good. No medium, no séance, no debunked ghost.

But then, the headlights of the car blinded Holly, shining right in her face. She tented a hand over her eyes to ease the glare from the light.

A car door slammed.

Footsteps crunched over gravel.

Misty rain blew across Holly's face.

"Angel?" Holly called.

If it was Angel, wouldn't she answer? An unease inched up her spine.

"Hello?" Holly's voice kicked up an octave.

More footsteps and then a dark figure holding an umbrella backlit by the car lights came into focus.

Holly took a few backward steps. "Who's there?"

The figure kept advancing at a steady pace.

Holly backed around the corner of the house and ran for the back porch, to the light. She yanked the screen door open, then latched it behind her.

The contrast of the yellow light on the porch made everything a foot past the screen pitch black. Her heart beat so fast it became one big continuous thud as she backed toward the door, keeping her eyes on the screen door. *Why don't they answer?*

The scuff of footsteps came from beyond the light.

She wrapped her hand around the doorknob behind her. All she had to do was open the door and she'd be safe. *From what? Mercy. Why don't they answer?*

"Can I help you?"

"You already have," Angel's voice came from the shadows before she pulled on the latched screen door. At the edge of the yellow light, Angel's pale face was all Holly could see. Her long black dress faded into the dark.

"You scared the bejesus out of me." Holly blew out a sigh then crossed the porch to unlatch the screen door.

When Angel stepped onto the porch, a faint static beat came with her. Heavy metal? She swiped her finger across her cell phone then wrapped the black earbuds around her phone.

*That explains why she didn't answer me.* "Where were you?"

"Cemetery." Angel stuffed her phone in her black purse.

"At night?" Holly shivered.

"Why not? They're just as dead, night or day."

"Seriously, why did you go to a cemetery?"

"I didn't plan on it." She sighed. "I planned on driving straight to New Orleans tonight."

"Why didn't you? If this thing goes bad for me, it'll be just as bad for your reputation."

"Sylvia told me you're worried Burl wouldn't show up. She offered me twice my fee to fake the haunting."

Holly widened her eyes. "The spirits didn't like that, did they?"

"She offered much more. When I refused, she fired me. She said she'd hire an actress if she had to, but there would be a Ghost in the Grove. Then she told me if I left immediately without speaking to anyone, she'd pay my regular fee and I could make any excuse I wanted to later."

"You could have had your fee and just gone home." Holly threw her hands in the air. "Why didn't you? They would have canceled. There are only a few days left on that option I signed."

"At the end of your driveway, a green orb flashed in front of me. That's sometimes how a spirit manifests itself." Angel looked into the distance as she often did. "That's not unusual."

"I've never seen it, and I've lived here all my life."

"Maybe you didn't notice or know what to look for. I come across lost spirits all the time. They're just passing through, but then it flashed to the right of me in the opposite of the direction I needed to go. I put my left blinker on and it flashed in front of me again and jumped to the right."

Holly shook her head. "And you turned right and went to a cemetery because a green light bobbed that way?"

Angel nodded. "I've had spirits follow me home if I ignored them."

"It led me a mile or so down the road to a beautiful old cemetery surrounded by a wrought-iron fence and behind a locked gate. In the beams of my headlights, I could see about twenty or so tombs, tilted and cracked. The grounds overgrown. No new tombs."

"No new tombs because no one has been buried there since my family sold it before my mother or even my grandmother was born. It's the old Holly Grove family cemetery. I tried to get the owner to let me take the people who stay here to visit the tombs, but he wanted to charge admission, which sounded kind of crass, so that didn't happen."

"Probably for the best. I sense a restlessness. Disturbance. The orb floated over the tombs. I sensed the spirit was trying to show me something important, but then the orb disappeared. I thought the spirit was just passing through until it signaled me to turn in at Holly Grove."

"Are you saying a spirit wouldn't let you leave?"

"Not alone."


Nelda opened the back door and stuck her head out. "Folks is lookin' for y'all."

Thomas stood behind Nelda with a distressed look on his face. Probably worried about his investment. "Is everything okay?"

Holly nodded. Though it wasn't okay. She had no idea how this séance would go. Potential unknown ghost. Sylvia testing her acting chops? A few well-placed traps to suggest a bit of haunting. Surely some of it would work. Maybe.

Angel took a deep breath and squared her shoulders. "The spirits are with me."

"I just hope they stay with you, especially if they're troubled," Holly said as she walked toward the door.

"I'm gonna pretend I didn't hear that." Nelda stepped onto the porch and hefted her purse over her shoulder. "I'm goin' home to my big fat recliner and my blessed house, where the only spirit is the Holy Ghost."

Holly and Angel slipped in the back of the darkened dining room unnoticed while Sylvia had the command of the guests who had congregated in the entrance hall.

"I can't believe that woman would just leave without a word. As much as I want to protect my good reputation, I'm afraid we're going to have to cancel this shoot," Sylvia said. "Unfortunately, my option expires in just a few days. We can't possibly reschedule."

Angel flipped the lights on, then off.

"Angel," Sylvia said with genuine shock in her voice. "We thought you'd abandoned us."

Without saying a word, Angel took her seat at the head of the table as Holly lit the votive candles.

Tru ambled into the dining room first. "Cold feet?"

"Not at all," Holly said. "A spirit called to her and she had to answer."

"Yeah, right." He settled into a side chair next to Angel.

Bob and Liz took their places in the corners of the room.

Sam checked his watch. "It's going to be midnight before we get this thing done."

"What's the matter?" Miss Alice asked. "Past your bedtime?"

"I did a little research, and midnight is often the time séances are held," Thomas said, sliding into a chair.

The familiar sound of the screen door slamming on the porch registered with Holly. Everyone who was supposed to be there sat at the table. Who was on her back porch? The flutter in her chest raised hope Jake had finally made it. A few more whacks against the screen door doused that hope. The wind must have caught the screen door. Nice touch for a séance if the wind keeps up.

"You better go latch that screen," Miss Alice said. "All that flapping will loosen the hinges."

*Well, horse hockey. That woman could hear a gnat break wind forty feet away.*

"You wouldn't want any false bumps in the night, or would you?" Tru smirked at Holly.

She stood and pulled her shoulders back, then glared at Tru. "Nelda just left. She couldn't possibly latch the screen from outside."

Holly spun on her heel and marched across the antique rug in the dining room. *Tru is trying to poison everyone's mind to believe I'm rigging the séance and I had nothing to do with the screen door. Largely, because I didn't think of it. Dang it.* When she charged through the kitchen door, Nelda jumped.

"Jumping Jehoshaphat!" She stood with her hand covering her heart, her hair blown wild, and a box of salt in her other hand. "Don't sneak up on me like that with a séance goin' on and all."

"I thought you went home." Holly pointed to Nelda's hair. "And what happened to . . ."

"My car quit right after I got out of the parkin' lot smack in the middle of the driveway at the front door." Nelda smoothed her hair. "The wind 'bout blew my hair off my head while I was trying to jiggle the cables on my battery. I poured a fully leaded Coke on it too."

"Are you going to try salt on the battery now?" Holly asked.

Nelda looked at the salt like she'd forgotten she held it. "Nah. I called one of my nephews to come jump-start the car."

"You should have come and gotten me."

Nelda grunted. "For what? I never known you to know much about a car 'cept where to put the gas."

"True." And sometimes she'd run her truck on fumes before she noticed the gauge.

"Besides," Nelda leveled an eye at Holly. "I didn't want to bust up in there and see somethin' I can't unsee."

"I'm so sorry that happened to you on a nasty night like tonight." Holly took Nelda by the arm. "You go up to my room to dry off and wait for your nephew."

"It ain't the weather that's bothering me tonight." Nelda waved her off and ambled toward the back door. "It's the ghost y'all might call up. Ain't no way, I'm stayin' in this house for that."

Holly followed her to the door. "You'd rather be outside alone?"

"I got protection." Nelda shook the box of salt. "I'm shakin' this 'round my car to protect me from any ghosts while I wait."

Holly sighed. Salt hadn't done a thing to keep Burl away, but she hadn't had the heart to tell Nelda that back then. "Suit yourself."

With a wave over her shoulder, Nelda stepped out on the porch and out the screen door.

Holly latched the screen behind her and took a deep breath before turning around to go back to the séance. She only hoped it had as much of a chance of conjuring up a ghost as Nelda thought it did or at least Sylvia could give a convincing performance.

"Are you okay?" Thomas asked, poking his head into the kitchen. A crease folded between Thomas's gray brows.

*Thoughtful or impatient? Hard to tell.* "I'm fine." Holly looked back over her shoulder. "Nelda had some car trouble."

"Anything I can do?" he asked.

"She has help coming." Holly crossed the kitchen to him. "We better get back in there."

Thomas trailed Holly back to the dining room and pulled her chair out for her, next to Tru and then sat across from her.

"Okay, now that everyone is here," Liz said. "A few ground rules."

Holly cast a glance at Sylvia.

She gave a barely perceptible nod.

"First, we'll have an intro," Liz said. "I've given you instructions about what to do at a séance." Liz zeroed in on Tru. "You are to stand in the back as an observer. We'll interview you after the séance for your rebuttal. Understood?"

"What?" He opened his mouth wide in fake shock. "I can't be in the circle, chanting and calling to the dead?"

"Your energy would not be conducive to a good connection with the spirit world," Angel said in a sedate tone.

Tru got up and leaned against the sideboard and crossed his arms.

"Take your position to make your entrance," Liz said to Sylvia.

She stepped out of sight into the entrance hall.

"In five, four, three, two." Bob counted down from behind the camera.

Sylvia paused for effect at the double-door opening. She stared right into the camera with her blue-tinted contacts. "Tonight, *Inquiring Minds* takes you back to 'The Ghost in the Grove,' where we met the ghost of B&B owner Holly Davis's husband, Burl Davis. Though the evidence was overwhelming, one voice challenged the story."

Bob aimed the camera at Tru.

"And," Sylvia continued her pitch-perfect monologue, "we accepted that challenge by Truman Jeremiah Stalwort, III."

*What a mouthful. No wonder he goes by Tru.*

Angel lifted her gaze above, then closed her eyes. "May the spirits be with us."

*Please make it so. One spirit. Any spirit. Or just a make-believe spirit. Don't let this be the end of Holly Grove.*

# CHAPTER FOURTEEN

Holly's throat tightened as Sylvia closed the pocket doors. The dining room fell to darkness except for the votive candles on the table and a slice of light peeking through the drapes from the gas lanterns on the porch.

It all came down to this night. Holly took shallow breaths to calm herself. She couldn't do anything else to save her reputation. Would Angel declare the house clear of spirits? Could Sylvia pull off a hoax? Should Holly just confess now and save herself the humiliation of being exposed as a fraud? Soon the séance would begin and the fate of Holly Grove would be sealed, for good or bad.

As Holly's eyes adjusted to the dark, the faces of everyone around the table came into view. Deep in the corner, a red dot glowed from Bob's video camera. She guessed Liz was nearby. All she could see of Tru was a shadow propped against her walnut sideboard.

Angel sat—eyes closed—as though deep in meditation at one end of the table. Sylvia sat at the other end staring down her opponent as though she were in a boxing match.

"If we are to welcome spirits, we must open our minds and hearts to their souls, for that is all they have to give." Angel said in a quiet but serious voice. She lifted her hands, palms up. "Join hands so that our spirits may work as one to summon the dead."

Thomas's cool hand took Holly's and she put her hand in Angel's warm hand. Miss Alice sat across from Holly and next to Sam. Sylvia sat at the other end of the table, completing the circle.

During the last séance, Holly had felt a definite sensation when they all joined hands. This time? Nada. Not good.

"Clear your mind of everything in the outside world," Angel said in a rhythmic voice. "It doesn't exist in this world. Let everything go and be present here as one."

Still nothing, although Thomas's hand did feel quite soft for a guy who considers carpentry therapy. *Maybe he wears gloves.*

"Please still your mind. I sense some of you are elsewhere." Angel closed her eyes and tilted her face upward. "We are one in seeking the spirits of this room. We are one." She rocked back and forth. "We are one. We are one. We are one."

Everyone chanted with her. "We are one . . ." But Sylvia's voice was the clearest and the loudest. She rocked back and forth in unison with Angel.

Sylvia couldn't want even a whiff of a ghost to show up more than Holly did.

"Close your eyes. Become one. We are one . . ."

Holly found herself rocking back and forth as

they chanted. A chill settled over her shoulders, right on time. The doors had been closed to the heating in the rest of the house for about fifteen or twenty minutes. She cracked an eye open to check out Tru. He wasn't there.

"We are one. We are one." The chant continued, minus one.

Holly squinted as she searched outside of their circle for Tru. The draft seemed to worsen around the back of her neck. Maybe something was happening? She glanced over her shoulder.

Tru stood, arms folded, close enough to breathe down her neck. The little troll tipped his fedora. The ire rushing through her veins cut through her prearranged chill.

*Concentrate, Holly.* "We are one . . ."

Angel stopped chanting. Her chest lifted and fell with each breath. "I sense a presence among us."

Thomas squeezed her hand.

Did he feel something?

Miss Alice craned her neck as she cased her surroundings, then turned to Angel and asked. "Do you see something?"

If Angel did, she saw it in her mind because she never opened her eyes. "I feel it."

"I don't feel a thing." Miss Alice leaned back in her chair.

"Don't break the connection," Angel whispered.

Holly studied her. Was she faking it? Which would be a good thing as far as Holly was concerned, but Angel had said the spirits she knew wouldn't allow that. Holly closed her eyes and tried to concentrate on probably the most boring séance ever. Her "Ghost in the Grove" was so going to get debunked.

Angel moaned. "Oh, spirit world. I am your servant. Please make yourself known."

*Yes please. If you're out there just pop in a minute. I'd be eternally grateful for a Girl Friday ghost or Guy Friday. A temp. Just for now.*

The candle in front of Sam sputtered out. "Did y'all see that?"

The water and heat had made just enough steam to snuff the candle. Holly held her lips together to hide her smile. *Science is a wonderful thing.*

Angel's eyes popped open. She stared straight ahead, above Sylvia's head. Angel's eyes widened and her breath came in shallow bursts. "I don't understand. Speak to me."

"Is he here?" Sylvia scooted to the edge of her chair. "Where?"

"The spirit is very weak. It cannot speak." Angel continued to focus on the space above Sylvia's head. "I sense desperate loneliness."

"That's right," Sylvia nodded. "Burl and Holly aren't speaking. I'm sure he does feel lonely since no one else can hear him."

She turned to Holly. "Speak to your husband."

"My ex. Well, nearly ex." *He just didn't live long enough to sign the papers.* Holly shifted in her chair. "Burl, I know we haven't spoken in a while, but please don't take your anger out on these good people who have come to see you."

That was just weird. If Burl were here, she'd see him. He'd never been shy about haunting her.

She'd feel him. If there's a spirit lurking about, it's not Burl.

"The spirit is weak . . ." Angel closed her eyes again. "Forgotten."

"I haven't forgotten you, Burl." Sylvia tilted her head upward and closed her eyes, mimicking Angel. "My body is strong. Use me to communicate."

Another votive candle sputtered out in front of Thomas. He gave Holly a side-eye and squeezed her hand harder.

Angel's mouth parted slightly and her eyes fluttered open. She fixed on something above Sylvia's head again.

A pinpoint green light flashed above Sylvia's head. Was that flash the orb Angel had followed earlier?

A collective gasp came from the table as they stared at where the dot had been.

Sylvia looked behind herself. "Was he here?"

Holly sat up straighter in her seat and willed the light to reappear.

"Just the remains of its aura." Angel shook her head. "The spirit is fading."

"He can't go." Sylvia's body went rigid. "Burl wants to use my body."

*Lordy.* That did sound like Burl, but it couldn't be.

Sylvia grabbed her throat. "He says he's lost his voice from not speaking for so long and will need to use mine."

"But—

"I can't stop him," Sylvia said, cutting off Angel. She flailed about and swayed.

*Could it be?* Holly exchanged glances with Angel, who gave a barely perceivable head shake.

Sylvia kicked her feet up on the table and splayed her arms over the chair back like a man. "My name is Burl Davis. I'm tired. I'm mad. I'm stuck here with the woman who owns this place." Sylvia nodded toward Holly.

*Way to make me look like a real witchy woman, Sylvia. Thanks a lot.*

"I'm only speaking through Sylvia because I have a connection with her from the last time she visited." Sylvia pointed to Holly. "She says we're divorced, but I never signed any papers, so I'm not speaking to her or anyone else until she stops calling me her ex."

*That does sound like Burl. Dang. Sylvia has his character down like she knew him.* There's a reason she's not a Hollywood star, but her acting was a better than Holly had expected. Maybe with some creative editing it will fool the viewers.

Sylvia pointed her finger at Holly. "Say it."

"Huh? Me?" Holly pressed her hand over her heart. She was no actress, but she'd better play along. "You're actually speaking to me now? Does that mean you'll start showing up to haunt once in a while?"

Sylvia folded her arms. "Say you're my widow?"

"Technically, I guess I am."

"That's all I wanted to hear." Sylvia's legs fell from their perch on the table and she slumped in her chair.

No one said anything. Holly checked their faces and no one made eye contact. They didn't buy it.

Angel folded her hands as though in prayer and just stared at Sylvia.

And Sylvia just lay there waiting for applause like she'd nailed a death scene in a play or something. Finally, she barely opened one eye.

"You should consider developing your talent as a medium," Angel said as she stood. "I have a long drive back."

Sam snored and Miss Alice elbowed him.

Startled, he opened his old eyes wide. "What?" He jerked his head from side to side. "What'd I miss?"

"All of it." Miss Alice stood and helped Sam up. "Come on. You need coffee, so you can drive home without killing yourself or anyone else."

Just as they exited the room, the chandelier blasted the room in bright light. Tru stood beside the light switch. He adjusted his glasses. "Not quite yet."

Tru strutted around the dining room table. "What a performance, don't you agree?"

He didn't wait for an answer. "I'll bet by the time the footage goes through the art of editing and special effects it will prove beyond a shadow of a doubt that a ghost was in our midst to anyone who wasn't here."

"I beg your pardon," Sylvia said. "Are you doubting that the Ghost in the Grove spoke through me?"

"I'm sure it did, since the proprietor of this establishment and you hatched him up for your own gain in the first place."

Holly shook her head. "That's not true. I never wanted Burl to come back. Of course, I didn't wish him dead, but—believe me—I never wanted him back. I swear on a stack of bibles."

Tru turned in a circle. "Burl? Burl? Is that true?" He cupped his hand to his ear. "Poor man, he can't defend himself, can he? Convenient, huh?"

"He's not here now," Holly said. "Look, all I know is he came back. Watch the YouTube video, talk to others who encountered him. He was here."

Tru leaned on the back of Holly's chair. "But he's not here now if he ever was."

Sylvia stood and pounded the table. "Are you calling me a liar?"

"More of an opportunist." He singled out Angel. "And she does it full time, or are you a barista by day?"

"You know nothing about me or my gifts," Angel said. "You would be wise not to challenge the spirits. They are more powerful than you know."

"*Right.*" He loaded the word with sarcasm. "I read about violence in the streets perpetrated by spirits all the time."

"This is supposed to be an interview," Sylvia said. "And this is my show. So, if you'll have a seat, I have questions for you."

*Go get 'em, Sylvia.*

"I like to think of it as more of a conversation the world needs to hear." Tru didn't sit down. "Do you know how much money is extracted from clueless people by charlatans like that medium, greedy owners of tourist traps, paranormal TV shows—like yours—magazines, and on and on? It's a multimillion-dollar business that preys on the one thing that everyone wants to believe: Death is not the end." He raised a finger in the air. "But it's a cruel lie."

"You'll soon find out," Angel said under her breath.

Tru whirled around to her. "Yeah, right."

"We all die," Angel said. "Some sooner than others. As my gift to you, I tell you that you must change your ways or your life will be short."

Tru chuckled and shook his head. "Did the spirits tell you that?"

"No. Your aura." She made the motion of a halo around her head.

"Something only you, the very gifted, can see, no doubt. Come on." He jabbed his hands in the air. "You can do better than that."

"That green glow we all saw back there earlier." Angel gave a nod to above where Sylvia had been sitting. "That was the remaining aura of someone who has passed on but is still lingering among us."

Tru threw his head back. "Ha! That's someone in here with a laser pointer."

"Think what you want." Angle kept a level tone. "I speak truth for the spirits."

Tru ambled to behind Angel's chair. He rested both hands on the back of her chair and leaned down beside her, then looked into the camera. "You colluded with your accomplices to rig a ghosting for TV, didn't you?"

"There is no laser pointer." Sylvia said.

"Oh, it's here," he said dryly as he straightened and eyed Holly. "It was a good effort. Just like lowering the temperature in here."

*Busted.* Heat rushed her cheeks. "I swear, I didn't

lower the temperature in here." Which was true. She just kept the heated air from getting in.

"It's a fact that when a spirit is present it chills the air around it," Angel said.

"Yeah, right." He rolled his eyes. "We all know when a ghost is present the temperature drops because people like you tell us so. But someone closed the vents and opened the windows in my room just last night. Of course, with a little time it gets cold. If I were gullible, I may have thought the chill proved the ghost rumor about Holly Grove true. But I'm not gullible."

"The windows are all closed. Check for yourself." Holly glanced at the windows. "For all we know, you closed the vents to make us look bad," she said to take the heat off herself.

"That's right." Sylvia stood. "You've made all these accusations with no proof."

Rain pelted down on the windows and flashes of lightning lit up around the edges of the closed drapes. "And why does it have to be dark or midnight to have a séance?" Tru asked. "Would a ghost care if it was night or day? All the haunting goes on at night, right?"

"Not necessarily," Holly said. "Burl showed up night and day."

"So you say, but who else actually saw him?"

He picked up a spent candle. "Funny how they all blew out one by one while the medium was conjuring up fake ghosts. Could these be trick candles or somehow rigged to go out?"

Holly slid a little lower in her chair.

"The darker the better, right?" He continued. "To be manipulated by a medium who tells you what to see in the dark." He tapped his temple. "The power of suggestion, right?"

"If it was light enough to shoot video in here, it was light enough for us to see what was going on," Sylvia said. "You're reaching."

"It's an easy reach." He shrugged. "The most obvious con was your performance."

Sylvia lifted her plucked brows. "Excuse me?"

"Wait." Tru looked skyward. Then lifted his arms. "A spirit wants to communicate through me. He's telling me something important. He's telling me." He paused for effect. "This whole séance, ghost thing is a big crock of steaming hot—"

"You can't say that on TV," Sylvia said. "And you can't possibly understand what happened to me when Burl entered my body. I would have never believed it if I hadn't seen it on video."

"You won't believe it when you see this footage." Tru smirked then looked into the camera. "Challenge over. 'The Ghost in the Grove' debunked." He turned to Sylvia. "You lose!"

"I never lose." Sylvia glanced at her cameraman and made a slicing motion at her neck.

"Cut." Bob gave a thumbs-up. The red recording light switched off.

"Let's get one thing straight," Sylvia said. "That will be cut from the interview. You will not attack my character on my show. The video will speak for itself."

Thunder rolled as the rain picked up.

"Yeah." Tru jabbed his hands in the air and rolled his eyes. "After a Photoshop-palooza you can make anything look believable."

"Every professional show is edited to frame the story we want to tell." Sylvia's lips curled in a triumphant grin.

"Even if it's a lie?" Tru drilled Sylvia with a stare.

"*Lie* is a rather harsh word, don't you think?" Sylvia slithered into her chair at the dining room table.

"And you're going to edit me?" He pointed his finger at Sylvia. "That's bull!"

"You signed a contract." Sylvia folded her hands in front of her on the dining table as if closing the conversation. "My show. My terms."

Tru sighed and looked down at the floor, then back at Sylvia. "I never had a chance of winning, did I?"

"Of course not. I told you the ghost was real and now I've proved it to the world on video." She folded her arms and cocked her head sideways. "Again."

"Did anyone here see a ghost? Hear one?" Tru asked.

No one answered.

"I didn't think so." Tru pushed his glasses up on his nose. "So, we all agree there is no Ghost in the Grove, right?"

Silence.

Holly almost felt sorry for him. The séance had been awful. By all rights, he should win, but . . .

"I have the raw facts—no spin—that totally debunk your ghost, right here." He tapped the side of his glasses. "I've recorded every conversation since I've been here, including all of tonight with these glasses."

He pointed to Sylvia and her crew, and then Holly. "You are all going down."

# Chapter Fifteen

"His glasses recorded everything?" Holly asked Thomas. Surely a guy who invests in tech would know. "Is that possible?"

"Possible?" Thomas shrugged. "The technology has been around a long time, but more recently for the public."

He seemed nonplussed.

"Bought them online for less than two hundred bucks." Tru adjusted his glasses. "Worth every penny to debunk this whole fiasco."

"It's not legal to record someone without their permission," Liz said. "I demand that you turn them over right now."

Thomas cleared his throat. "I believe we all gave permission to be recorded for the show."

"That's right." Tru made his way to the corner of the room where Liz and Bob stood. "I tell you what. I'll make a deal with you."

Sylvia marched over and stood by Liz and Bob. "What kind of deal?"

Tru pointed to the camera. "You give me the raw

footage and I'll just show that. *Inquiring Minds* gets their show. I get the truth. We all win."

Sylvia gave a nod to Bob and he pressed a few buttons, then looked back at Tru. "Looks like the video is corrupt, man."

"Right." Tru lunged for the camera. A clap of thunder shook the house and the lights went out.

"Back off, man," a male voice said. Holly guessed it was Bob.

Then scuffling sounds, grunts, followed by a crash in the dark and chair backs hitting the floor. The lights flickered back on for a minute. Bob had his tattooed forearm pressed against Tru's neck.

Tru's legs flailed as he clawed against Bob's arm.

"Stop!" Holly screamed. "You're going to kill him."

"If I wanted him dead, he'd be dead," Bob said. "Nobody gets in my face like that."

Tru's eyes bulged. "Okay. Okay. I'm sorry. Get off me."

Bob yanked Tru up by his collar then slammed him onto the table before backing away with his hands in the air.

*Whoa. I've always heard to watch out for the quiet ones.* Holly helped Tru up. "Are you okay?"

"Yeah. Not that you or anyone else here would care." He lifted his shirt and it seemed to stick to him. "Other than candle wax melted to my clothes." He looked at Sylvia. "You should keep that guy on a leash."

Tru felt his face. "My glasses. Where are my glasses?" His mouth hung open as he frantically looked at the table and the floor and then accusingly at Bob.

"I don't have your glasses, and you don't want any more of this," Bob said, taking a step forward.

Tru backed up and drilled Holly with a stare. "You were right there."

"I don't have them." Holly held her hands up. "I swear."

"Over here." Thomas bent over and picked up the glasses.

Tru rushed to Thomas and snatched the glasses from his hands. After turning them in every direction, he put them back on his face and slid his fingers across the frame. He let out a breath. "I know you guys will be glad to know they still work and you still lost." He turned and started walking out of the room.

*Mercy. My business. My home. My reputation. All shot to hell. I really did have a ghost, but who'll believe me now?*

"You really don't understand. This is all a huge mistake. I can explain," Holly said.

"No." Tru shook his head. "You don't understand. It's over." He turned and started walking out of the dining room with enough footage to ruin Sylvia. Angel. And Holly.

"Wait," Holly called.

He didn't.

"You realize this is all your fault," Sylvia said to Holly.

"*Mine?*" Holly pointed to her chest. "I told you my ghost was MIA."

"And you," Sylvia turned her wrath on Angel. "You should have taken my advice. If he releases that video, you'll never work again."

"*You* may never work again," Angel said in an unusually calm voice. "The spirits are with me."

Sylvia made a beeline for the stairs. "Tru, I want to buy that video."

"You don't get it," he said without slowing down. "I don't do this for the money. I do it for the truth, something you can't afford to buy."

"Everyone needs to calm down," Thomas said. "Videos taken with glasses like his are often very poor quality. He probably doesn't have anything."

"But what if he does?" Holly's voice cracked.


After everyone stormed off to their rooms, Holly walked past the five generations of women who had managed to hold on to Holly Grove. It would all end with her. Her throat tightened around sobs as she climbed the stairs. If her B&B failed, she couldn't afford to keep it.

They'd always found a way to keep Holly Grove through the worst of times. Wars, depressions, floods, all worse than anything she had to deal with. She'd let them all down, and now she'd lose everything they'd fought for.

As if in a trance, she walked down the hall she'd taken her first steps in, as had her mother and grandmother, and on back probably. If she ever had any children, they'd never know Holly Grove because she'd have to sell it. She couldn't even pay the taxes and utilities with the little bit of money she got from leasing out the few acres she had left to a sugarcane farmer. Every generation had sold off a little more of the land to keep the family home. By the time her grandmother inherited it, there wasn't much left to sell. Even if Holly sold that last bit of farm property, how long would it last with the constant maintenance of a 150-year-old house? How in the world had her mother managed to keep it as a single parent on a schoolteacher's salary?

When she reached the middle of the hall, she noticed the mystery portrait was crooked again. Surely the little bit of hammering she'd done on the widow's walk above hadn't jarred it loose? She sighed. *And if it's the weak ghost Angel says is here, it could have at least moved a tiny votive candle or something at the séance. What a disaster.*

Rhett trotted to her side, probably ready for bed-time. She scooped him up and sighed. *I need my bed and sleep to forget the day.* She dragged herself to her room and sprawled across her four-poster bed with the only male she could count on. Rhett snuggled up to her side, but it was little comfort. She kicked off her heels and they clattered to the floor.

*If having a ghost go viral put Holly Grove B&B in the company of the most successful B&Bs anywhere, this debunking and the buzz with it will be the end of my business.* There was no way to fix this. She stared up at the ceiling.

*If only Tru understood that I really wasn't lying. If only Burl could come back for just a few minutes to explain. If only I could have told Sylvia Burl was gone for good. If. If. If.*

Holly rolled out of the bed and wrapped her coverlet around her. She put her slippers on and shuffled to the French doors and looked outside. The storm had passed. She opened the French doors and stepped out onto the balcony into a calm night. Rhett trotted out with her. She sucked in the scent of fresh rain. The moonlight shone over the twin row of oaks, as old as her home, which led to the Mississippi River. Any other night, she'd find comfort in their strength. Tonight, she saw the future of Holly Grove, and it wasn't good.

She tightened the coverlet around her shoulders and sat with Rhett on the swing that she and Grandma Rose used to sit on every night drinking hot chocolate after Mama died.

Tears welled in her eyes. Every memory she had was tied to Holly Grove. It was a piece of her grandmother and mother. It was more than a house. It was the memory of all she loved and all who had loved her and Holly Grove.

Now, Tru and his spy video were going to take all that away. For what? To prove he's the biggest debunker that ever lived? What does he get out of that? *All because I didn't tell everyone, oh by the way, my ghost moved out.*

He'd probably cost Sylvia, Bob, and Liz their jobs, not that she felt all that sorry for Sylvia. She'd probably already started planning legal action to stop him from posting the videos. *Good luck with that.*

All because of Tru digging up trouble, they'd all be out of a job and his video would live forever on the Internet. She stood and walked to the railing. She hoped karma bit him in the rear with a vengeance.

Remnants of rain spattered to the ground with the slight breeze. and with that breeze came a hint of a charred scent. Holly sniffed. Cigar smoke.

She flung the coverlet off and charged for the

door with Rhett at her heels. *It's not good enough that he's trashing my reputation and my business, now he wants to chance burning it down. He's out of here tonight, if I have to call the cops to evict him.*

A crash and a several thuds clamored above. Either a tree branch fell on the house or worse—Tru.

Heart pounding, she bolted from her bedroom for the stairs and to the widow's walk.

Surely he didn't fall through another soft spot on the decking. She and Thomas had checked it for weak spots. Didn't find any. She'd warned Tru the railing was too low. He'd know better than to get close, wouldn't he?

Taking the steps two at a time, she reached the door to the widow's walk and flung it open. She was blinded by the change from the lighted hallway to the night sky outside. The clouds raced across the moon.

"Tru!" she called out. She held her breath as she listened for his reply.

It didn't come. As her eyes adjusted to the dark, she scanned the widow's walk. He wasn't there. The remnants of his cigar smoke hung in the air. He could be hiding behind one of the chimneys. The clouds parted enough for a sliver of the moon to shine through as she walked toward the closest chimney.

A woman's scream from down below pierced the eerie silence.

Holly turned toward the sound coming from the lawn below.

A flashlight beam bounced along the pathway below. The beam grazed the wrought-iron railing of the widow's walk. Then shouts.

Holly trembled. She closed her eyes and imagined Tru's mangled body on the ground below. "Oh, Tru."

She stepped back from the edge of the widow's walk. Why didn't he listen to her and stay off the widow's walk? She turned and ran down all three flights of stairs and prayed for a miracle with every step.

Maybe he'd survived. Maybe the balcony or tree limbs broke his fall. She'd thought the worst when Mackie fell through the roof, and he'd walked away from his tumble. Tru could too. He had to.

When Holly reached the front porch, she found Miss Alice hunched over Tru performing CPR. Between breaths she shouted at Nelda to start compressions.

"Lord, Lord, Lord." Nelda stood in front of her car mumbling, then shrieking, then mumbling some more, all the while clutching her chest. "That man just fell right out of the sky, Lord help him."

"Nelda!" Miss Alice shouted. "Snap out of it. I need some help."

*Poor Nelda.* She wasn't going to snap out of that any time soon.

"I'll do it." Holly said, jogging over to Miss Alice.

Tru lay there motionless, his limbs contorted in unnatural positions. She covered her mouth to hold back her gasp. "Just tell me what to do."

"You've done enough," Miss Alice said with a quick glance toward the widow's walk.

"You don't think—

"Press on his chest like this," Miss Alice barked as she pressed on his chest, palm over palm. "One compression per second."

*Did she see me on the roof? Blame me for not securing the widow's walk better?* An ever-expanding puddle of Tru's blood circled his head. Her stomach curdled. How much blood could a person lose and not die? She copied Miss Alice's hand placement on Tru's chest and started chest compressions.

Gasps, hushed whispers, and then the clicks of a camera came from behind Holly. She looked over her shoulder. Sam squatted behind her snapping pictures in rapid-fire succession.

"Sam!" Holly yelled between compressions. "What are you doing?" Not that she was shocked, but it just felt wrong.

"Same thing any newsman worth his salt would?" He held his camera out and checked his screen. "Get the story."

"Did you at least call 911 first?"

"Thomas is calling," he said, as he turned his camera lens toward the widow's walk.

Thomas raised his hand. His other hand held his phone pressed to his ear. "Yes, the roof. Holly Grove B&B on Highway . . ."

Everyone filed out onto the porch. Angel clutched her black shawl so tightly her knuckles had turned white. Sylvia stood, arms folded, wearing the same thing she had on during the séance. Bob sat with his head in his hands on the front steps, and Liz paced back and forth, on the phone. Nelda stroked Rhett as she held him and seemed to have calmed down a bit. Holly had never thought of Rhett as a therapy dog, but he seemed to have risen to the occasion.

Headlights flashed across Tru and Miss Alice as a sheriff's patrol car rolled to a stop in the driveway.

Holly grunted as she pressed down on Tru's chest. "Where's the ambulance, for crying out loud?"

Coming up for air, Miss Alice grabbed Tru's limp wrist and pinched it between her thumb and fingers as she looked at her large-face watch.

"Is he—?" Holly winced.

"Don't stop," Miss Alice said. "The paramedics may be able to bring him back."

"Back?" Holly froze mid-compression.

# Chapter Sixteen

Buster Fuller, the former member of the nerd squad in high school and now temporary chief deputy sheriff, slammed the patrol car door and hitched up his pants. Even in his thirties, he'd never filled out his frame from their high school days. "What's going on here?"

"Where's the ambulance?" Holly yelled still doing the best she could with her half of the CPR. "We need paramedics now!"

"I was just down the road when I heard the call on my radio," Buster said. He shook his head. "This one looks like the real deal."

"Seriously. You want to bring that up now?" Three false alerts and every 911 call from Holly Grove was suspect now. Sweat beaded on Holly's brow as she continued chest compressions on Tru.

"What happened to him?" Buster asked.

He must not have listened to the 911 call very well. "He fell off the roof," Holly said, glancing up at the widow's walk.

The chief deputy let out a long whistle and kicked back his hat as he scratched his head.

Miss Alice huffed. "I'm getting dizzy from blowing. We're going to have to switch."

Tru's mouth, somewhere between purple and gray, hung at a slight angle as though he'd had a stroke. Holly choked back her dinner. "I think I might be sick."

"Get over it and do what I told you or he doesn't have a chance," Miss Alice barked.

"I didn't say I wouldn't do it." She couldn't live with herself if she didn't, but she didn't have to like it. Her stomach curdled as she leaned over him. "How exactly do I do this?"

"Pinch his nose shut, then take a breath and blow it in his mouth," Miss Alice said as she placed her wrinkled hands over his heart. "If he starts breathing, stop."

When Holly touched Tru's cold nose, a shiver ran through her, but she pushed it aside. She leaned over the last lips she would ever want on hers and sucked in a breath. The next one would be for him.

*Just breathe, Tru. I wanted you gone, not dead.* Somehow she felt responsible, even though she'd warned him to stay off the roof.

Sirens blared as red lights strobed across the oak trees and lawn. Holly looked up as a fire truck and ambulance pulled to a stop on the driveway. *Thank goodness. What took them so long?*

"Over here." The chief deputy directed them with his flashlight. "Real deal this time."

"What happened?" Sandy Wright jogged over with an EMT right behind her. It had been a while since

Holly's first ride in an ambulance, and the false rumors about a drug overdose had almost died out. She'd heard Sandy stepped up to paramedic since then.

"He fell from up there." Holly looked up at the widow's walk.

"Head trauma. Possible internal injuries. Broken bones," Miss Alice reported.

Sandy took his pulse. "How long on the CPR?"

"Ten minutes," Miss Alice said. Her knees creaked as she stood. "He needs a shot of adrenaline or whatever newfangled drug medics use these days to shock his system, ASAP, then—"

Sandy already had a needle in Tru before Miss Alice could finish her instructions. "I've got it from here, Miss Alice. Thanks for stepping up."

"All right," Buster said, herding back Miss Alice, Holly, and the guests who'd gathered around the tragedy. "Give the professionals some room to work."

"I am a professional." Miss Alice huffed and stood her ground. "A registered nurse."

The chief deputy tipped his hat. "Yes, ma'am."

Holly's legs may as well have been Jell-O as she watched Sandy and the other EMT poke and prod Tru. *Just open your eyes, Tru. They can put you back together. It may take a while, but you'll be just as obnoxious as ever.*

Buster sidled up to Holly. "That wouldn't be Truman Stalwort, would it?"

"Yes," Holly said. "He's one of my guests."

Sandy and the other EMT covered Tru with a sheet.

"Was," the chief deputy said.

"No." Holly staggered and sat on the grass. "This can't be happening."

"Seems pretty surreal to me, too." The chief deputy rested his hand on his gun. "I just talked to Mr. Stalwort a few minutes ago."

"What?" Holly's head was in a fog. She couldn't have heard Buster right. "What do you mean, you talked to Tru a few minutes ago?"

She trailed after Buster as he weaved his way through the EMTs, firemen, and police officers at the scene. The red and blue flashing lights pulsing across the grounds made her feel disoriented and dizzy.

"Yep." He stopped short and Holly nearly plowed into the back of him.

"Why?" She took a backward step to gain a little personal space from Buster, who'd planted his boots like he was guarding ground. "What did he say?"

"Privileged information at this time." Static came across the radio strapped to his collar. Buster spit some numbers out and ended with "ten-four." He tipped his hat to Holly and strutted away like he was a five-star general.

*Well, I'm not in the army and he's not my general.* "Buster, wait up."

He didn't.

She caught him by his sleeve. "I need to know what's going on. This happened on my property."

He looked down at her hand holding a wad of his sleeve, then back at her. "Ma'am, release my uniform and step away. Failure to do so could result in arrest."

"Seriously, Buster? I've known you since we were

at Fulton Elementary." She let his shirt go. "I just need to know what's going on."

"At this time, I have nothing to confirm." He dusted off his uniform sleeve as though they were in sixth grade and she had cooties.

"Fine," she said to his back as he walked away. *Nothing to confirm. Tru is dead. Confirmed. What kind of power trip is Buster on that he couldn't say why he'd talked to Tru? Whatever it was, it can't be good.*

The ground spun beneath her and her legs weakened. She plopped down on the grass and noticed she was missing a slipper. She groaned. How could any of this be happening? She pressed her hands to her head. It seemed impossible. Tru knew the railing was too low. Why would he chance getting so close? She should have evicted him for smoking in a no-smoking area or for just being a total pain in the tush, contract or not. At least he'd be alive.

"I knew he was near the end of his life," Angel said as she approached Holly. "I just didn't know how close."

"He didn't believe you anyway," Holly said. "If he had, he would've never chanced going up on the widow's walk. I told him about Mackie falling through the decking. I told him the railing was too low and rusted."

"His path was written into his soul." Angel squeezed her shoulder. "May he rest in peace."

Holly nodded.

"I'm going to pack up and drive back to New Orleans." Angel glanced back at the house. "I won't be able to sleep in there tonight. The spirits are restless."

"The laser pointer ghost?" Holly asked.

"The forgotten one and others. You should have me back for a private session."

Holly held her hand up like a stop sign. "Thanks, but no thanks. I've had it with ghosts. If that ghost doesn't bother me, I won't bother it."

Angel's long black skirt swished as she turned around and walked toward Holly Grove, then looked back over her shoulder. "It seems one ghost was very good for both of our businesses." She paused. "And Sylvia's."

"You mean *is*," Sylvia said. Her stilettos poked holes in the grass as she walked up to them. "He didn't really debunk 'The Ghost in the Grove.'"

"Really, Sylvia?" Liz said as she padded along in her Birkenstocks. "The man fell to his death. Can you have a little respect?"

"I'm only saying what we're all thinking." Sylvia put a hand on her hip. "He can't release his recordings from the grave."

"I wasn't thinking about that at all," Holly said, but now that she had she couldn't help but feel relieved and guilty for it. *Jeez.*

Angel ignored Sylvia. "I've got to pack," she said as she walked toward the front door.

Little lines creased between Liz's brows. "But what are we going to put in that slot now?"

"'The Ghost in the Grove Revisited,'" Sylvia said, then flashed her thirty-two perfect teeth. "After some creative editing, of course."

"We should shelve it," Liz said. "We can tell the producers the video is corrupt. That's what you told Tru."

"I really don't think you should do that." Holly stood and dusted off her skirt. "I mean, that was his last work, and he did debunk 'The Ghost in the Grove.'"

Sylvia's face morphed into shock. "Did you not notice your ex-husband invaded my body and made me speak for him?"

"Yeah," Liz said. "According to the tabloids, she's in therapy because of the last time he did it."

"And my fans eat it up." Sylvia turned her attention to Holly. "And you don't have any say in what we do with the show anyway."

Sylvia glanced at Holly's feet. "By the way, you're missing a slipper."

# CHAPTER SEVENTEEN

Jake McCann gunned his new-to-him motorcycle as he rolled down the highway to Holly's place. He'd lucked into the bike a few months ago when a buddy of his with ICE in New Orleans decided to sell it—or his wife did—after they brought home baby number three. *His loss. My gain.*

After all, Jake needed his own transportation if Delta Ridge was going to be his physical address between assignments. With his line of work, it would probably be a virtual address. He could be called out on an ICE undercover assignment any time.

He'd spent half the night and part of the day in taxis, trains, and planes to get back to Holly, but this was the way to go. The only thing better would be to have Holly riding on the back with her arms wrapped around him as soon as she got over being ticked off, which would take some effort on his part, but he looked forward to that challenge.

The blacktop glistened with a recent rain. If he hadn't had to wait out the storm under an overpass, he would've been at Holly Grove for dinner. He could almost taste Nelda's smothered pork chops, gumbo, and bread pudding.

He leaned into a curve lined with political signs. BUSTER FULLER FOR SHERIFF. The old white water tower stood out against the night sky. His heart did a little uptick. Had it really been more than fifteen years since he'd painted that red heart on the tower for Holly? He squinted. Was it still there? Too dark to tell.

The chilled night air blasted his damp leather jacket. *Man, I hope Holly doesn't put me in Abe's cabin.* He sped up. A lone streetlight on the highway glowed, marking the turnoff to Holly Grove just ahead.

When he turned off on the gravel road, red and blue lights flashed from a fire truck, ambulance, and sheriff's patrol car. What the—? He goosed the gas.

It was most likely one of Holly's older guests had a heart attack or broke a hip, but it could be Nelda. She was getting up in age. He couldn't even think about if anything had happened to Holly. Especially since the last time he'd talked to her he'd ticked her off. *Oh, man, I don't want anything to happen to either of them.*

He gunned it to the end of the driveway, then dropped his kickstand and hopped off his bike. He worked his way through the crowd. A body lay covered in a white sheet on the ground. A couple of medics and an officer stood over the body, which appeared to be too big to be Holly's but not big enough to be Nelda's. *Body?* What the hell?

He strode up to the officer. "Who's the victim?"

"Back off." The ninety-pound county mounty put

his hand on his gun and his palm to Jake's chest. "This area is restricted."

Jake's jaw tensed, but he fought back the urge to disarm the joke of a cop. "My . . . friend lives here."

*Friend? How lame can you get, Jake?* He frantically searched the faces for Holly. When he spotted Sam behind a camera snapping pictures, he strode his way. "Sam!"

The old man's bushy brows slammed together. "You old son of a gun, what are you doing here?" He wrapped Jake in a hug, but he shook Sam off and looked past him for Holly.

"Where's Holly? She's not . . ." In trouble again. Jake nodded behind him to the body under the sheet.

"Nah. Freak accident." Sam waved him off. "One of her guests."

Jake's muscles relaxed as he blew out his breath like a release valve.

"You didn't think—

"I didn't know what to think." Jake scrubbed his hand across his forehead. He hadn't exactly expected a warm welcome, but this . . . This beehive of activity looked way too busy for an accident investigation. All he wanted to do was wrap his arms around Holly if she'd let him. "Where is she?"

Sam pointed at the group of people Jake had passed through earlier. "Over there."

"Where?" Through the legs in the group, he spotted Holly, sitting on the ground hugging her knees. She rested her headful of crazy curls on her knees and she was beautiful. A beautiful mess.

What kind of trouble had she found this time?

\* \* \*

"Well, look who's here," Sylvia said, practically purring. "I thought you said Mr. Delicious was out of the country."

Holly followed Sylvia's stare to Jake as he strode across the grass. He wore a leather jacket, worn jeans, biker boots, and a smile aimed right at her. Her heart did gymnastics that could cause a coronary until she remembered he'd been MIA for almost three months. As much as she wanted to jump into his arms, she stood planted on the ground. *Now he shows up in the middle of all this! Mercy. And none for him.*

"Jake," Holly said, her voice calm and level as she extended her hand. "I see you finally made it."

He took her hand and then leaned in and brushed a chaste kiss on her cheek, the way most Southern gentlemen greet a lady.

She allowed it but didn't reciprocate because that's what ticked-off Southern ladies do.

His smile faded a bit. "I've been traveling since the butt crack of dawn to get here."

He could have finished that out with *to see you*, but he didn't. And that said all she needed to know.

Sylvia extended her hand and wrapped her arm around his neck as she plastered a kiss on his cheek. "I love how you guys say hello."

*Gag me. What does she know about Southern traditions?*

He didn't reciprocate, but Sylvia didn't seem to notice.

*Bless her heart . . .*

"Ain't you a sight for sore eyes," Nelda said, waddling up to them and giving Jake a quick hug and a peck on the cheek. "Can you believe that debunker fell off the widow's walk and killed himself?" She made the sign of the cross. "God rest his soul."

Buster stepped from behind Jake like a short noon shadow. He gave a sharp nod and straightened his belt. "That's under investigation."

"Investigate what?" Nelda asked, hands on hips. "I told ya 'xactly what happened. He fell off that roof." She glanced up at the widow's walk and then to the ground where he lay. "I saw him land, God rest his soul, right in front of my eyes." She shook her head and stroked Rhett's head. "And I can't unsee that."

"I received a call at zero one sixteen hours from Mr. Stalwort to report a theft."

"What time is zero one sixteen hours?" Nelda scrunched up her brow. "Nobody knows what time you're talkin' 'bout. Just spit out the o'clock."

"Sixteen minutes after one this morning," Jake said, but he seemed to study Buster. "Military time leaves no room for error in official reports. The chief deputy here is a seasoned professional." Jake gave Buster one of those good-ol'-boy nods men exchange.

Buster offered a man-nod back and puffed out his chest like a rooster at daybreak.

*Yeah, right, and I'm a five-star chef. Give me a break.* Why was Jake sucking up to Buster? Did he remember who he was in high school? *Investigation, my foot.* "Wait. Tru called you? What theft?"

"Confidential." Buster hitched up his belt again. "I—"

"Not if it happened on my property." Holly's mind whirled around the fact that Tru had called the sheriff's office moments before he fell to his death. Why didn't he report the theft to her? She gulped, recalling the knock-down, drag-out in the parlor after the séance. *Of course, he wouldn't call me.* "What was stolen?"

"Privileged information at this point." Buster cleared his throat. "I arrived here at zero one twenty-six hours and he was unresponsive. Dead at zero one thirty-one hours." He adjusted his belt. "I think we've got us a murder here."

*Murder?* "That can't be." No sooner than the words left her mouth, she questioned them. Which of her guests hadn't had an altercation with Tru? But murder?

"Whoa." Jake jumped in. "Buster, right?"

"Chief Deputy Sheriff Fulton." He jacked his chin up. "Of St. Agnes Parish."

Jake rubbed his hand across his mouth. "Soon to be duly elected if you solve this murder quickly, and I'm sure you will." Jake shoved his hands in his pockets. "How'd you figure it out? There's a big leap between theft and murder."

"Not if the victim said the property was worth hundreds of thousands of dollars." He dipped his chin down and eyed Jake. "And Mr. Stalwort felt his life may be in danger."

"The guy only checked in with a duffel bag. What was in there? Gold bars?" Holly asked.

"What did he report stolen?" Jake asked.

Buster hitched up his pants. "His glasses."

"Oh." Holly swallowed hard. The video evidence that Tru had debunked her ghost, Angel's reputation of communicating with the dead, and *Inquiring Minds*'s credibility. And every altercation any of them had had with him if he'd recorded everything like he'd said he had.

"Nobody leave until I get statements from everyone." Buster shone his flashlight on Angel, who was standing on the porch with her suitcase. "That includes you, ma'am."

Holly glanced around for Sylvia. Where had she gone? Hmm . . . She must have slipped away just about the time Buster mentioned the investigation.

Lights flashing, two sheriff's deputy patrol cars screamed down her driveway. The entire sheriff's office was now on the case, and probably Jake, too.

*Mercy. What now?*

Holly plopped down on the porch steps as Buster and his officers swarmed Holly Grove. Her stomach rolled as flashlight beams zapped down from the widow's walk to the grass where Tru's body lay covered in a sheet. Buster barked orders as he climbed the steps past where she sat.

She propped her elbows on her knees and rested her head in her hands. Her palms cooled her forehead as she stared at the hypnotic basket weave of the brick sidewalk and let her mind wander.

Could it really be murder? Sure, Tru had made a few enemies tonight, but why would anyone kill him if they had his glasses with all the recordings? Surely his death was a terrible accident. She blew out a long breath. This publicity wouldn't be good for her business. And just when business was picking up.

Big black boots stepped into her view. She looked up. Six feet of delicious man who had just sucked up to Buster while he claimed there had been a murder at Holly Grove.

"You okay?" he asked.

Holly sighed. "Just peachy."

He pointed to her feet. "You're missing a slipper, Cinderella."

"I know." Holly rubbed her bare foot over the top of her remaining slipper. "I must have lost it in this disaster."

"I can see how that could happen."

"On top of the terrible accident, Buster thinks Tru was murdered. And you do, too!" Holly shook her head. "Why were you swallowing everything Buster said? Don't you remember him from high school?"

Jake shrugged. "This is probably the biggest excitement he's ever seen."

"You mean your new best friend?" Holly huffed. "The guy who washed your jock and everyone else's on the football team. The guy who thought he was a coach because he typed the playbook. The guy who took hall monitor to a level that nearly got me suspended for responding to the call of nature."

"Yeah, I remember." Jake rubbed a hand over the handsome stubble of his two-day beard.

She blinked and shoved that thought to the back of her mind where it belonged. "Could have fooled me."

"We called him Bust-a-jock." Jake gave a so-what shrug. "That was high school. He's the chief deputy sheriff now. People change. Why not give him the benefit of the doubt?"

"Because he hasn't changed." She flapped her arms at her side. "You know why he's chief deputy sheriff? Parish charter. That's why. The charter dictated the longest serving deputy be appointed interim sheriff after Sheriff Walker was forced to step down."

"Makes sense to have the most experienced man step up until the election. Do you think he'll win?"

"On what? His career record?" Holly sat up straight. "I've got a collection of Buster's police work over his ten-year career—signed and paid for. Parking tickets and speeding tickets. Twenty-seven to be exact, for parking the least bit out of the lines or going as little as five miles per hour over the speed limit. We all have them. He'll never get elected."

The left side of Jake's mouth kicked up. "Unless he solves a murder or does something newsworthy."

"You think that's why he's screaming murder? To get elected?" She rolled that thought around a second. "It has to be."

Jake shoved his hands in his pockets and rocked back on his heels. "Maybe. Maybe not."

"Buster always overreacts."

"But what if he's not? Wouldn't you want one of us to be on his good side?"

"Is that what you were doing?"

"Call it insurance. I've dealt with guys like him. If I feed his ego, he'll eat out of my hand before long." He sat down beside her. "One of us needs to be on his good side, and it's not going to be you."

And just like that, Jake was inching his way back on her good side.

"Now tell me what happened here."

"Oh, Jake, this is awful. Tru came here to debunk my ghost." She rubbed her arms against the cold. "He was nothing but trouble from the time he walked through the door, but I didn't wish him dead." She sighed. "Gone. Definitely. But murdered? By one of my guests?" She pressed her palm to her head. "I just can't believe it."

"So, you think it was an accident?"

"I hate to tell you this, but Mackie fell through the floor up there just before this crazy train started."

A crease pinched between Jake's chocolate eyes. "Is he okay?"

Holly nodded. "He's a little banged up. Sore back and some scrapes, but nothing serious. Miss Alice checked him out."

A shadow of a grin slid across Jake's face. "If she didn't call an ambulance, he's fine." He glanced down. "How about otherwise?"

"He's not drinking, if that's what you mean. I think he's staying sober for you. You really should let him know when you're coming. It gives him something to look forward to."

"It'd also give him a chance to sober up before I get here."

"He was crushed when I told him you weren't coming. You should have let him know yourself."

"How? He doesn't even have a phone. It's hard for me to make calls when I'm undercover, especially just to leave a message for him at Dottie's Diner."

"Unless you're sleeping with your target, you

should be able to get away for a phone call sometime."

"It's not just the time. If the target gets jittery, he
may ask to look at my phone, bug my room. They've
got ways. The less communication with people I care
about the better."

*Like me, maybe.* She studied Jake but he gave nothing away.

"I'll go see him tomorrow."

"No need. He told me he'd be back to finish the
job tomorrow, but now it's the scene of a crime according to Buster."

"We'll see about that." Jake took off his jacket and
draped it over her shoulders. "You need to find your
other slipper before you catch a cold. I'm going to
see if I can find out more about why Buster is
jumping to that conclusion." He winced. "Pardon
the pun."

With a quick squeeze of her shoulder, he stood
and followed Buster's trail up the steps.

*Mercy.* Jake had only been here a few minutes and
was already getting back in her good graces. It was
so much easier to stay mad when he was far away.
That's the problem. He won't stay. *Remember that.*

Jake may be able to get some answers out of
Buster, but Holly couldn't count on that. She had
to act, and she knew just who to call to nip this in
the bud.


One patrol car shined its spotlight over Tru's
body while two deputies removed the sheet that covered it. They laid down some kind of tape around

Tru's contorted body. Holly shivered on the brick steps of her B&B. *Holy Mary, Joseph, and baby Jesus, how could this have happened?*

Police car radios blared codes from a dispatcher over the muffled voices of Delta Ridge's finest as they collected evidence. It all seemed like a dream, a bad one. She couldn't wrap her mind around the thought of one of her guests pushing Tru off the roof. Maybe they didn't. Maybe he fell. Look what happened to Mackie. He nearly fell off the roof. Why had she wanted to open that widow's walk up anyway? Just the name sounded depressing.

Holly propped her elbows on her knees and stared at Tru's body. As obnoxious as he was, he didn't deserve this, accident or not.

The wind kicked up and she glanced at the sky. Clouds raced across the almost black heavens. Another storm was brewing.

When she looked back at Tru, his mop of red hair whipped around with the breeze and the flaps of his coat fluttered at his side. It reminded her of when the wind blew the door open, and she'd tried to make him think her ghost had done it. She sighed. He'd dismissed it as predicted weather. He'd had an explanation for everything, but he wasn't here to explain this. *He couldn't have predicted this, but Angel did.*

The sounds of footsteps and voices morphed around her into a faded cacophony as she stared at Tru's corpse. The deputies must have finished marking out his body position, because Sandy and an EMT loaded him on a gurney and covered him with a sheet again.

Her tension eased a bit with Tru's body out of

sight, but a little pang of guilt pinched her gut. On TV shows and movies, the gesture seemed heroic—protecting the dignity of the dead and all that.

Not so much in real life. Covering the body hid the vulgar truth of what death looked like.

The wind rippled across the sheet that covered Tru, and Holly pulled Jake's coat a little tighter around her shoulders.

Holly hadn't wanted to see Tru's body and now she couldn't unsee it, as Nelda had said. *Death ain't pretty before it's all cleaned up, painted up, and laid out in a coffin, and it's only tolerable then.*

She fidgeted with her nails to keep from chewing them off. His poor family would find out soon. Would they come here? How could she face them? She glanced back at the gurney where Sandy was securing Tru's body.

Tru sat straight up, right through the sheet.

Holly gasped and slammed her back against the steps.

Sandy didn't seem to see Tru rise from his body. The deputies didn't either. No one saw him but Holly. Her heartbeat hammered through her body and echoed in her ears. *Oh, hell no! Not again.*

Tru dusted off his clothes and looked up at the widow's walk. Then he watched as Sandy strapped his body on the gurney. "Hey," he said to Sandy.

She didn't answer.

He turned in a full circle, taking in all the commotion, and stopped dead when he saw the body outline on the grass. He grabbed the first deputy he came to. His hand went right through him. Wild eyed, he raced to the body and snatched at the sheet, but his hand went right through that, too.

*Well, stick a fork in me and call me done.* Tru the paranormal debunker *is* a ghost. Holly stood and brushed off her hands, then walked over to Tru and whispered, "Debunk this."

# CHAPTER EIGHTEEN

Tru dug at his face with his hands. His expression twisted from confused to bewildered to panicked. "It's not possible." His mouth hung open as he shook his head. "Ghosts don't exist."

Holly nodded toward the widow's walk and then to the body, careful not to speak to him in front of anyone. The whole town would have her certified if she talked to another ghost. It was one thing to think there was a ghost hanging out at Holly Grove, but chatting to thin air didn't sit well with the good people of Delta Ridge.

He stared at his former body for a moment, then his mouth gaped open in a silent scream. He stood in a red-hot glowing whirlpool that sucked him straight down. As he clawed at the earth, his image melted. In an instant, the earth filled in the charred hole as though it had never been there.

Holly stumbled backward, panting. She held her hand over her runaway heart. *Holy, moly. That never happened with Burl. What the—*

A hand touched her shoulder.

Holly jumped and nearly took off running.

"Sorry," Angel said. "Has the chief deputy sheriff questioned you yet?"

"No but I had a," she drew quotation marks in the air, "visitor."

Angel's dark eyes widened. "Anyone we know?"

Holly dragged Angel over by the azalea bushes at the corner of the house, away from the action. "Tru. He's back."

"Did he tell you if someone pushed him off the widow's walk like the chief deputy sheriff seems to think?"

Holly shook her head. "He was only here for a few minutes, but he doesn't believe he's a ghost. He still thinks that's impossible." Holly leaned in closer to Angel. "Do ghosts ever kinda spin and melt into a hole of fire in the ground?"

Angel sucked in a breath. "He may not be coming back."

"Burl used to fade out all the time. He always came back." Holly lifted a shoulder. "Until he didn't."

"Burl didn't go to . . ." Angel glanced down. "Hell."

Jake stepped out onto the widow's walk, and the night sky felt unnaturally close. Tru had jumped, fallen, or been pushed off the roof. If there was evidence to prove what had happened up here, Jake intended to find it or find out about it. At the very least, he wanted to know exactly why Buster was so convinced Tru was murdered or if he was looking for headlines to win an election.

Buster and his deputies pored over Tru's last

stand like a high school band in Chinese fire drill mode at a halftime show. The beams from standard-issue flashlights darted across the worn floorboards as the local flatfoots combed the area. Jake's size-twelve shoes gave him a steady footing as he peeked over the side of the widow's walk. *Man, that's a long drop.*

He'd puked three times when he left that bill-board-size love note to Holly on the St. Agnes Parish water tower before he left town after graduation. It was their secret. Still was. He lifted a heavy foot. *Mind over matter, man.*

If he hadn't climbed that tower, he'd have never made it through basic training or his first jump or snagged his dream job. He wasn't afraid of heights, but he respected the danger.

Old Tru had hammered that home tonight, whether he'd fallen or had been pushed to his death. All Jake had to do was get a few answers from Buster and check the scene out for himself.

Jake sucked in a breath. His dark clothes and lack of a flashlight would let him blend in for a minute or two in the chaos, maybe long enough to assess the scene. He glanced around at the plywood patch on the floor, sawhorses, a wooden crate, and two random buckets filled with sand beside a chimney. Enough trip hazards for a lawyer's wet dream *if* Tru fell to his death.

All that was surrounded by a rusted row of munchkin-size wrought-iron railing with a three-foot section broken off. That section faced the side of the house where old Tru had met his end.

Two flatfoots stood over one of the sand buckets. The shorter of the two men held a flashlight while the other plucked spent stogies out of the sand and dropped them in a clear evidence bag. Among the stumps of cigars, three lipstick-stained cigarettes lay at the bottom of the bag.

A beam from a flashlight skittered across the railing and the glint of something shiny about a foot outside of the railing caught Jake's eye.

He eased over to the railing, then squatted in front of it. With the ambient light and the occasional swipe of a flashlight beam, he spotted a slender metal cylinder about two inches long resting in a drain trough just out of his reach. Jake took out his phone and snapped a photo without a flash. A grainy image showed up on his phone, but it would have to do. The flatfoots would find it sooner or later. He slid his phone in his pocket and stood. "Hey, Buster."

Buster spun around and nearly blinded Jake with his high-powered flashlight. "That's Chief Deputy Sheriff Fuller. I don't go by Buster anymore, and don't touch anything."

"Got it, Sheriff." Jake said, shielding his eyes and adding rank to stroke Buster's ego. It couldn't hurt.

"This is all a crime scene," Buster said from behind the light. "Official personnel only."

Jake fished his ICE ID from his pocket and held it in the air. "Immigrations and Customs Enforcement. Is that official enough?"

"No jurisdiction in this," Buster called out. The beam darted to the left of Jake's face, giving him a bit of relief. "You know where the door is."

Jake glanced over his shoulder at the spotlight on

the door, then back at the wannabe sheriff. "I'm following up on a bust I did here a few months ago."

Which he was, but only for his own peace of mind. There had been no intel of activity at Holly Grove or nearby on the Mississippi River. Mostly, he wanted to look out for Holly, and that could be a full-time job some days.

"Yeah, I remember that." Buster aimed the high-powered beam back at Jake.

Jake tented his hand over his eyes. "Could be connected. I don't want to find any loose ends involved with this. Mind if I ask you a few questions?"

"Hadn't thought of a drug angle." The blinding beam clicked off. "What ya got?"

*How's that bait taste, Bust-a-jock?* Of course, a murder connected to a drug bust would be even better for the wannabe sheriff's ambitions. Jake held back a grin and ambled over to Buster. "Murder you said, right?"

"Definitely." Buster licked his lips and his eyes lit up as though he'd been called off the bench for his one chance to play in the game. "First degree."

"No kidding." Maybe it was and maybe it wasn't. Buster had probably never investigated a murder. "How'd you eliminate the other possible reasons for his demise?"

"Oh, I, uh . . ."

*Either he hadn't thought of that or didn't want to for political reasons? Neither competent reasons. The reported theft and concern for the victim's safety could have been a cover for a suicide. Someone else could have made the call and fed the dispatcher a phony story to throw them off the real murderer's trail.* "My first thought was a jumper."

"Nope." Buster's thin lips flattened out in a proud grin. "No suicide note. No goodbye posts on social media. No depression or anxiety or any other meds in his room."

*Just what I wanted to know.* "And there's no possibility he simply fell off this thing?" Jake glanced around. "Lots of trip hazards here and not much to keep him from going over the edge."

"Tell me about it," Buster said, tipping his hat back and scratching his forehead. "That's why I told my men to be extra careful up here."

"They should be. You see that hole in the floor? Mackie fell through that a couple of days ago when he was prepping to raise the railing." Jake nodded toward the door he'd come in through. "You noticed all those construction notices and keep-out warnings on the door, right?"

"Hard to miss." Buster pulled his hat back in regulation position. "Didn't keep the victim out, obviously."

"Why do you think Tru came up here against all those warnings, or do you think he was lured up here by his killer?"

"My deputies found a cigar on the floor over there." He pointed to the edge of the railing near where Jake had found the canister. "More in the sand bucket and three of the same brand in the victim's pocket. We've got a parish ordinance against smoking inside historic buildings. The victim probably came up here to smoke."

Being a Boy Scout paid off for old Buster. "Alone or with his soon-to-be killer?"

Buster shrugged. "No way to know."

"It's the difference between an accident and murder. Alone, he had an accident."

With a downward glance, Buster shifted his weight before making eye contact again. "Well, he wasn't alone then, was he?"

Textbook body language of a lie in action Jake had seen too many times. Buster had nothing. Tru could have known his killer or someone could have laid in wait for him knowing he'd be up there for his nightly smoke. "No sign of a struggle."

"That's because he knew his killer."

"So, he just let the killer push him off the roof?"

"Look." Buster folded his arms over his scrawny chest. "He told me he feared for his life at this place. His property was stolen." Buster hitched up his utility belt and stared up at Jake. "Then someone pushed him over the edge."

"What was stolen?"

"It's pretty unusual, but he said it was worth a fortune."

That's relative, but Jake didn't want to press Buster too hard. "What was it?"

"A memory card with videos on it. Said it was worth big bucks."

"Legal videos or . . ."

Buster shrugged. "Worth killing for, but keep that confidential until I finish my investigation."

Jake cocked his head to the side and hammered the county mounty with a stare. "Suspects?"

"Unless they can provide an alibi, everyone who was here at the time of the murder."

"Everyone?"

"You mean Holly, don't you?" Buster dropped his arms to his side and shook his head. "You never got over her, did you?"

"Would you?" He'd thought he had until an investigation called him back a few months ago. He'd tried to get over her since. Buried himself in his assignment. Limited his calls, but it didn't work.

A thin-lipped grin crossed Buster's face. "Probably not."

"Hey, Chief," a deputy called from the other side of the widow's walk. "I've got something."

The deputy trotted over to them with a clear evidence bag that held the cylinder Jake had found earlier. "I don't know what it is and couldn't open it up 'cause I might bugger up the prints. Got any ideas?"

"Good job," Buster said. "What's in it is probably more important than the container. Put it with the other evidence and bring me exhibit number one." Buster gave a turd-eating grin. "Agent McCann needs to see it."

*This couldn't be good.*

A few seconds later the deputy returned with another evidence bag. Jake knew exactly what that bit of evidence was and what it meant.

Holly had some explaining to do. She'd really stepped in trouble this time.

# CHAPTER NINETEEN

"There you are." Thomas's voice came from behind Holly. "I've been worried about you."

She twisted around from her perch on the steps. His gray brows slanted over eyes filled with concern. Her heart drank up the gesture, too, probably because she was an emotional mess right now. "Thanks, but I'm fine. I'm just so sorry this happened. I know this was a bucket list trip for you and that's ruined. And Tru . . . I-I don't know what to say except how sorry I am this happened to him."

"It's not your fault." Thomas coated her in a sympathetic gaze. "He had no business up on that widow's walk. I saw all the notices you'd put up there. He took that risk, forewarned."

"I still feel responsible. After what happened at the séance, I knew my business would take a hit, but this." She held back tears. "This could end it once and for all."

"It was an accident, and I don't think anything is going to come of the recording tonight out of respect for the dead."

"Have you met Sylvia?"

Thomas chuckled. "What a night, huh?"

"You don't know the half of it." A shiver ran up her spine as she recalled seeing Tru raise from the dead and then go straight to . . .

Thomas sat beside her on the steps and watched the coroner's car ease out of her driveway, which left one lone officer standing duty and the rest canvassing the widow's walk for evidence.

"Do you really think someone pushed Tru off the roof?"

"Buster seems to think so." Holly pulled Jake's jacket closed across her chest and hoped he was able to get more information out of Buster.

Thomas tilted his head to the side and a fine line pinched between his brows. "Buster?"

"The temporary sheriff. Tru reported something stolen from his room not long before he fell. Buster thinks the theft and the murder are related." *Crapola. I should have asked Tru what happened when I had the chance.*

Thomas's Adam's apple rode up and down his throat as he stared into the distance. "And you told the sheriff about the theft?"

"No. Tru didn't report it to me. We weren't exactly on speaking terms after what happened at the séance. He called the sheriff's office to report it before he fell. I didn't even know about it until Buster told me."

"What was stolen?"

Holly stood and dusted off her backside. "Buster wouldn't tell me, but I've got my suspicions."

The static of a police radio crackled from the

deputy guarding the driveway. He covered his mouth and spoke into his radio as he walked across the driveway toward them. "Ten-four."

"Any suspects?" Thomas asked.

"Ma'am." The deputy tipped his hat as he approached them. He looked barely of legal age to vote, much less enforce the law. "The sheriff says you're needed inside."

Holly saluted the kid cop, then turned and climbed the brick stairs to the front door with Thomas at her side. "I guess we'll find out."

Thomas fell in step behind her. "Guess we will."


"Glad you could join us, Mrs. Davis." Buster stood as though he was holding court on the fifth step on the entrance hall staircase at Holly Grove.

*Jeez, Burl may be gone, but his last name is still haunting me. I've got to go back to my maiden name.*

Murmurs came from all six guests gathered near the staircase as she hung Jake's jacket on the coatrack.

*This can't be good. Did Buster really have enough evidence to prove murder? Here at Holly Grove? Surely not. Sure, Sylvia is a pill, but I can't imagine her or Angel getting their hands dirty enough to murder anyone. Liz and Bob didn't have their reputations at stake. Thomas had nothing to gain. It just didn't make any sense.*

*Think positive. Buster has been on the widow's walk. He's seen the hazards up there and the signs I put on the door. Maybe he's decided it was an accident after all.*

Behind Buster was his band of merry men and

Jake. Holly squinted. He had either gone rogue on her or succeeded in buddying up to Buster.

Jake winked at her.

Heat spiked her cheeks.

*Mercy.* Another reason he was dangerous to her heart.

"I came as soon as I got the invitation." She glanced over her shoulder at the baby-faced deputy, then folded her arms across her chest and stared at Jake. The least he could have done was given her a heads-up.

Thomas and the deputy filed in beside her.

A bright white flash lit up the room. Sam stepped out of the crowd and crouched in front of her and went all paparazzi.

"Lordy, Sam. You're about to blind me." Black spots blanketed her vision. She held her palm up to block the rapid-fire flashes.

Sam looked at the view screen of his camera, then gave a thumbs-up to Buster. "Get on with it," Sam said. "It's past my bedtime and I want this story in print for the *Gazette's* special edition tomorrow."

"When can we leave?" Angel asked, sitting on her suitcase. Long lashes batted over blue eyes. "I can't possibly stay here another night after what happened. The spirits are not pleased with any of this."

Holly shivered. Tru certainly hadn't been happy, but he was gone now. Who was Angel talking about? The green orb that Tru had said was a laser pointer? The ghost that was so weak Holly hadn't seen hide nor hair of it?

"You can't keep us here." Sylvia cast a rallying look around the hall at the other guests. "We have rights."

Liz and Bob sat in the S-shaped courting chair and exchanged glances.

"For Pete's sake." Miss Alice peered over her glasses from her perch on a folding chair. "It's two o'clock in the morning. Say what you've got to say and let us go to bed."

"If any of us *can* sleep," Thomas said.

Everyone was there except Nelda. Maybe Buster had given her a pass since she'd been so upset. If he had, she certainly deserved it. Holly would give her the day off tomorrow. Nelda was too old for all this. So was Miss Alice. "My guests have had a difficult night, Buster. Can we finish this in the morning?"

A faint siren sounded in the distance. Holly held back a grin and tried to be patient.

Buster cleared his throat. "May I have your attention, please?"

"Why on God's green earth do you think we're here?" Miss Alice stuffed her knitting in a basket on her lap and huffed.

"As you know." Buster raised his voice over the approaching siren. "Truman Jeremiah Stalwort, III, fell to his death on these premises tonight. After inspection of the crime scene and review of other evidence, the St. Agnes Parish Sheriff's Department will be investigating this as a murder."

A collective gasp echoed through the room followed by dead silence as Holly's guests eyed each other.

"What evidence?" Holly marched to the foot of the stairs and glared at Buster.

"Shortly before he fell to his death, the victim

reported a memory card with valuable information on it had been stolen. I'll give more details as the investigation progresses, Mrs. Davis." He directed his attention to the rest of the crowd. "I expect all of you to remain here until we can take your statements."

"Here with a murderer among us?" Sylvia asked.

"My deputies will be here at all times. After you retire for the night, one of them will be stationed at each building to make sure no one is roaming about. You'll be perfectly safe."

"We might as well be in jail," Angel said.

Buster adjusted his utility belt. "Besides, there is nowhere else to stay in Delta Ridge unless you would like to spend the night at the city jail." He eyed Angel.

"I'm certainly not paying for my room tonight," Sylvia said. "I doubt I can sleep at all after this."

"No one is paying for their rooms tonight," Holly said. "Comping your rooms is the least I can do. I'm just so sorry this happened to Tru and all of you were here for it." *And one of you may have done it.*

Buster ripped open a manila envelope and pulled out a document. "This is a search warrant for the entirety of this establishment and the rooms of all registered guests. I'll be taking statements from Nelda, Miss Alice, and Sam first. They were in the company or vicinity of one another when the death occurred, therefore, they are not under suspicion." He paused. "Any questions?"

*Yeah. Plenty.*

The siren blared outside Holly Grove then stopped, followed by the slamming of a car door.

Everyone turned toward the sound.

Baby-face opened the front door and peeked out, then pulled the door wide open. It groaned on its hinges.

Retired Judge Masion, the interim sheriff of St. Agnes Parish, trudged up the brick steps. The tail to his pajama top hung out from under his khaki uniform. Wisps of gray hairs in his comb-over flapped the wrong way in the crisp wind before he tugged his hat in place. He carried a large manila envelope in one hand, his hat in the other, and wore a scowl on his face.

This could be good or this could be bad. When Holly had awakened him from a dead sleep about thirty minutes ago, the first thing he'd asked was what kind of trouble she was in. She'd told him what had happened and said something about Buster being Buster—making a mountain out of a molehill. The last thing he'd said was he'd look into it.

Judge Maison nodded to Baby-face as he walked through the door, then delivered his scowl to Buster.

Buster's eyes widened. His Adam's apple rode a deep swallow all the way down.

Holly held back a grin. *This is gonna be good.*

"I understand there's been a tragedy here tonight." Judge Maison's Baptist-preacher baritone voice hung in the air. He removed his hat and held it over his heart. "My condolences to all concerned."

"Judge, I-I mean, Sheriff," Buster said as he made his way down the stairs.

"If you good people will excuse us a minute," the

judge said, putting his hat back on his head. "I'd like to confer with my deputy sheriff and the owner of this fine establishment, so we can better inform you of the situation at hand."

Holly rushed out the door following the judge with Buster behind her. The judge stopped and turned to them at the far end of the porch.

He pulled the envelope from under his arm. "It's nearly two o'clock in the morning, and I get a call from Judge Verret. Then he sends me this, which I had to print half-asleep." He shoved the photos at Buster.

Holly looked over his shoulder at the photos of the widow's walk under construction and poor Tru, downright dead on the lawn.

The judge pointed at Tru's photo. "And Judge Verret tells me you think this guy was murdered because someone stole a memory card that goes in some sort of spy glasses."

"Yes, sir. The victim was a debunker. He'd recorded a séance last night to prove there was no ghost at Holly Grove." Buster jacked his chin up. "There *was* no ghost, but someone stole the proof and pushed him off the roof."

The judge shook his head. "Son, you didn't watch that show everyone in town watched this week because Holly's place was on it, did you?"

"*Inquiring Minds,*" Holly said. "Millions of viewers."

"No, sir." Buster said. "I work the night shift."

"I'm aware." The judge blew out a slow breath. "According to my wife, almost everyone in town now believes Holly has a ghost."

"That's right," Holly said. "I do have a ghost." Or she did.

"I watched the show. Candles blew out in the dark. The medium seemed to communicate with the dead. The host of the show appeared to be possessed by the ghost. I did not *see* a ghost. No one did. But they felt like they did."

"Of course, he didn't capture an image of a ghost on video. If he had, that would have been valuable."

"But—"

"I understand *Inquiring Minds* recorded the séance too. Why was his video valuable enough to steal when neither video has photographic evidence of a ghost?"

"I, uh—"

"Furthermore, why would anyone push him off the roof if they had what they wanted anyway?"

Buster scratched his head.

"Look at the photo of that rooftop," The judge said. "Do you see one or ten things that could trip a man up in that picture?"

The judge turned his attention to Holly. "You, young lady, need a lawyer, because I can smell a lawsuit cooking right now."

"But he wasn't supposed to be up there. I warned him and put up signs and everything."

"Tell that to your lawyer." The judge tucked his pajama top in his pants. "I want no more talk about murder just to get your name in the paper unless you have hard evidence, a witness, or a confession. You may be running for sheriff, but you answer to me until then."

"Yes, sir," Buster said.

"And Holly, if you see your ghost, why don't you ask him if he saw the victim fall off the roof or if someone pushed him? He's the only one who will know."

Holly nodded.

"If you'll excuse me, I have to make a few official comments to your guests."

"Thank you all for your patience on this very stressful and tragic night," Judge Maison said to Holly's guests still gathered in the entrance hall. "As you know, Chief Deputy Sheriff Fulton has been conducting an investigation into the tragic accident that led to the death of a young man far too soon. It's standard practice to investigate all accidental deaths, and we will continue to do that. His family will need closure, and we want to be prepared to answer their questions. I'll need you to make yourself available to give your statements."

"How long will this take?" Angel asked.

"We should be able to get the paperwork finished in a day. It takes as long as it takes." Judge Maison scratched his balding head. "Doesn't really matter. All this rain today pushed Bayou St. Agnes over the only road out of Delta Ridge. That's the problem with being a small town situated in the oxbow of the Mississippi and no bridge across it for miles. It'll be a day or two before it retreats to its banks."

"What?" Sylvia shoved her way to the front of the group. "There's got to be a way out of here."

"I'm so sorry," Holly said. "I'll comp your rooms, and we have plenty of supplies."

The judge nodded. "The only way out will be by boat or high-water vehicle, but those are reserved for emergencies."

A collective groan stretched across the entrance hall.

# CHAPTER TWENTY

Holly's bare foot was practically blue from the cold by the time she made it to her room to put on a pair of shoes. *Lordy, what a night.*

She staggered through her bedroom to the bathroom in the dark. Something just wasn't right about this whole thing with Tru, but who was she to argue with the judge or Jake about evidence?

Tru had obviously fallen from the widow's walk, which was a whole other problem. A legal one. Acid bubbled in her gut. But she couldn't think about that right now. She had guests to take care of and more questions to answer downstairs.

She shucked out of her skirt and blouse, then kicked off her remaining slipper on top of the pile of clothes in the corner of her bathroom. She tugged on a pair of yoga pants and a T-shirt she'd left hanging on a hook on the bathroom door.

As she washed her face, she tried to make sense of what had happened. *It had to be an accident. If someone pushed Tru, I would have seen that person in the hall or on the widow's walk, wouldn't I? Yes, I would.*

Holly dried her face then pulled her bathroom door open and flipped on her bedroom light.

A scream was trapped in her throat as she jumped in a spasm backward and hid behind the bathroom wall. Her heart thudded in her ears.

Wait. I couldn't have possibly seen what I saw. No way. She peeked around the door frame.

*Jumping Jehoshaphat!*

Standing in the middle of her bedroom, Burl stood dressed in a white tuxedo like he'd worn for their wedding ten years ago. Not a translucent ghost of her nearly ex husband but a solid image with a silver glow all around it. Holly blinked and clutched her chest.

He had to be a hallucination from the stress. Exhaustion? Maybe she'd fallen asleep and didn't know it. She rubbed her eyes.

Burl was still there. Just like last time he came back. *Oh, crapola.*

"Bet you didn't expect to see me here again, did you?" He opened his arms and gave a sly grin.

"B-B-Burl?" She stammered.

"In the flesh." He glanced down at his body. "Kind of."

She gripped the doorframe like a vise. "What are you doing here? Why are you here?" She shook her head as though that would clear her vision. "I don't understand. You're supposed to be . . ."

"In Heaven?" He lifted his hands, palms up, and eyed the ceiling.

"Yeah. It's a one-way ticket."

He dropped his hands to his sides. "I'm on furlough, kind of."

"Who gets a furlough from Heaven?" She pinched her brows together. "Why?"

"I asked for it," he said, stuffing his hands in his pockets. His brows slanted down over sad puppy eyes. "Guess you're not as glad to see me as I am to see you."

"Wait. You came just to see me? Can you do that?"

"Not exactly." He dug a white patent leather shoe into the rug.

Holly took a tentative step from the protection of the bathroom door. "Did you get kicked out of Heaven?"

"No one gets kicked out." He thumbed his chest. "Not even me."

"Lucifer got kicked out." But Burl was never that bad, although she wouldn't be totally surprised if Burl was a heavenly washout.

"Contrary to what you may think of me, I'm no Lucifer." He ambled to the French doors and looked out the window. "I came here of my own free will."

Holly took another step into the bedroom. "You get free will in Heaven?"

"Up to a point," he said, but didn't turn to face her. Could he lie on furlough like the old Burl?

"Spit it out, Burl." She slammed her hands on her hips. "Why are you here?"

He turned on his heels to face her. "I want to earn my wings."

"Seriously?" She all but rolled her eyes. He's got

to be making this up. "Like Clarence in that old black-and-white movie we used to watch with Mama at Christmas. *It's a Wonderful Life,* right?"

"Not exactly like that, but sort of." He sat on the edge of her bed, but the mattress didn't sag.

*Creepy.*

"Okay." Holly folded her arms over her chest. "I'll bite. How do you earn your wings, and do I have to do anything to make that happen?"

"Glad you asked." He eased off the bed and paced as he talked. "It's no secret I barely made the cut to get in that mile-high club, right?"

*Oh, no, he didn't just refer to Heaven as the mile-high club.* She stared at him with her mouth hanging open. "Burl! Do you know what you said?"

Thunder clapped and shook the house.

His eyes widened. He slapped his hand over his mouth and looked skyward. "Freudian slip." He held his hand to his heart. "I swear. You can't count that one."

"Count? What are you talking about?"

He looked back at her. "Nothing."

An old distrust inched up her back. *Same Burl. He's not telling me something and I know it.*

"I'm just saying I know what it's like to stare down the gates of Hell. Saint Peter thinks it makes me uniquely qualified for an important job that can help me earn my wings."

"What job is that?"

"Fixer." He puffed out his chest and laced his thumbs under his lapels. "I mean Heaven is great and all that, but I want something to do." He winked at Holly. "And wings are really cool. You know how I loved to fly."

"Okay," Holly said, drawing the word out. "What does a fixer do?"

Burl grinned. "I thought you'd never ask." He held up a finger. "Stay right there. I'll be right back."

He disappeared.

*Whoa.* Was that real? She staggered to the slipper chair and eased onto it. He'd come back as a ghost once. She shook her head. Why should she be surprised he'd come back as an angel? Or did he?

*Couldn't be. I'm asleep. That's it.* She rubbed her cold foot. *Or, I've finally lost my mind. Of course, Nelda always said that if you think you're crazy you're probably not. And if you are crazy, you don't know it because you're crazy.*

She sighed. *I may not be ready for the psych ward, but this is not normal. Even for me.* She leaned back in the chair and closed her eyes. Just very, very tired.

A chill settled over her as the acrid scent of smoke filtered into her senses. She popped her eyes open and gasped.

# CHAPTER TWENTY-ONE

Burl stood grinning and as proud as a cat holding a twitching mouse for his owner in the middle of her bedroom on her best heirloom rug. He held a semi-translucent Tru by the collar.

"I'm b-a-c-k," Burl said in a singsong voice.

"What the . . ." Holly stammered as she skittered behind her slipper chair for protection. "Why? And why on earth did you bring him back?"

"I heard you needed a ghost."

She shooed them away with both hands. "Take him back right now!"

"You!" Tru lunged for Holly.

She shrank into the corner. *Holy moly.*

Wild eyed, he fought against Burl's grip.

"Relax, bud." Burl tightened his grip on Tru. "I'm one of the good guys." He threw a glance her way. "She is too."

"I don't care who you are." Tru clawed at Burl's grip with blackened fingernails. "Get your hands off me."

"Ingrate." Burl held him at arm's length and eyed Holly. "Can you believe this little pile of . . ."

Tru's singed hair stood on end as though he'd stuck his finger in an electrical socket. Soot marked his cheeks and forehead, and his coat hung in tatters.

"Mercy!" Holly grabbed two fists full of her hair and mashed them to her skull to keep from pulling her hair out by the roots. "Why did you bring him back?" Was this payback for faking a ghost? *Oh, good gravy.*

"He didn't bring me back," Tru shouted. "Look at me. I'm dead."

"But you're in a better place," Burl said.

Tru screwed up his brows. "Huh?"

"Get it?" Burl slapped his knee. "Better place. Haven't you heard that before at a funeral?"

Tru hung his head and sighed. "Not funny, man."

Holly almost felt sorry for Tru.

"Sorry, bud. Afterlife humor." Burl let go of Tru's collar and slapped him on the back. "You'll get used to it."

"When?"

"You've got all of eternity. That depends on you." Burl nodded toward Holly. "And her."

"Me?" She pointed to her chest and shook her head. "Not again. How can you do this to me?"

"You're kidding me, right?" Tru said. "She's the reason I'm dead."

"How can you say that?" Holly wagged a finger at Tru. "I told you it wasn't safe up there. I warned you about what happened to Mackie. If you hadn't broken the rules, you wouldn't have fallen off the widow's walk."

"I did not fall." Tru glared at her. "I was pushed."

Holly froze for a second. "But . . ."

She slumped against the slipper chair. The last sliver of hope that this was all just a terrible accident rushed from her. So it was true. One of her guests was a murderer. She'd suspected it all along but didn't want to believe it. "Who did it?"

"If I saw the person, do you think I would've let anyone push me off the roof without taking that person with me? Some coward sneaked up behind me and pushed me over." He scowled at her and took a step forward. "It could have been you."

Burl grabbed him by the collar. "You can rest easy on that one, bud. If she was ever going to kill anyone it would have been me." Burl's eyes softened. "But she didn't."

"What do I have to do to get Tru where he needs to be?" Holly asked.

"Here's the deal." Burl clapped Tru on the back. "Old Tru here couldn't accept the fact that he was in that place where he could go either way." Burl made a thumbs-up, then a thumbs-down motion.

Holly recalled Tru being sucked into a red-hot hole in the earth and shuddered.

Tru groaned. "I wasn't exactly prepared to die."

"Who is?" Burl quipped. "Anyway, he got sucked down under, and I don't mean to Australia. Saint Pete wasn't ready to let him go, so he sent me to fix it."

"You're going to fix," Holly gulped, "him?"

Burl gave Tru the once-over. "Not exactly."

"So why am I still here?" Tru picked at his singed

hair. "Why didn't you just fly me up to Heaven with you?"

"Don't rub it in, bud. I'm going to get those wings," Burl cocked an eye at Tru. "Unless you belong where I found you."

"You mean I could go back down there?" Tru asked.

"Or take the highway to Heaven." Burl shrugged. "Or hang out as a ghost forever. Not my call."

"Wait a minute. You don't mean he could be stuck here with me."

"That's above my pay grade, too," Burl said. "All I know is I made a deal with the gatekeeper down there. He'll trade Tru for the soul of whoever is responsible for his death." Burl tilted his head forward and eyed her. "He'll collect on his time. Y'all figure that out any way you can." Burl glowed a moment, then disappeared leaving her with the ghost of the worst houseguest she'd ever had and a murder to solve.

Just peachy.


"I don't trust you," Tru said, as he followed Holly across her bedroom.

"Well, I don't like you," Holly said without so much as a sideways look at him on the way to her bedroom door. She didn't have time for any of this. Jake needed to know right away that Tru was positively pushed off the widow's walk and one of her guests did it. Her stomach pinched a bit. She wasn't looking forward to telling him she had another resident ghost and Tru's death was no accident. With her hand on the doorknob, she looked over her shoulder.

Tru stood, arms crossed, with a pout of a two-year-old.

Holly whirled around to face him. Sucking in a breath, she matched his body language as they had a stare down.

He snorted. "That's brutal."

"I'm working on honesty because lying gets me in trouble." If she'd just admitted Burl was gone, would Tru have come to debunk her ghost? Nope. He'd still be alive. Even though she didn't push him off the roof, she *felt* responsible. Somehow, she was going to make this right, even if she didn't like him one iota.

"I can handle it." Tru faded a bit. "No one likes me."

Holly patted her foot. "No one? What about your mother?"

"Dead." His image flickered.

"Father?" She asked.

"Dead," he said matter-of-factly.

"Do you have any family?"

"Nope."

Her heart dipped into the pool of loneliness she'd felt since she'd lost Mama and Grandma Rose, the last of her small family. *Crapola. I don't need to feel sorry for this guy.* "Friends?"

"Real or online?"

"Real."

"Just my fish." He shrugged. "Guess they'll die too."

"Fish. That's it?" No need to ask about a girlfriend. At least she didn't have to face his family after what happened. "I'm not surprised. You could really use some work on your social skills."

"Social skills are overrated."

She had to get rid of this guy fast. "I'll call an animal shelter and see if I can get your fish rescued."

"Why would you do that?"

"It's the right thing to do. Just like figuring out who pushed you off the widow's walk." She cocked her head to the side. "Speaking of which, we need to set a few rules if we're going to work together to get you where you need to be."

Tru's image faded a bit.

"Are you okay?" she asked.

"Do I look okay?" He bugged his eyes out and swept down his singed clothes with a flourish. "I'm a freakin' ghost, which do not exist according to metaphysical science."

"See, you should trust me. You thought I was lying about Burl, but—

"Duh." He shook his head. "Don't rub it in. I got it, but I don't have to like it."

"It's just when Burl was a ghost and he faded like that, he— he disappeared for a while."

"Where did he go?"

Holly shrugged. "He said it was like a black hole or something."

"As long as it's not where I was."

"I want you out of here, so I need you to help me figure out who pushed you."

"You could have knocked me off the roof as easily as anyone else here."

"A testament to how many people you've totally teed off and why you don't have any friends."

"Ha. Ha. What if you don't want to find my killer because it's you?"

"They do have the death penalty here in Louisiana." She pointed a finger at him. "You are not worth dying for, a life sentence, or my eternal damnation."

"You probably didn't plan to get caught."

"You don't have to believe me or trust me."

"Good, because I don't."

"Not that you care, but whoever murdered you is under this roof. I'm not letting anyone get away with murder at Holly Grove."

"Unless it's you."

For the last time, you're not worth killing to me."

"Someone thought so."

Holly blew out an exasperated sigh. "What good would it do for me to kill you since I'm stuck with you, anyway?" Holly eyed Tru. "Temporarily."

"Good point." A little ash fell from Tru's hair as he scratched his head.

"First, we need to lay down a few rules if you want me to help you."

"I don't know why I need your help. No one can see me and I can go anywhere and listen to any conversation. I'll have this figured out in no time."

"No one can hear you either, except me." Holly said. "You know that, right? No one but me saw you or heard you scream before you got sucked down to you-know-where."

He screwed his lips to the side and looked away.

"You've got to work with me if you want your side of the story told, so you can go to . . . wherever."

Tru nodded.

"These are the rules." Holly counted them off on her fingers. "I will not talk to you in public. Ever." Lesson learned from her last ghostly encounter. "You will never go in my bathroom when I'm in there."

Tru bugged his eyes out. "I'm not that kind of creeper."

"Just sayin'." Another lesson from experience. "You will not mess with Nelda or Rhett in any way."

"If they can't hear or see me, how can I mess with them?"

"Just don't." Holly shoved a hand on her hip. "It's a rule."

"I won't bother Nelda unless she killed me."

"She didn't." Holly sighed. "You landed in front of her car with her in it."

Tru shook his head. "Good alibi, if it's true."

"You *do* realize you are dead because you *didn't* believe me in the first place."

Tru kicked his head back. "Oh, yeah."

"And most important, you will do what I say."

"And if I don't?"

"It may be very hot where you're going."

A knock sounded on the door.

Holly glared at Tru. "Follow the rules."

She crossed the bedroom and cracked the door open.

Six feet of delicious Jake stood with his arm resting on her door frame. "Just checking on you."

She yanked him inside. "I've got proof someone pushed Tru off the widow's walk." She winced.
"Sort of."

"Huh?"

"Well, you might not be able to see him, but you
did see Burl just before he, you know . . ."

Jake tilted his head to the side and crinkled his
brow. "See who?"

"Never mind. Just look." She whirled around and
pointed to the empty room."

Tru was gone. *Crapola.*

Jake followed her gaze, then looked back at her.
"Um, am I missing something?"

"Tru. He's back." She waved her hands as though
she could erase what she'd said. "I mean he's a ghost
like Burl."

Jake cut his eyes to where she'd pointed. "He's
here now?"

"No." She walked to where Tru had stood and
could feel the chill of his presence. "He was right
here, but he, uh . . ." She flopped her hands by her
side. "It's a ghost thing."

"Ghost thing?" Jake's brows slanted over his chocolate eyes. At least this time he didn't think she was
crazy.

"Burl used to just fade out or disappear all the
time. He didn't know why or he didn't tell me if he
did." She wagged a finger at Jake. "But I'm telling
you Tru was here."

"As a ghost?"

Holly nodded her head.

"Déjà vu." He scratched his head. "What is it with you and ghosts?"

"I don't know, right? Be careful what you wish for." She sighed. "I thought Burl was a one-off thing, but maybe once you see one ghost you can see them all." She shoved her hands in the air. "I don't know, but Tru told me he did not fall off the widow's walk. He was pushed."

"Who did it?"

"He didn't see the person. He said someone pushed him from behind." She shoved her hands on her hips. "It was *not* an accident."

"Oh, boy."

"We've got to figure out who did it."

"We?" Jake shifted his weight.

"You know I can't tell anyone Tru's ghost told me someone pushed him until I have proof. What did you find out?"

Jake flashed his jacket open, showing his St. Agnes Parish Sheriff's Deputy badge. "What do you think?"

"How'd you get that and why?" Holly asked, staring at the badge.

"I've got my ways of weaseling my way to where I need to be." He melted her with his chocolate gaze. "Part of my skill set."

Among other things.

"The judge deputized me since they're short-handed and to keep an eye on Buster. I'm the newest deputy for the St. Agnes Parish Sheriff's Department. Looks like I'm working undercover for you, sweetheart." He winked at her. "I'm also here on official police business."

"What's that?"

"Buster sent me to escort you downstairs to give him your *official* statement."

"Now?"

Jake nodded. "And I don't think a voice from the grave is going to help your case."

"Case?" Holly swallowed hard. "He doesn't really think . . ."

"He found your missing slipper on the widow's walk."

"Mercy."

# CHAPTER TWENTY-TWO

"State your name for the record." Buster said, sitting across the table from Holly in her dining room.

"Good grief." Holly waved him off. "You've known me since kindergarten."

"Legal name," he said, stone-faced.

"Holly Lane Davis." She squirmed on the embroidered chair. "I've already answered questions once. I really need to take care of my guests." And figure out which one is a murderer. *Mercy.*

"This won't take long," he said, pencil in hand hovering over a clipboard.

Wind from the storm outside rattled the windows. Would the rain ever stop? She rubbed her arms against the chill coming in with the weather.

Buster glanced outside. "Coming in from the north. That's gonna push water in some low-lying places." He pushed a button on a radio clipped to his shoulder. "404 to dispatch. Any calls about more flooding?"

The radio crackled and a female voice spit out a few numbers and garbled words.

The gasolier over the table swayed a fraction. *Mercy.* She hadn't seen it do that since the last hurricane. The medallion around the base of the fixture bowed.

Two well-worn loafers bled through the medallion, followed by blue jeans and the rest of Tru Stalwort. His shoes, which had been to Hades and back, touched down on the Queen Anne walnut table that every generation in her family had gathered around for meals. *He really, really can't stay here.*

Tru held his hands palms up, out to his sides, and bobbed his head. "How cool is this?"

She realized her mouth hung open and she closed it.

A voice came into her consciousness. "Are you willfully ignoring my questions?"

Holly snapped her attention to Buster. "Huh? I mean . . . I'm sorry. My mind must have been on something else." Or someone. How could she carry on a conversation with this sideshow?

"Did you think the widow's walk was unsafe?" Buster asked.

"I-uh," She stared at Tru as he passed his hand through the gasolier.

"This part of being dead is awesome. Physics is way wrong," Tru said, whipping his finger back and forth through a dangling crystal on the gasolier.

*Until I get my hands on him.* She motioned with her eyes to get off the table.

He tiptoed around the votives on the table and

squatted in front of Buster, then waved his hand in front of his face.

"Wow," Tru drew the word out in a long breath. "You're right. He can't see me."

*Just ignore him.* "I'm sorry, Buster. What did you say?"

"At the scene of the . . ." He hesitated and eyed Holly. "Accident."

"Accident? You mean murder!" Tru whipped his head around to Holly, and soot peppered out of his red mop of hair, then disappeared as it fell. "Tell him!"

Rule number one. Do not talk to him in public. Holly clenched her jaw. *And I won't pay attention to his temper tantrum either.*

Buster tapped his pencil against the walnut dining table as though waiting for her to say something. He huffed. "Accident is what the judge called it and we'll go with that unless proven otherwise."

It sounded like Buster still wanted to prove otherwise. How could she persuade him he was right about the murder but it wasn't her? She couldn't. At least not yet.

Tru slammed his fist on the table but it sunk into the surface. He lost his balance and fell right through the table.

Holly covered her mouth to hide her grin. Tru had a lot to learn about being a ghost, but she had to admit his skills were progressing faster than Burl's had.

She nodded at Buster to keep from saying something stupid such as Tru's ghost had told her he was pushed off the widow's walk. If she knew Buster, he'd have her locked up at the St. Agnes Clinic until they could transfer her to a padded room because she was obviously out of her ever-lovin' mind. And that was the best-case scenario. Her slipper put her on the widow's walk around the time of Tru's murder, and that's all Buster could see or understand right now. He gave parking tickets for one inch of a bumper over the yellow parking line. He couldn't see past the obvious.

Tru pushed through the surface of the table and waded out of it. "Aren't you going to tell him? He can help us figure out what coward did this to me."

The sooner she got out of that room, the sooner she could explain to Tru why she couldn't push for a murder investigation right now, not that he'd understand. At least, he'd be aware.

"I took several photographs of the warning signs you had on the door to the widow's walk. Why did you feel they were necessary, and when did you put them up?"

*Is he setting me up for something?* "When Mackie fell through the decking the other day, I knew it wasn't safe. I put the signs up after I caught Tru smoking a cigar up there."

"Come on." Tru huffed. "You made that rule up. If I could smoke on the balcony, why couldn't I smoke on the widow's walk? Open air. Same thing." Tru tossed a look at Buster. "And why does he care?"

"But you've lived in this house your entire life and never felt it was dangerous, right?" Buster said.

"Of course not." Holly did her best to ignore Tru

as he looked over Buster's shoulder at his clipboard. "I used to play with my dolls up there."

Tru rubbed his chin. "Want to know what he's writing?"

"After you converted to a B&B, you weren't concerned your guests would wander up there and fall off?"

She nodded at Tru.

"So you did know the danger?" Buster jotted something down.

"No." *I wasn't nodding at you. Mercy.*

"He wrote negligence," Tru said.

*The very idea!* She sat up on the edge of her chair. "Look, none of my guests knew the widow's walk was up there until I renovated the attic. When I added two more guest suites up there they could see the door at the end of the stairs. Before then, they would have had to go through the attic." She cocked an eyebrow. "That was a hazard. Now that you mention it, I did find two little old ladies rummaging through the attic once. They didn't even know what they were looking for. They just thought they may see something interesting." Holly gave a weak smile. "It never crossed my mind that anyone would go up there."

"When did you decide it was dangerous?" Buster asked.

"It wasn't dangerous if you watched where you walked, and I did," Tru said in Buster's ear, then shook his head and paced around the table. "Unless someone sneaked up behind you and pushed you off. That is *not* an accident."

"When the inspector visited last month to give me a permit to renovate the widow's walk for stargazing.

I thought it would be a draw for guests if I installed a telescope up there. He told me I needed a higher railing to meet the public code and a handrail on the stairway up to it. I hired Mackie to build a Plexiglas barrier at the right height. Then I found out the floor had a rotten spot in it when Mackie fell through it. That's when I knew it was dangerous."

"I see," Buster said. "And when did you put up the warning signs."

"After I caught Tru smoking a cigar up there." She stood. "I really need to check on my guests." *And get Tru out of here.*

Buster pointed to her chair. "Not before?"

Holly shook her head but didn't sit. "Can I go now?"

"Just a few more questions," Buster said. "Did you feel that posting that notice protected you if anyone fell from the roof?"

*He's setting a trap, and I'm not going to fall for it.* "No. It protected them." She sighed. "Or it was supposed to." She cut an eye at Tru. "Some folks don't follow rules."

"Some rules are stupid," Tru said.

Buster made a few more notes. "Did you tell him the area was restricted?"

"Yes, but he went back up there multiple times until he . . ." She glanced at Tru.

"Fell?" Buster said, scribbling on his clipboard.

She didn't confirm. Holly gave herself a virtual pat on the back. She'd carefully made it through the interview without telling one lie.

Tru jabbed a finger toward Buster. "Tell him someone pushed me. He's a cop. You know, the kind that actually solves crimes."

While Buster wasn't looking she held one finger up to Tru for rule number one. *I will never talk to you in public.*

Tru rolled his eyes. "You are purposely misleading that cop, and you're supposed to be working on telling the truth. Ha! I know you can go to jail for doing that to the FBI. Whose side are you on?"

Buster shifted in his chair but didn't look up from his clipboard. "Did you or anyone else see him fall?"

*The sneaky little devil still thinks I did it because he found my flippin' slipper.* If she could convince him he's right about the murder but not about her, he could help her figure out who really did it. How could she do that? She eyed Tru. Buster would never believe Tru's ghost told her.

"Didn't you talk to Nelda? He landed right in front of her car. When I heard her screaming and he wasn't on the widow's walk, I knew what had happened."

"I've taken her statement." Buster stole a quick glance at Holly, then fidgeted with his pencil. "Did *you* see him fall?"

"No." She drew the word out for emphasis.

Buster hooked his arm over the back of the chair as though he had all day to hear what she had to say.

"I smelled cigar smoke on my balcony and I knew he was up there. I was on my way to make him come inside when I heard the thuds. When I got up there, I heard Nelda scream. I looked over the side and saw Tru on the ground."

"Is that when you lost your slipper? Since you were only wearing one slipper when I drove up, it's logical the mate we found on the widow's walk belongs to you, correct?"

"You!" Tru screamed and shoved a blackened finger at her face. "You pushed me!"

Holly leaned back and sucked in a breath. *Oh, boy.* She shook her head. "He wasn't on the widow's walk when I got there," she said, focusing on Buster and doing her best to ignore Tru, who looked like he was about to self-combust.

"You suck at lying." Tru kicked at the air. "And you're supposed to help me. I don't have a prayer."

"Are you interrogating me?"

"No, ma'am." He scribbled across his clipboard. "Just getting all the facts down for the accident report. I don't believe for one minute that the victim fell off the widow's walk." Buster reared back on two legs of his chair. "But what I believe doesn't count. Evidence does."

"What if I told you I knew for a fact Tru was murdered?"

Buster's chair wobbled and he waved his arms to keep from falling backward. The front chair legs came down with a *clomp*. He leaned forward and leveled a serious stare at her. "Are you making a confession?"

# CHAPTER TWENTY-THREE

"Confession?" Holly stood up so fast she knocked over the Queen Anne armchair. She took a few steps back from Buster. "No way. All I'm saying is I believe someone pushed Tru off the widow's walk, but it wasn't me." She lifted her right hand. "I swear."

"Says the women who's trying to stop lying." Tru turned to Buster and got on his knees. "Come on, man. Please. Arrest her."

Buster stood and yanked up his pants. "Unless you saw someone else making a getaway, you were the only one with opportunity."

"Now you're talking." Tru jumped to his feet.

She glared at Tru. "But I wasn't the only one with motive."

"Doesn't matter." Tru banged his palm to his head. "I've seen enough TV to know it takes motive and opportunity. I exposed your scam. You are two for two. And guilty."

"It was dark," Holly said, careful to keep her voice calm. "Someone could have hidden behind one of the chimneys."

Buster threw his pencil on the table. "If it wasn't for the judge, I'd arrest you right now."

"Who's this judge? What is this? Good-old-boy justice?" Tru looked at the ceiling. "Where's that wannabe angel? This isn't even close to a fair chance to keep from roasting for eternity."

Thunder rattled the house.

Burl materialized beside Tru and grabbed him by his collar. "You called, bud?"

"My work here is done, man." Tru pointed at Holly. "She did it. Take her. Go make the deal and set me free."

"You think you've earned your get-out-of-Hell-free card just by pointing a finger?" Burl gave an exasperated sigh. "Come with me. We've got to talk."

Well, at least Burl believed her. There was no doubt in her mind Buster would arrest her if the judge hadn't said it was an accident until proven otherwise.

Holly tipped up her chin at Buster. "I've got nothing else to say to you without a lawyer."

With that, she spun on her heels and marched to the door. She slid the pocket doors open with more gusto than necessary.

Miss Alice and Sam stood inches from her face. Sam cleared his throat and took a step back. At least he pretended he wasn't listening. Miss Alice folded her arms and eyed Holly.

What had they heard?

Holly closed the pocket doors behind her then held her finger to her lips. "None of that can go in the paper or anywhere else, do you hear?"

"The public has a right to know if we have a murderer in our town," Miss Alice said. "Isn't that right, Sam?"

Sam's bushy gray brows twisted across his forehead like they didn't know which way to go. "Darn straight."

"For once, I need y'all to keep a secret." Holly grabbed them each by an elbow and towed them toward the porch and privacy. "I know what I'm doing, believe it or not."

Miss Alice huffed. "If you call getting yourself almost arrested knowing what you're doing."

"Shh," Holly said as they walked past the parlor doors."

Miss Alice huffed. "Don't you shush me?"

*No need. It won't work anyway.* As they passed the parlor, Holly cased the guests. Bob had manspread over most of Holly's Victorian settee. Liz dozed, resting her head on Bob's meaty shoulder. Sylvia paced behind the settee while she talked on her cell phone. Kneeling on the floor in front of the hearth, Thomas tended an impressive roaring fire. But where was Angel?

Holly paused and scanned the parlor again. Maybe she was in her room. Had she left? And where was Jake?

Miss Alice wrestled her arm loose. "I can walk on my own."

"Fine." Holly took the final steps to the back door and held it open. "Just hear me out."

Miss Alice gave Holly a side-glance as she walked ahead of Sam.

Old school all the way, Sam grabbed the door and motioned Holly ahead of him. "This is going to be interesting."

"No." Holly faced both of them. "This is going to be boring if you just hear me out."

"How long is this going to take?" Miss Alice ambled to a wicker rocker. "My feet are killing me from standing on that hard floor."

"You could have been sitting in the parlor like everyone else." If she wasn't so nosy, but Holly hoped that would be a good thing for once.

"That has nothing to do with it." Miss Alice dusted off the cushion on a wicker rocker. "I've been in these pumps since yesterday at five."

Sam stood in front of another wicker chair, waiting for Miss Alice and Holly to sit.

Did anyone under sixty do that anymore? "I'm too antsy to sit."

Miss Alice balanced her purse on her knees. "Get on with it."

"Neither of you think I murdered anyone, do you?" Holly asked.

They eyed each other.

Sam scratched his head. "There was that time she nearly killed Jake."

He would bring that up. "That was an accident, and I don't have to point out that Jake is not dead."

"I'll give you that," Sam said. "But there was that time—"

"The point is I've never *tried* to kill anyone." Holly put her hands on her hips and patted her foot.

*Mercy. Like I've got a string of bodies in my past. Well, there was Burl, but still.*

Miss Alice peered at Holly over her glasses. "Not on purpose. But what about Mackie?"

"Okay. He did fall through my roof, but it's not like I tripped him or anything." Holly flapped her hands at her sides. "Really, you both know I wouldn't kill anyone."

She took their silence as agreement or as close as she'd get to agreement by either of them. "All I need you to do is just not even breathe the word *murder* until after checkout time today."

"Why would I suppress that story?" Sam asked.

"So, I can prove I didn't do it and who did before they all leave at checkout time today. Just give me twelve hours."

"Lord help us all," Nelda said stirring a pot of the homemade hot chocolate on the 1928 gas stove at two o'clock in the morning.

The sweet, rich scent of cocoa hung in the air as the swinging kitchen door flapped closed behind Holly. Rhett lay curled in a ball dead asleep under the planter's table.

No Jake. A niggle of disappointment worked its way through her. Where could he be? "What are you still doing here?"

"Those poor folks can't even go to bed, not that they could sleep if they did." She rapped her favorite wooden spoon on the side of the pot. "I know I can't."

Holly noticed a platter stacked with crustless peanut butter and jelly sandwiches, cut in perfect triangles. "You made midnight PB&Js like Le Pavillon in New Orleans."

Nelda nodded. "Ain't we fancy."

"I guess we could call it an early wake for Tru." Holly snagged a sandwich. Maybe Jake had gone to bed. He'd told her he'd been traveling all day and night.

"Poor Tru." Nelda crossed herself. "God rest his soul."

Tru's soul was nowhere near at rest, but Nelda didn't need to know that right now. Holly wasn't sure if she should warn Nelda about Tru or hope he followed rule number three: Don't mess with the cook.

Nelda glanced toward a cabinet. "Get some of your grandma's blue willow cups down for the hot chocolate."

"Have you seen Jake?" Holly asked, grabbing stacks of cups and saucers.

"Not since he came in earlier lookin' for you." Nelda turned the flame off under the hot chocolate. "Why?"

"Oh, just wondering." She'd expected him to want to know how the interview went.

"Uh-huh." Nelda batted her lashes at Holly. "Don't you lie. You know you're glad he's here."

"I haven't even thought about that." Heat rushed to Holly's cheeks as she put the blue willow cups on the counter next to the stove.

"Uh-huh." Nelda poured a ladle of hot chocolate

in a cup. "I'll tell him you're looking for him when I see him."

Holly spread a white linen napkin over a hundred-year-old silver tray. After Nelda dropped a dollop of whipped cream on a cup of hot chocolate, Holly placed it on the tray. She laced her fingers through the baroque handles on the tray.

"You just back away from that liquid chocolate." Nelda elbowed Holly aside. "I don't want to be mopping up that sticky stuff."

"Really?" Holly faked insult. She couldn't count the number of times she'd let things slide off trays attempting to help Nelda serve her guests. Just this week it had been orange juice.

Nelda lifted the tray of hot chocolate and motioned with her head to the cute little PB&Js. "You grab those. This ought to put everybody out for what's left of the night."

Holly followed Nelda to the kitchen door.

Nelda bumped the door with her hip and held it open for Holly. "I hear Buster still thinks it was murder?"

"He thinks I shoved Tru off the roof." Holly barely squeezed by Nelda without tipping her tray.

"Humph. He's all for show." Nelda let the door go and it flapped closed behind her. "Buster's just doin' all that for attention 'cause he's runnin' for sheriff. I think I'd know if I was feedin' a murderer."

"I read somewhere that we walk right past a murderer multiple times a day and don't know it." Holly still couldn't wrap her head around the idea that one of her guests could be a killer.

"Maybe in New York City or Chicago but not in

Delta Ridge," Nelda said, without as much as a slosh of the cups of hot chocolate as she made her way down the entrance hall.

"My heart still ain't right after Tru just dropped from the sky in front of my car. Then the sheriff was thinkin' one of us shoved him off the roof, 'cept not me 'cause I saw that poor boy fall. Not Miss Alice or Sam either 'cause they were on the ground, too."

"It's just awful," Holly said, falling in behind Nelda.

"Couldn't have been your Jake either 'cause he wasn't here yet when that terrible thing happened."

*My Jake.* Nelda couldn't get it into her head that Jake was not the kind of guy anyone could possess, much less Holly.

That left Sylvia, Liz, Angel, Bob, and her in Holly Grove when someone shoved Tru off the roof. One of them was a cold-blooded killer. "I'm so sorry you had to see that," Holly said.

"At first, I thought it was a big tree limb, on account of all the wind we've been havin' 'cause that front is movin' in. But when I got out my car, I saw him all crumpled up there on the grass, God rest his soul."

"You really should have gone home after all that," Holly said. "I thought your nephew was coming to get you."

"Humph." Nelda stopped just before the wide doorway to the parlor. "Buster said I couldn't go nowhere 'til I give a statement, so I told my nephew I'd call him when I was ready. I figured I'd stay busy to calm my nerves."

"Have you given your statement yet?" Holly asked.

"Yeah, but I was almost finished with the PB&Js when it was my turn. After all that, I decided I might as well wait until six when my nephew gets up for work. No need for both of us to lose a night's sleep."

Holly noticed the deputy who had been guarding the front door had left. "Where'd the deputy go?"

"Oh, they all left 'cept Buster not long after the judge said it was an accident and not murder."

"And Buster?"

"He left after he took about a book full of notes on what everybody saw, but he still said no one could leave 'til tomorrow after he files his report with the sheriff."

"Then why is everyone still up?"

"'Cause I told them I was makin' something to help them sleep."

They stepped into the parlor. Hushed conversations stopped, leaving only the crackle of the fireplace. Sylvia stood warming her backside against the fireplace. Thomas had joined Bob and Liz on the settee, and Miss Alice and Sam sat in the matching Victorian chairs across from the settee.

"Who wants PB&Js and hot chocolate?" Nelda asked.

Sylvia groaned. "I was hoping for something stronger after the night we've all had."

"Me too," Sam said pulling himself up to the edge of his seat."

"Nonsense." Miss Alice put down her knitting. "The melatonin in the warm milk will help you sleep. Not alcohol."

"Speak for yourself." Sam stood. "I'll take a shot of bourbon in mine if you've got some."

"That's Holly's department." Nelda held the tray of steaming hot chocolate in front of Bob, Liz, and Thomas.

"Hope you enjoy," Nelda said as Bob and Liz each took a cup. Liz's cup rattled and a little of the hot chocolate sloshed out onto the saucer.

*At least, I'm not the only one with trouble balancing cups and saucers.*

Thomas smiled and took a cup of hot chocolate. "Smells wonderful, Nelda."

She all but turned her nose up at him. Holly had never seen Nelda take an instant dislike to anyone like that before.

Sylvia stepped away from the fireplace and snagged a cup of hot chocolate. She lifted it to Holly. "I'll take some of that bourbon Sam is having in mine, too."

"No problem." Holly held out the tray of PB&Js. All she really wanted to do was find out where they were when Tru was killed. She had so many questions that would be better asked privately, but how could she get them alone?

"It's really thoughtful of you to make a snack for us after such a trying night," Thomas said, taking a PB&J from the tray.

"Nelda made them." Holly handed him a starched napkin square embroidered with the Holly Grove initials in white on white. "It's the least we could do after what y'all have been through tonight. It happened right in front of Nelda, bless her heart."

Thomas shook his head. "I heard her scream. At first, I thought it was you. I ran as fast as I could to the sound, and then I called 911."

"So, you were the first to get there," Holly said. "Were you still downstairs when it happened?"

"I wasn't first." He glanced at Sam and Miss Alice. "They were already there. I'm not sure who else was there. I was just the first to call 911. I felt like I needed to do something."

Holly tried to remember who was standing on the front porch when she made it down from the widow's walk. Was everyone there except her?

Liz took a PB&J and her hand shook as she nestled the sandwich on the saucer with the hot chocolate cup.

"Are you okay?" Holly asked. Was she traumatized from the night or was something else going on? Was this more traumatic for her because of a guilty conscience? Liz didn't seem like the type to get mad enough about anything to raise her voice, much less do bodily harm.

Liz nodded. "It's just I've never seen anyone dead. Have you?"

"Unfortunately, yes." She glanced around the room for Tru. If he was like Burl, he could show up anytime.

"I just want to go home," Liz said to Bob as Holly held the tray of PB&Js in front of him.

Bob leaned back and held his hand up like a stop sign. "Allergic."

"Oh, I'm sorry," Holly said, pulling the tray away from him. "I didn't know. I'll get you something else."

He shook his head. "I'm not hungry anyway."

Had he lost his appetite because of the murder or because he'd murdered someone or because she just waved potential death in front of him? *Am I letting my imagination take over?*

"I'll eat his." Sylvia licked her lips while looking at Bob. She pinched a sandwich triangle between her French-manicured fingertips.

His lips parted just a fraction, then he quickly looked down at his cup of hot chocolate. Had he been trapped in her spell for that second? Was something going on there?

Liz sipped her hot chocolate and didn't seem to notice, or maybe she was used to it.

"If anybody wants seconds, I've got two cups left," Nelda said as Sam and Miss Alice each took a cup of hot chocolate from the tray.

Those two cups belonged to the only guests not present, Jake and Angel. Her imagination jumped into overdrive. Were they together?

Sam loaded four PB&Js on his napkin. "Might as well eat a whole sandwich."

Miss Alice passed. "Peanut butter isn't just peanuts, you know. It was originally made with Crisco. Years ago, I wrote letters to the FDA to demand that be taken out. They said they did but I don't trust what they replaced it with."

Sam smacked. "I liked it with Crisco and I like it now."

Holly turned to Bob. "Why don't you come with me to the kitchen and see what we can find to make a sandwich for you."

"No thanks. Like I said, I'm not hungry."

*Crapola.* How was she ever going to get anyone alone to talk to them?

"Suit yourself." Holly headed to the kitchen to get a bottle of bourbon.

A few minutes later, she rummaged through the liquor bottles in her pantry. She shook a half-empty bottle. It'd have to do, but she could have sworn she had a full bottle behind it just the other day.

Just as she closed the pantry door, she heard the deep rumble of a motorcycle. Jake.

She rushed to the door and stepped out on the porch. The motor pulsed as a single headlight meandered toward Holly Grove.

And just like that memories of their night rides in high school popped into her head. She'd slip out of the house and meet him at the highway. Then she'd hop on the back of his motorcycle and wrap her arms around his waist. They rode like one. They were one. Back then.

Now he didn't even tell her or evidently anyone else he was leaving. She folded her arms across her chest. Well, he'd better be able to tell her more about what Buster learned by interviewing her guests about the so-called accident since he was a deputy now.

A few seconds later, Jake rolled up to the porch. He wore a solid black full helmet and Angel, dripping wet, was plastered to his back. What the . . .

# CHAPTER TWENTY-FOUR

Jake hit the kill switch on his motorcycle and everything went as black as the night sky except for Holly. Under the porch light, she stood strangling the neck of a bottle of bourbon and staring him down. It hadn't taken but a glance to see something was wrong, and whatever that something was had to do with him.

Angel slipped off the back of his bike like a mad wet cat. She swiped the rain off her face and marched toward the house. Evidently he was two for two for ticking off women today. He knew why Angel was mad at him, but Holly? He had no idea.

He pulled off his helmet and stuffed it in the compartment under his seat.

"He's crazy," Angel said as she stomped past Holly on the way in the house.

Jake had been called worse for doing less. He brushed the rain off his leathers, then strode toward Holly and whatever wrath she had in store for him.

"Crazy, huh?" She met him at the screen door. "Must have been some ride."

"Wet." He stomped the mud off his feet, then scrubbed his soles across the not-so-welcome mat. "And eventful."

"I bet." She looked over her shoulder. "What did you do to her? Pop wheelies or do doughnuts?"

He could see Angel drying her hair with a towel through the window.

"That would have been more fun, especially with you on the back of my bike."

"You didn't ask me to go for a ride." Holly spun around and paced double-time into the kitchen.

"You're jealous, aren't you?" Jake followed Holly into the kitchen about the time Miss Alice walked in carrying a cup and saucer.

"Don't you touch me," Angel said, pointing a finger at Jake.

Miss Alice stepped between them. "What's going on here?"

"He kidnapped me." Angel glared at him.

"He what?" Miss Alice put her cup on the counter. "Did he do anything to you?"

"Hold on there," Jake said. "Let's not jump to any conclusions."

Miss Alice put her arm around Angel, then lifted it and looked at her sleeve. "Child, you're soaked."

"His fault." Angel shot Jake a drop-dead look. "I left because the spirits are restless here. I can't stay in this environment, but he followed me. He had no right to haul me back here against my will."

Holly turned to face Jake. Her brow knitted and her lips parted like she was going to say something, but she didn't.

"Remember, the judge deputized me to help out

temporarily." He shoved his hands in his pockets. "Just following orders."

"What orders?" Miss Alice demanded. "You can't just manhandle a woman like that."

"The judge asked everyone to stay put until tomorrow in case he had any more questions."

"Yes, he did," Miss Alice said. "It's our civic duty since this was a—"

"Terrible accident." *Mercy.* Holly didn't trust Miss Alice to keep a secret. *That may not be possible for her.*

"The sheriff wants to give a full and accurate report of what happened to console Tru's family," Jake said.

"That's right," Miss Alice said. "And Holly even waived our room fees for the inconvenience."

"I never agreed to stay here another night," Angel said.

"You didn't disagree either." And he didn't buy the whole restless spirits in the house thing. That woman was hiding something. "You left and I followed you, and it's a good thing I did."

Angel all but rolled her eyes. "I could have gotten across."

Jake shook his head. "Then why did your car flood out right before I pulled you out of the St. Agnes Bayou?"

"How deep is it now?" Holly asked.

"About four feet deep just before it meets the highway," Jake said.

Holly covered her mouth, but he could see her grin. Why would she be happy about being flooded in with this crew?

"You had no right to bring me back here and you'll regret it." Angel stormed out of the kitchen.

"Bless her heart." Miss Alice clicked her tongue. "It's fools like her I read about in the newspaper every year who drown trying to drive through high water on roads."

Jake shucked out of his leather jacket. "No one at Holly Grove or anybody who lives along this dead-end blacktop is going anywhere as long as Bayou St. Agnes is backed up over the road."

"It floods every hurricane or frog-strangling rain and sits there for days," Miss Alice said. "It's ridiculous the parish doesn't fix that problem. I'm going to call the mayor in the morning and tell him we almost had a tragedy over the parish's lack of initiative." Miss Alice shook her head and pushed on the swinging kitchen door, then turned back to them. "Oh, Sam wanted the bourbon."

Holly handed over the bottle, and Miss Alice left.

"Was wondering if all this had driven you to drink." Jake winked at Holly.

"Not yet, but I'm not making any guarantees." She peeked out the kitchen door, then turned back to Jake. "This is the break we needed."

"Break?" Jake didn't like the sound of being marooned at Holly Grove being a break.

"Yes. Burl made a deal with the gatekeeper in Hell to trade the name of whoever killed Tru to erase his name from the book of the damned. If no one can leave, I can figure this out. I can free Tru and make things right."

"Maybe Tru needs to make things right. Whoever

did this may not blink an eye at killing again. This could be dangerous."

"Maybe, but I couldn't live with myself if Tru goes to Hell because I got him involved by lying about still having a ghost. You know lying is a sin. If I don't save Tru, could my name be added to the list?"

"You're going to get in the middle of this no matter what, aren't you?"

"If I saved Burl, I can save Tru. I think I've found my calling."

"I think you're in over your head."

Holly now knew she'd been given a gift and a curse. *Jake has no confidence in me, but I'm going to prove him wrong or earn an orange jumpsuit trying.*

Either way, Angel had told Tru he'd be dead soon. Holly needed to know all she could about Angel. Why had she made that prediction? Why was she so desperate to get away from Holly Grove? And did she have an alibi for her whereabouts when Tru flew off the widow's walk?

Holly took a fortifying breath outside Angel's door. She carried a tray that held her peace offering of PB&Js, a cup of hot chocolate, one of Nelda's pralines tucked in a wax-paper sleeve, and a bag of sage.

"Turndown service," Holly called through the door.

No answer. Had Angel slipped away again? But where could she go?

Holly put the tray down and pulled her master key out of her pocket. She knocked. "Housekeeping."

Still silence. Holly unlocked the door, then opened it a crack. "Angel, are you in here?"

Holly pushed the door open and stepped into the dark room. She flipped the light on. The bed was made and Angel's wet clothes hung from all four posts on the rice planter's bed. The bathroom door was open. The cord to the blow dryer was strung across the lavatory like Angel had a death wish. A couple of towels lay in a pile in the corner. "Angel?"

Holly eased into the bathroom. The luxury bathrobe she kept on a hanger on the back of the door was gone. So were the washable slippers that should have been in the basket near the pedestal lavatory.

*Huh.* Wherever she was she'd be wearing a bathrobe and slippers. She had to be somewhere in the house.

Holly eyed the French doors to the balcony. *Aha.*

She scampered across the room and flung the doors open. A blast of damp winter air bit her as she stepped outside on the empty balcony.

*Crapola. Where is she? I'm really not in the mood for hide-and-seek.*

A light fog floated from Holly's mouth as she rubbed her arms to fight off the cold. The scent of smoke drifted to her nose. She sniffed. Not cigar smoke. Cigarette smoke.

A memory flashed in her mind. A plastic evidence bag. Three lipstick-stained cigarette butts. She'd seen the baby-faced deputy carry it down from the widow's walk.

Holly took off for the widow's walk. Her heart beat like a locomotive as she eased the door open under the cupola on the widow's walk. The overcast night sky blocked out the moon and stars to almost total darkness. She sniffed the air. Cigarette smoke? Or was that something else?

As her eyes adjusted to the darkness, a figure came into focus. A woman with long black hair sat cross-legged, facing away from Holly. Angel?

A faint glow from in front of Angel cast a yellowish light, framing her as a dark silhouette. She held her hands, palms up, out from her sides almost like an Egyptian princess.

"Angel?" Holly whispered.

She didn't answer.

"It's not safe up here." Holly took a tentative step onto the widow's walk. Her stomach swirled with anxiety.

Everything told her not to get any closer. Angel could be dangerous. Holly chewed on a fingernail.

*But what can I do? Call Jake or Buster and say Angel is on the roof and won't come down? Would that get the answers I needed?*

Holly swallowed hard. She was a little taller than Angel, but with those curves she probably outweighed Holly. Could she fight Angel off if she needed to?

*Lordy. I'm borrowing trouble. Even if she pushed Tru off the widow's walk, why would she want to do me in? Especially if I pretend to be on her side, and maybe I am. We both lost when my ghost didn't show up. Strap on your Teflon big-girl panties and talk to her.*

"I'm worried about you," Holly said as she inched out onto the widow's walk.

Angel didn't move.

Holly crept forward until she was parallel to and about six feet from Angel.

Eyes closed, Angel sat still. If not for the tiny puffs of foggy air escaping from her nose, Holly would swear the woman wasn't breathing. Was she in one of her trances?

One of Nelda's small iron skillets sat in front of Angel. Embers glowed in the skillet and smoke curled into the night air, drifting into the darkness. Nelda would be none too pleased if she found out what Angel had done with her skillet. Holly sniffed the air again. What was that, sage? Was this some sort of yoga meditation for mediums or what?

"I've been looking for you," Holly said, trying to sound casual.

"You are not the only one." Angel's voice came out smooth and calm. She didn't open her eyes.

"Who else is looking for you?"

Angel scooted to the side of the skillet and faced Holly. "I think you know."

"Tru?" Holly hated to say his name for fear of calling him back. "Did you see him, too?"

Angel pulled a mottled cigarette out of her robe pocket and a box of kitchen matches.

Holly squinted. That box looked very familiar. No telling what kind of snooping around Angel had done while Holly wasn't looking.

With the cigarette between her lips, Angel struck a match, then held it to the tip of the slender cigarette until it glowed red. She tilted her head back and took a deep drag. The smoke billowed out in a long cone as Angel stared at the sky. "He thinks I pushed him off the roof."

"Really? He thinks I did it, too."

"The truth is if he'd posted that video without any context, it would have gone viral. You, me, Sylvia, we'd all be known as scam artists worldwide. We all had reason to make sure that didn't happen."

"There are other ways besides pushing the guy off from up here."

Angel took another drag. "Some people aren't very creative."

"I didn't know you smoked."

"Closet smoker." She took another drag. "It relieves stress. I'm overly sensitive to the emotions of spirits, and most of the time they're stressed."

"Ghosts stress me, too," Holly said, trying to find mutual ground. "Did you smoke after the epic-fail séance?"

"Yes, but I didn't push Tru off the roof. His aura had deteriorated so fast after the séance, I knew he may not make it through the night. I came up here to tell him he needed to be careful or maybe even go to a hospital and get checked out."

Holly remembered Angel had warned him about his aura before the séance, but Holly had no idea how prophetic that was at the time. "What did he say?"

"He said, and I quote, 'You're full of it.'"

"Sounds like Tru."

Angel gave a hollow laugh. "Oh, that's not all. He asked me how much it would cost to fix it."

"Can you do that?"

"Unfortunately, no." She lowered her thick lashes and thumped the ash off her cigarette in Nelda's skillet. "If I could do that I would have never lost anyone I loved."

"What did you tell him?"

"That only he could change his life path, but he needed to do it soon. He said his life path was going to be just fine as soon as his video, debunking 'The Ghost in the Grove,' *Inquiring Minds*, and me, went viral. The only thing that could change that path was a big fat check."

"How much?"

"I didn't ask because I wasn't willing to pay. I'm up front about my services. It's all over my website. I never guarantee a ghost to show up or that I can get rid of one. All I can do is help listen when they speak and share that with those who cannot hear them."

"Do you think you were the last person to see Tru alive?"

"When I left him on the widow's walk his aura was paper thin, but he was alive."

"Did you see anyone on the stairs or in the hallway when you left?"

Angel shook her head. "But when I was packing my bag, I heard a door slam across the hall."

*That would be my room . . .*

"And then I heard footsteps running down the hall." Angel snuffed out her cigarette. "I hear they found your missing slipper up here, but who am I to judge?"

# CHAPTER TWENTY-FIVE

Sam had told Jake that he was nuts to sleep in a dead man's room before the body was cold, but Jake needed to stay in the main house. The judge had deputized him to keep the peace in the event Tru's accident was no accident. Holly may see ghosts, but he didn't, usually, and what he couldn't see wouldn't bother him.

Then why was he still awake before dawn? He stretched and rubbed his back against the spindly chair he didn't trust with his weight. He'd pushed it up to a fairly solid table next to the bed. People back in the 1800s must have been smaller. Holly did a good job of keeping Holly Grove authentic, but he wished for a regular old hotel desk tonight. He'd reviewed all the statements collected by the deputies and had narrowed the suspects down to four, excluding Holly—Buster's main suspect.

Jake yawned and looked at the bed. He'd put those fresh sheets on himself after St. Agnes's finest had combed the room for evidence and secured

Tru's belongings. He yawned again. Fresh sheets, but still a dead man's bed.

He hadn't believed Holly a few months ago when she'd told him her B&B was haunted by her dead husband, but he wouldn't make that mistake this time. He'd believed Holly when she told him Tru had come back from the dead as a ghost and that his fall was no accident. Too bad Tru didn't get a look at the guy or gal who pushed him. This would all be over by now.

Jake had researched the likely suspects after reviewing their statements and still didn't have a gut feeling about who the perp may be. There was only so much he could tell by reading the reports. So far, Angel was the only one with motive and a weak alibi. Her determination to flee the scene of the crime didn't make her look innocent either.

A light tap sounded on the door.

Any reason for knocking on his door at this time of night could be trouble. He slipped his shoulder holster back on and dashed for the door, then cracked it open.

Two big blue eyes framed by familiar wild curls stared back at him. "Did I wake you?"

She was trouble all right but worth every bit of it. He swung the door open and Holly stepped into his room. That would have been a dream come true back in high school. "Nah."

"Wow." She pointed to his holster. "What's with the gun?"

"Habit." He lied. "I'm legal, so why not? According to you and Tru, we have a murderer on the premises."

"Shh." Holly held her finger to her lips, then closed the door behind her. "I'm trying not to panic the guests, but I feel guilty for not letting them know what happened tonight wasn't an accident. If I say anything, whoever killed Tru will be tipped off we know. That's why I can't sleep."

Jake yawned. How could she talk this much at this hour? "You can sleep in here if you're scared."

"Like I'd get any sleep here. Besides, I'm not scared. Whoever did this to Tru was after him because of what he did. Heck, Buster thinks I did it for the same reason."

Jake yawned again. She needed to wind down. "Have you been drinking coffee?"

"Hot chocolate." Holly gave a sheepish grin. "Nelda's homemade hot chocolate probably has more caffeine than coffee."

"You really need to get some sleep."

"But I wanted to tell you that I talked to Angel. She admitted to being on the roof with Tru after the séance, but I don't think she did it."

"She didn't say she'd been on the roof in her statement." Jake walked over to his makeshift desk and pulled up her statement on his computer.

"Are people always truthful in their statements?"

"Usually, unless they have something to hide or just don't remember correctly." He read over her statement. "Says here she was in her room packing when she heard a scream."

"Holy moly." She leaned over his shoulder. "You've got everyone's statements. How did you get all this?"

"I told you the judge made me a temporary

deputy on this case. It's a perk. The judge is one savvy lawman. I'm here to protect the innocent and investigate a death under suspicious circumstances on the QT."

"I thought he was convinced it was an accident."

"He's convinced Buster will overreach and spook the perpetrator and the public. I'm assigned special duty here to keep an eye on the investigation and you."

"Me?" She put her hand to her chest and blinked. "He doesn't think I—"

"Killed Tru?" She caught Jake with her deep blues. Those eyes were dangerous all right, but not like that. "Under these conditions he thinks you need supervision."

She huffed. "Seriously?"

"Do I need to list what happened the last time you decided to investigate on your own?"

"Hey." A blond curl rested on her forehead. He resisted the urge to tousle the rest of her curls. Why did he think she was so darned cute? "Results count more than method."

"If you live to tell it," he said and meant it.

She pointed to the laptop. "Give me the lowdown on the statements."

"Will you go get some sleep if I do?"

"Promise," she said, crossing her heart.

"It's mostly a string of alibis." He tapped the screen. "Sylvia was with Bob reviewing the footage in his room."

"Where was Liz?" The delicate skin between her eyes pinched together. "She's the producer. It seems like she should have been there, too."

"It says here that she was breaking down the equipment in the dining room."

"What about Thomas?"

"According to his statement, he was on his computer in his room."

"Hmm." She pushed a curl behind her ear. "Let me see Angel's statement."

He scrolled to Angel's statement.

Holly leaned over his shoulder and read from the screen. "Where were you at 12:40 a.m.?" She squeezed Jake's shoulder. "Seriously, who knows where they were at an exact time, unless they have an appointment or something?"

"Some people do." *Responsible people do.*

"All she said was she was in her room packing. I'm pretty sure she was in her room though, because she heard me slam my door on the way to the roof after I smelled Tru's cigar smoke. In a way, she confirms her own alibi by hearing my door slam and me running down the hall. She wouldn't have heard that outside the house and two floors up. She couldn't have been on the widow's walk when Tru took that dive."

Jake rubbed his hand over the stubble on his face. "Why do you suppose she left that out but wanted you to know she'd heard you in the hall?"

"Let's hope she doesn't tell Buster the rest of her story or he'll have the cuffs ready for me."

"Right." Jake scrolled to the bottom of the list. "Sylvia and Bob say they were together. That leaves Liz and Thomas without alibis."

"Or a strong motive." Holly paced to stand beside the desk and face Jake. "Someone is not telling the truth, but who?"

"I've been doing a little research that may give us some context but not really a motive."

She yawned.

"Why don't you get a couple hours of sleep and we'll talk about this tomorrow?"

"It is tomorrow." She walked over to the bed and stretched out, then propped her head up on her elbow. Jake swallowed hard. All of a sudden that bed looked much more inviting.

"What did you find out?" she asked.

"Not a lot." He took her in. Why did he wait so long to come back? "Mostly background stuff. Sylvia has been married three times. Divorced three times."

"No surprise there."

"Her contract expires the end of this season, so she couldn't afford bad PR with Tru's debunking."

"Liz told me that." Holly folded her hands under her head.

"Um, this sharing info goes both ways, right?" Jake motioned between him and her.

"I didn't know that tidbit would be part of an investigation then."

"Don't hold back."

"Sylvia was convinced Tru wouldn't be able to debunk my ghost. I think she bet her career on it. Unfortunately, she gambled with the reputation of all of us involved in the 'Ghost in the Grove' episode."

"Including the crew." Jake leaned in to read the screen. "Looks like Bob has never married. He had a long-term relationship with a trainer. Did you know he was a champion bodybuilder?"

Holly's eyes looked heavy. "Doesn't surprise me. Have you seen that guy's arms?"

A twinge of jealousy pricked Jake. If he left her in Delta Ridge for months at a time, would she eventually find someone else? "Did you know he started training at a federal prison?"

Holly jerked up and propped on her elbows. "For what?"

"He and his brother ran a chop shop of some sort and got busted for chopping stolen cars. His brother is back in prison and Bob went straight. Not even a speeding ticket in the last five years."

"How'd he go from chop shop to videographer?"

"He was the assistant videographer for the prison TV station while he was there and liked it. *Inquiring Minds* has a policy to hire convicts as part of their PR. He's been there ever since he got out of prison."

"Hmm." Holly twirled a curl around her finger. "No violence in his record?"

"Unless he has a juvenile record." Jake lifted a shoulder. "I can't see that."

"What about Liz?"

"Never married. Cat lover according to her Facebook page. Runs marathons. Ivy League. BA in journalism. She dabbles in writing. No criminal record. She doesn't even have a driver's license."

"Sounds pretty nonviolent."

Jake nodded. "Thomas is married to Chris St. Claire."

"Is it a law enforcement thing to mention the marital status first?"

Jake shrugged. "It's pertinent information."

"I guess so."

"He isn't on any social media. Considering his age that's not surprising."

"But a little odd since he's invested in tech companies. I hear some tech people don't use social media because of privacy concerns. Do you think he has something to hide?"

"No criminal records. No records or newspaper mentions prior to about thirty years ago, which I find odd. He should at least have an employment record. His birth certificate is sealed, so I guess he was adopted."

"Hmm." Holly gnawed at her pink lip. "He told Miss Alice he was from somewhere around Natchez."

"I'm going to dig into that. The past thirty years he's been in tech startups and done well. Low-profile guy. His retirement hobby is building airplanes and traveling, according to a magazine article." Jake glanced over at Holly.

Eyes closed, she lay sound asleep on fresh sheets that now looked very inviting.

Holly woke to the doorbell and Rhett barking. Rhett sounded far away, but he always slept with her. Still groggy, she rolled over to look at her Seth Thomas clock. She came face-to-face with Jake.

"Morning, sweetheart," he said as though it was the most natural thing in the world."

Holly shot out of bed. "What are you doing here?"

"I *was* sleeping." He lifted up on an elbow and the sheet fell from his shoulder, exposing a well-toned chest.

She licked her lips. *Well, that's not something I usually wake up to.*

*Holy moly.* She looked around the room. Not her room. A guest suite. She'd been stone-cold sober last night. How'd she get in bed with Jake and what did she miss?

Holly looked down at the same clothes she'd had on last night. Relief trickled through her. *At least, I didn't miss that.*

She reviewed the last things she could remember before she passed out. Angel on the roof burning some sort of herb. Her alibi. Knocking on Jake's door. Oh, yeah. "I must have fallen asleep."

"More like passed out," he said with a sly smile.

She wiped her hand over her mouth, hoping she didn't have drool running down her chin. Lordy, she couldn't imagine what a rat's nest her hair was. And her breath! No man should witness any of this without the benefit of sex.

The doorbell chimed again followed by a flurry of Rhett's barks. Poor thing had slept in the house alone in all the chaos last night.

She dashed for the door and trotted down the hallway as she fished her phone out of her pocket. Nine-thirty! Was she the last person up? She picked up her pace. Maybe all her guests had been as exhausted as she was and slept in, too.

The delicious scent of bacon hit her as she jogged down the stairs. *Bless Nelda's heart, she must have cooked breakfast.*

She peeked in the empty parlor on the way to the door. *Whew. Maybe they are all still asleep.*

Rhett bounced around her feet like she'd been

gone a week. She scooped him up and rubbed his head. "I'm such a bad mommy. I'm so sorry you had to sleep in the wild by yourself."

A loud knock came from the door. Rhett wiggled out of her arms and barked some more.

She opened the door and found Mackie and Dog standing on her porch.

Rhett bounced around Dog and ran through her legs.

"What happened to you?" Mackie asked. "If I didn't know better I'd say you were hung over."

"Worse." Holly opened the door wider and Mackie picked up his toolbox and came inside.

"Come on, girl," Mackie called to Dog. Dog lumbered in with Rhett still bouncing all around her. She sniffed Holly, then snorted.

"Progress," Holly said. "At least she didn't growl."

"She's been under the weather lately." He patted Dog on her back. "She wouldn't eat this morning. That's why I brought her to work with me."

Dog had packed on some weight since Holly last saw her. "She looks like she's been eating to me."

Mackie shrugged. "Maybe I just didn't notice if she ate or not when I was on the bottle."

"Rhett has days he doesn't eat much. I don't think you need to worry." She eyed Mackie's toolbox. "You have no idea how glad I am you feel like finishing up the widow's walk. You probably haven't heard, but Tru fell off the widow's walk last night."

"Whoa." Mackie shook his head. "Not just through a soft spot like I did? You mean off the whole thing?"

Holly nodded.

"Guess he's downright dead then."

*Not exactly.* "It was awful." *And I feel responsible.*

"What was he doing up there?"

"Smoking a cigar after I told him it wasn't safe up there. I even told him about how you fell through the decking into the attic."

"Now that's addicted." Mackie sniffed the air. "Is that bacon I smell?"

"Yeah. Nelda must be cooking breakfast." Holly motioned for him to come in. "Would you like some?"

"I thought you'd never ask." He put his toolbox on the floor next to the staircase. "I couldn't get to Dottie's Diner this morning because the bayou is over the road. I can't even get TV to see what's going on in the world. That storm blew my antenna off."

"You're probably the last person on earth who has an antenna." She closed the door behind Mackie. "Why don't you get cable?"

"Because antenna TV is free. I don't watch it much anyway. By the way, how was your show the other night? It wasn't on free TV."

"A big hit." Holly made a note to check her website for reservations. She was booked through the spring for now. Who knows what would happen after this thing with the debunking and Tru's murder.

Mackie's face brightened as he looked past her.

"Hey, Mackie," Jake said, as he ambled down the stairs. "How's it going?"

"Hot dang!" Mackie grinned from ear to ear. "You're a sight for sore eyes."

Her eyes weren't sore and she liked what she saw.

Jake's bare feet, bed head, sleepy eyes, and two-day scruff on his face tweaked a sweet spot in her. *Mercy*.

Mackie wrapped Jake in a hug. "Just over one hundred days sober."

Jake slapped him on the back. "That's awesome."

"One day at a time." Mackie's eyes moistened. "My goal was to stay sober until you came back."

"Glad you did, because I need you to help me with something." Jake guided Mackie outside to the front porch and closed the door behind them.

She obviously wasn't invited. Holly peeked out the window as they walked into the yard talking. What was Jake cooking up that he didn't want her to know?

A clatter of pots and pans came from the kitchen. Nelda probably needed help with breakfast. She would fuss at her about sleeping late. All Holly wanted to do was give Nelda a hug for being there.

Holly pushed through the swinging door and stopped short.

Thomas wore Holly's "Domestic Diva" apron and was on his knees digging through Nelda's collection of what she called "dead people pots and pans."

"What are you doing?" Holly said as she marched across the kitchen.

Thomas stood, holding a huge skillet by the handle. "Cooking breakfast."

"Why?" Not to mention Nelda would have a cat if anyone was cooking in her kitchen but her.

He grinned. "We have to eat."

"You're a guest. You shouldn't have to do anything here."

"I might as well be useful." He put the skillet on the gas stove and straightened the "Domestic Diva" apron.

"No," she said with a little more gusto than necessary, which she blamed on a lack of sleep. "I mean, I really appreciate the gesture and everything, but Nelda gets really testy when anyone is in her kitchen."

"If you don't tell her, I won't" He dropped a glob of butter in the skillet and lit the flame on the gas stove. "Everyone needs to eat, and I know Nelda was here yesterday early in the morning." He eyed Holly. "And we all know what happened right in front of her last night. I'm sure you weren't expecting her to work today."

"Of course not, but . . ."

"So, it's settled." His cheeks lifted with a smile. "I'll cook breakfast."

She did have hungry guests who'd had a rough night. There was no way she could even get to Dottie's to pick something up. "Okay, but you better hope Nelda doesn't catch you cooking in her kitchen."

"I did work as a short-order cook once upon a time." The butter sizzled in the pan. "I'm fast."

"You better be," she said, stretching her hand out to him. "Give me that apron in case she walks in. I'll take the rap for you."

"This should be *Divo* for me anyway." He handed over the apron.

"I'll help you make it go faster." Holly tied the apron on. "Just tell me what to do."

"Help me find things. If Nelda has a nonstick pan I couldn't find it."

"If it was made in the past hundred years Nelda probably doesn't have it."

"How about a glass bowl to break these eggs in?"

Holly dug out a large glass bowl and put it on the counter. "Anything else before I set the table?"

Thomas cracked an egg in the bowl. "Would you look at that."

Holly peered in the bowl. "What?"

"It's so fresh."

Looked like any egg to her. "How can you tell?"

"See how bright the yolk is and how high it stands and how the white of the egg is tight?"

"Not really."

"These eggs are only days old."

"Nelda is picky about fresh eggs. She gets them from an organic farm down the road." Holly lifted a shoulder. "Eggs look like eggs to me."

"When I was a kid, my mother raised chickens," he said as he continued to crack eggs. "The difference is amazing."

"I'm amazed you're small-talking with this old dude." Tru materialized and propped his elbow against the kitchen counter next to Thomas.

Holly jumped.

Thomas turned down the flame under the sizzling butter. "Did it spatter on you?"

"Uh, no. I mean maybe a little." Who doesn't jump when a ghost pops in for breakfast? She hoped he remembered rule number three if Nelda showed up soon.

Thomas pointed the spatula at Holly. "Why don't you stand back a bit? I don't want you to get burned."

"Burned?" Tru shoved off his perch on the countertop. "Aw, want me to kiss it?"

Holly took a step back and eyed Tru. She should have known he'd show up again. Most of the soot had worn off, but his hair still looked a little fried.

"Why don't you ask him something important like did he kill me?"

Behind Thomas's back, Holly held her finger up to Tru and said, "Rule number one." Then she covered her mouth and pointed to him.

"Right." Tru dragged out the word. "Your rules."

Holly nodded.

"Pardon me?" Thomas turned around holding a knife.

Tru threw himself on the knife then stumbled away, grabbing at his stomach.

Holly cringed.

"Gotcha." Tru held his hands up to Holly. "No blood."

"Are you okay?" Thomas took a couple of steps toward her holding the knife.

"You only die once, right?" Tru slapped his thigh and laughed.

Not funny.

Thomas stood within inches of her with the knife. "What's the matter?"

"Uh . . ." She cleared her throat. "I'm not myself. I was just thinking about everything that happened last night."

"And you've got a guy who could be a murderer in your kitchen holding a knife. Possibly poisoning your food." Tru scratched his head. "And you're chitchatting about eggs? Who is this guy anyway? What do you know about him? Don't cozy up with the enemy."

"If there is anything I can do to help you get through this," Thomas waved the knife through the air, "just say the word."

"Tell him to confess," Tru said.

"I'm okay." Holly swallowed hard and took a step back from Thomas. "Why don't you let me do the chopping so you can concentrate on cooking."

He flipped the knife around like a Japanese chef and handed it to her handle first. "Safety first."

"Right," she said in a croaky voice as she took the knife from him. Why had she let her guard down with this guy? Sure, she'd liked him, but Tru had been murdered.

Thomas returned to the stove and stirred the eggs, leaving her with her thoughts.

Tru was right. Just because Thomas was likable and nice, she couldn't be less suspicious of him than the others. She really didn't know much about him.

Jake had said there was no record of Thomas the first thirty-five years of his life. Was he in the witness protection program? On the lam?

"I just want to know what really happened," Holly said.

"Me too." Thomas dumped the eggs out on a plate. "I heard someone pushed him because of what happened at the séance, but why would someone do that if Tru didn't have the memory card to debunk the ghost? It makes no sense to kill him."

"That's what the judge said." Holly wrinkled up her brows. "But how did you know about the memory card?"

"Bingo." Tru snapped his fingers. "That guy is the one who picked up my spy glasses from the floor after the camera goon decked me. He knows because he stole it."

*But Bob had knocked them off. He could have stolen the card, too.*

Holly eyed Thomas. "Who told you a memory card was stolen?"

"We've all been talking." Thomas shrugged. "Some of it is pretty far out there."

"Like what?" Had Miss Alice been talking? Buster?

"Oh, just talk." He pulled a tray of biscuits out of the oven.

A banging sound came from upstairs.

Thomas stopped and listened. "Did you hear that?"

Mackie must have started working on the widow's walk.

The kitchen door swung open and Liz poked her head in. Tension pinched her face. "You've got to open Bob's door," she said, breathless. "He's not answering his phone or his door."

# CHAPTER TWENTY-SIX

"Have you looked everywhere in the house and on the grounds?" Holly asked as she trudged up the stairs with Liz. Bob had to be around somewhere unless he had a pirogue to get across the end of the blacktop.

"I've looked," Liz said. "Besides, he'd have his phone."

Sylvia met them at the top of the stairs. She wore a white satin robe and matching slippers.

"I hope you brought coffee," Sylvia said in a tone as flat as death. "Bob is going to need a cup when you wake him up. I know I'd still be asleep if someone hadn't beaten on my door." She pitched a pointed glance at Liz.

"I really don't want to open the door and wake him up," Holly said.

"I've looked everywhere, and you know we can't leave," Liz said.

"What do you mean we can't leave?" Sylvia arched

a perfectly plucked brow. "I thought the judge said we could leave after he files his report today."

Holly did a double take at Sylvia's face. How does anyone wake up with perfect pink lips and a thin line of smudge-free eyeliner? Tattooed makeup. She'd heard of it but never seen it. "Actually, he said the report would probably be ready in a day, but it would take as long as it takes. We're not going anywhere as long as Bayou St. Agnes covers the only road from here to the highway."

"Um, you're kidding, right?" Sylvia crossed her arms.

"Um, no." Holly said, mocking Sylvia as she walked past her on the way to Bob's room on the attic floor. "It usually goes down in a day or two."

"Coffee." Sylvia groaned. "I need coffee."

Angel stepped out of her room as she tied her complimentary Holly Grove robe in place. "What's going on?"

"Liz thinks Bob is passed out in his room, which he probably is." Sylvia gave a sarcastic snort. "I think we drank the entire bottle of bourbon in the hot chocolate last night."

"Correction. Not we," Liz said. "You, Bob, and Sam drank almost the whole bottle."

Holly stood in front of the Bob's door and pointed to the DO NOT DISTURB sign. "Did you see this?"

"Yes, but it's nearly ten o'clock and he won't answer." Liz looked over her shoulder at the gathering crowd. "Everyone else is awake."

"I wonder why?" Sylvia rolled her eyes. "Because you woke us up."

"Look," Liz said. "I'll take all the blame if he's asleep in there. Just open the door."

"Bring Bob a cup of coffee when you wake him up for nothing. And while you're at it bring me one, too." Sylvia shook her head at Liz. "Let the man sleep. I know I wish I could."

Holly tapped on the cypress door with her key. "Housekeeping."

Nothing.

"I told you," Liz said, looking over Holly's shoulder.

"Bob, are you in there?"

Holly took a breath and knocked harder. She hated to impose on her guest's privacy, but under the circumstances she had no choice. She slid the key in the lock. The familiar click of metal on metal sounded as the lock released, but her muscles tensed. This could be an embarrassing situation. A bad situation. Or nothing.

"Bob," she called again as she eased the door open to the dark room.

Liz brushed against Holly's back as she tried to peek into the room.

Holly took a step into the room and flipped on the light. She stared at knotted sheets on an empty bed. The tension rushed from her.

Liz gasped and pointed at the floor.

A foot with a tattoo of barbed wire around the ankle stuck out on the floor behind the far side of the bed.

Holly's mouth went dry. *Joseph, Mary, and baby Jesus.*

"Is he dead?" Sylvia whispered, holding on to Holly's T-shirt.

Liz crept over to where Bob lay.

"I-I don't know," Holly whispered, still staring at Bob's foot. This couldn't happen again, could it? She stumbled backward into Sylvia and Angel, then out into the hall.

A wail came from Bob's room. "I think he's dead," Liz said between sobs.

"Go get Miss Alice in the carriage house," Holly yelled. Feeling her pocket for her phone, she realized she was still in her clothes from last night and her phone was on her dresser in her room. "Someone call 911."

"I'll go get Miss Alice," Angel said, then ran down the hall.

Sylvia whipped out her phone from her robe pocket and dialed. "What's the address?" Sylvia asked.

"Just tell them Holly Grove. They know where it is." Unfortunately, she'd had to call 911 all too frequently lately.

"What do you mean you can't get here?" Sylvia shouted into the phone. "You want me to do what?" She covered the phone. "Someone else is going to have to do this. I don't do CPR."

"Yoo-hoo," Miss Alice called from down the hall. Her pink terry cloth robe flapped as she padded down the hall wearing gold slippers. "Where is he?"

Holly ushered Miss Alice to Bob's side.

Miss Alice's knees creaked as she kneeled over him and grabbed his swollen wrist.

And that wasn't all that was swollen. His face was so swollen he looked almost alien.

Miss Alice shook her head. "No pulse, and his body is cold."

Angel made the sign of the cross and took a step back.

"How long?" Holly asked.

"Can't say." Miss Alice pulled the sheet off the bed and covered Bob's body. "Looks like anaphylactic shock."

"But he didn't eat any of the PB&Js," Liz said, wiping her nose on her sleeve. "He knew better, besides he had an EpiPen. He always had it with him."

"He could have had the reaction in his sleep and didn't wake up." Miss Alice pushed down on the side of the bed to help herself to her feet.

An EpiPen rolled across the bed. Holly covered her mouth. Had he tried to counteract the reaction and it didn't work?

"Don't touch it," Jake said, as he brushed her arm and strode into Bob's room.

Jake stooped by the body and pulled back the sheet. His face hardened as he studied Bob's body. "I'll have to call the sheriff."

"You don't think . . ." But Holly had already thought it. *How could someone slip him something with peanuts in it in his bedroom? Was she letting her imagination go wacky?*

"All deaths outside a hospital have to have a police report," Jake said matter-of-factly, not looking at her or anyone.

Was this another murder? If so, why?

* * *

The distinctive *whop-whop* of a helicopter pounded the sky above Holly Grove as Holly waited at the airstrip with Jake for the judge to land. She was just glad they'd figured a way to get Bob's body out of Holly Grove.

"I get why Sylvia or Angel would want Tru and his debunking six feet under." Holly gnawed at her lip. "I even get why Buster would think I would want Tru dead. But Bob was just a cameraman. There's got to be more to this."

Jake shielded his eyes from the sun. "Maybe he'll come back and tell you."

"I asked Angel about that. She doesn't," Holly drew quotation marks in the air, "sense him."

"You mean she doesn't see ghosts like you do." Jake tracked the helicopter as it circled the landing strip.

"Oh, yeah." Holly raised her voice over the noise. "She sees ghosts, but she can sense spirits when they can't or don't want to be seen. She tells me I have a forgotten spirit at Holly Grove that I can't see. I just hope she stays forgotten."

"She?" Jake cocked his head sideways. "Angel can't see this spirit but she knows the thing is female?"

Holly raised her hands. "Hey, I'm new to this. I don't know all the rules." So far, the rules she'd tried to make had been about as useful as a castrated bull, as Grandma Rose used to say.

"Well, if Bob doesn't come back and tell us what happened, we may never know. How do you prove someone slipped the guy a peanut or, more likely, how do you know he didn't accidentally get a taste?"

"In his bedroom? In the middle of the night? I don't know." Holly's head ached from thinking about that. "But I think if we figure out why, we can figure out how."

"Look, Sherlock." Jake's jaw tensed and his eyes narrowed. "You're off this case. If, and it's a big *if*, Bob's death was intentional, this is out of your league even with your special assistant."

"My ghost." Holly blew out a breath. "You know, the deal is he's got to get whoever killed him to take his place on the devil's roll call. I thought Tru would be right in the middle of this, and I haven't seen him. Maybe Bob pushed him off the widow's walk and he's where Tru was?"

"Why would an hourly guy do that?" Jake started walking to the helicopter.

"If not for money, maybe he did it for love," Holly shouted. The wind blew her hair to next Sunday.

Jake cupped his hand over his mouth and yelled. "That leaves Sylvia, Liz, and Angel."

"Angel? I guess that's possible, but I haven't even seen him speak to her. He hardly spoke to anyone except Liz and Sylvia."

Buster jumped off the helicopter just before it touched down. "Did you preserve the scene?" he yelled over the chopper.

"Sure did," Jake said. "I've got Mackie guarding the door now."

Buster gave Holly a nod but didn't speak. Surely, he couldn't blame her for this one too. She supposed she'd find out, but she had questions of her own about what had happened to Bob.

They all climbed in her Tahoe and drove back to Holly Grove. When they walked through the door, she heard Nelda's voice from the kitchen.

Holly stopped on the first step, held the newel post, and listened as Buster and Jake climbed the stairs.

"Who told you that you could cook in my kitchen?" Nelda's voice rang from the kitchen.

Holly shook her head. She pitied Thomas for his sin of a good deed. And worse, she'd bet no one had an appetite either.

As she followed them upstairs, it occurred to her Thomas was the only one in the main house who didn't come upstairs to see what was going on.

Surely, he'd heard the commotion or had heard about it by now. Nelda didn't like to leave her cooking, but there was no doubt she would've hustled upstairs if she thought something serious was going on.

*Was it possible he already knew? Again, why? What stake would Thomas have in this?* Holly just couldn't see a decent guy like him doing a deadly deed.

Holly reached the landing and turned down the upstairs hallway. The three rugs that broke up the twelve-foot-wide hall were crooked. She yanked on one to straighten it, but it was too heavy to move alone.

*How on God's green earth did the rugs get all wompy-jawed? Just walking on them wouldn't cause that and it never has before.* At the end of the hall, the mystery portrait had jumped off its hanger again. *Hmm. Was Tru learning tricks?*

"Psst."

Holly turned to find Angel motioning for Holly to come to her room.

Angel grabbed Holly by the arm and yanked her into her suite. "Tru is out of control. Look what he's done to my room."

The bed stood naked at an odd angle, and all the pillows and blankets were strewn across the room. "I guess that explains the hall."

"That was not him." Angel picked a pillow up off the floor and hugged it. "That and all this is why I can't stay here. That's why that brute you think is your boyfriend should have let me swim across that bayou if I had to."

"First, Jake isn't my boyfriend. Second, he's not really a brute. He's actually a gentleman." Holly tucked her chin in and eyed Angel. "After all, he didn't let you drown."

"So I could contend with this." She made a flourish with her hand at the disaster in her room.

"Welcome to my world." Holly looked around the room. "Where is the little poltergeist anyway?"

"I have no idea, but he is going to be dangerous if he figures out his full strength."

"What do you mean?" Holly rubbed her neck. "Burl could only blow a little. Well, he did take over Sylvia's body once. That was pretty impressive."

"Burl was sent back from a different place." Angel swept her hair over her shoulder. "He had a different reason for being here."

"All I know is Tru was in line for Hell because of some mix-up about his time to go. Saint Peter sent Burl to bring him back and give him a chance to make things right, but that required a deal with the devil."

"And he made it?" Angel looked up and seemed to mentally count to ten. "That's the problem."

"It's better than roasting until the end of time."

"What was the deal?" Angel asked.

"He has to give the name of whoever killed him to replace his name on the devil's roll call."

"So that's why he's so upset."

"Don't tell me Bob came back too. I know good and well everyone doesn't come back or I'd have Mama and Grandma Rose here with me."

Angel lifted her face upward and closed her eyes, then shook her head. "I don't sense that Bob has a path back."

"Good to know." If she does. That looked like a cursory check.

"You see," Angel tossed a pillow aside and sat on a Victorian rocker, "Tru thought since Bob died under suspicious circumstances that maybe the same person who killed Bob had killed him."

Holly had wondered the same thing. "But what does that have to do with you?"

"He thinks I did it." She placed her hand over her heart and looked into Holly's eyes. "But I didn't, and we both know who did."

Holly blinked. "We do?"

# CHAPTER TWENTY-SEVEN

Holly closed her bedroom door and felt a draft. Her French doors stood wide open. As she crossed the room to close them they flapped back and forth. She pulled on the handles but they slipped out of her hands.

The wind swirled in her bedroom like a compact tornado. The coverlet and sheets flew off the mattress and the bed lifted and spun. All the while the French doors banged against the wall.

Then, everything stopped and fell to the floor. Holly held her hand over her racing heart. "What just happened?"

Tru fell from the ceiling and landed wobbly but on his feet. He walked toward her like a drunk man, his hair wild and his clothes disheveled. "I happened."

Holly now understood what had happened to Angel's room. "Why? And how'd you do that?"

"Why?" He staggered as though he were dizzy. "Because I can."

"Okay." Holly crinkled her brow. "But why to

me? I'm trying to help you. Didn't Burl talk to you about that?"

"Yeah." He bent in a low bow. "Please forgive me, your most wonderful guide."

"Guide?" She tilted her head. "Like a spirit guide?"

"Whew!" He steadied himself by holding on to the bedpost. "That stuff makes me dizzy."

"I'm really not a, um, guide. I just happen to be able to see certain ghosts. I helped Burl because I would have been stuck with him for life if I didn't. I'm helping you because I feel partly to blame for what happened to you."

"I'm over that." He waved her off. "I know you didn't push me."

"That's not the part I feel responsible about." She sat on the bed beside Tru. "I feel responsible for you being on the widow's walk when it wasn't safe."

"Yeah. I sailed right over the little two-foot railing, but I wasn't supposed to be up there." He shrugged. "I don't know why but if someone tells me I must do something or can't do something, that's exactly what I want."

"Maybe you should work on that."

"No need to work on anything now. What worse can happen to me?" He gave a weak chuckle. "I've been to Hell."

"I'm to blame for you coming to Holly Grove in the first place. If I had just said I didn't have a ghost anymore, you would have never come to debunk 'The Ghost in the Grove.'" She cringed. "That lie is why I'm trying to stop lying."

"That whole 'the truth will set you free' thing." He looked down at his singed loafers. "It's a lie."

"I'm still going to try."

"Not me." He swung around her bedpost. "Here I was. Trying to keep a promise to the devil to give him the name of the guy who killed me, so he can take my place on the devil's roll call. Then Bob turns up D-E-A-D. Does he come back as a freakin' ghost with conditions? Nope. That guy is gone and I'm still here. I'm pretty ticked about it." He shoved off her bed. "Sorry about your room, but I've got to get some of this anger out or it could be really bad."

Holly now understood why Tru could be dangerous—and possibly useful.

"All right, people. Listen up." Buster rested his hands on his utility belt as he stood in front of the fireplace in the parlor. "I called you all in here, so I only have to say this once."

Holly leaned against the back wall with Jake and Mackie. Sylvia had dressed in a black dress for mourning, Holly guessed. The deep neckline and slit up the side suggested she wasn't all that sad.

"Sam isn't here yet," Miss Alice said. "He went to get his camera."

Buster relaxed his stance and Holly almost wished she'd brought in a folding chair. It wasn't likely Buster would say a word without Sam there to write it down and put it in the *Gazette*.

Liz blew her nose loudly and stuffed the used tissue in her cargo pants pocket.

Angel wore her signature black flowing dress and stared at the floor.

Miss Alice had staked out the wide-bottomed wing chair by the window. Thomas sat in the matching chair next to her.

Sam came in at a brisk pace for an octogenarian. He framed Buster in a shot and snapped the photo, then gave a thumbs-up. Sam had slept in the *garçonnière*, so he'd slept right through the second death at Holly Grove in two days. Holly's stomach quivered a bit. At that rate, even the ghost hunters may get nervous about checking in here.

Buster clapped his hands. "Here's what we've got, people." He swung his hands back and forth as he spoke. "As Deputy McCann told you, it's standard procedure to investigate a death at a residence. And that's what we're doing here. But," he raised his finger, "because there have been two deaths at this establishment in two days, I've raised the level of my investigation to death under suspicious conditions."

"What does that mean?" Sylvia asked.

"It means I'd like to take your statements as before, and St. Agnes Parish would greatly appreciate it if you would make yourself available for questioning at least through tomorrow."

"You do realize you can't hold these people here without charging them with a crime," Thomas said.

"Yes, sir. I do. Unfortunately, or fortunately, the only way out of here at least for today is by air or water. Unless there is a medical emergency, we are not obligated to evacuate you from these premises.

I've checked with Holly and I believe you were all scheduled to stay here through the weekend. So, this won't change your plans.

"But what if we don't want to stay here?" Angel said. "It's not safe."

"Are you saying you suspect foul play with these accidents?" Buster asked.

She shrank back into her seat.

Buster motioned to Holly. "Would you like to say a few words?"

Holly pushed off the wall. "First, I'm deeply sorry for the loss of Bob and Tru. This kind of thing has never happened here before, and I hope it never happens again. I apologize for any inconvenience this may have caused you and I'll comp your rooms."

Buster hitched up his pants. "Nelda, Miss Alice, and Sam are free to go. They were not in this establishment when these tragedies occurred and therefore cannot add to the investigation."

"We can't leave either unless we want to swim," Miss Alice said.

Sam stood and snapped another photo. "I'm staying. At my age though, I could be the next one to drop dead."

"You're all dismissed except Holly. I'll send my deputy to fetch you when it's time to take your statement."

*Oh, crapola. I'm first.*


"For the record, my name is Holly Lane Davis until I can legally change my name back to my maiden name." She took her place across from Buster at the dining room table again. There was no way he could suspect her this time. She'd stay cool and calm. *Ahem . . . You have nothing to hide.*

Buster scribbled across his clipboard. "Don't you find it odd that there have been two suspicious deaths at your place of business over the last two days?"

"Considering there had only been one in the 150 years prior, I think Holly Grove is a pretty safe place." She smiled just to get at Buster.

"I understand the deceased had a peanut allergy." Buster held his beady eyes on her. "Were you aware of that?"

"All of my guests fill out a registration form, and there's a box to check if they have any allergies. If they do, they write them down in the comments." She straightened in her chair. "I checked my records and Bob did not check the allergy box."

"I see." Buster cleared his throat. "Do you have peanut butter here at Holly Grove?"

"Of course." Holly huffed. "I keep it on hand to serve children if they don't like our regular meal."

"And did you have any minors as guests yesterday?"

Holly tried an upward glance and mentally counting to ten like she'd seen Angel do earlier. It didn't work. "Buster, you know everyone here, have interviewed them all, and have a copy of their registration cards. You know there are no children registered here." She flopped back against her chair.

Buster tapped his pencil against the table. "Just

answer the questions. Did you serve peanut butter last night?"

"Yes."

"Even though there were no children present and you knew the deceased had a peanut allergy."

Holly pointed to his clipboard. "You need to go back and fix that. I said I didn't know he had a peanut allergy because he didn't put it on his registration card."

He scrubbed his eraser over the form. "Why did you serve peanut butter?"

"Because we were still up at two o'clock in the morning because of what happened last night. We served PB&Js cut in cute little triangles and hot chocolate, too, but no one was allergic to that."

"Did the deceased eat a, um, PB&J?"

"He did not, and that's the end of this. I don't know if he had a nutty candy bar in his room or what. But when he told me he was allergic, I offered to serve him a different sandwich. He said he wasn't hungry."

"So, you did know he had a peanut allergy?"

*Lordy. If I counted to one hundred it wouldn't be enough to keep my cool.* "I knew when I offered him a PB&J and not before."

"Who else knew he had a peanut allergy?"

"Everyone here." She hesitated. "Wait. Except Angel and Jake. They weren't there for the PB&Js."

Tru's head rose through the walnut dining table. Holly shivered. She would never get used to seeing that creepy stuff.

Tru thumped the side of Buster's ear.

A giggle slipped past Holly's lips.

Buster swatted at his ear. "Is something funny here?"

Holly shook her head.

Tru yanked on Buster's gun with all his might and managed to pull the snap loose.

Buster felt for his gun and secured the snap.

"I could do this all day long," Tru said.

Holly snorted.

"What?" Buster flattened his brow out.

"Are we finished here?" she asked.

"Not quite." Buster reached for his pencil and Tru thumped it away.

Buster watched it roll across the table. "What's going on here?"

Holly lifted her shoulders. "You've heard Holly Grove is haunted, haven't you?"

"Right." Buster smirked and closed the cover on his clipboard. "I think we're done here."

Holly saluted him and stood.

"But I'm not finished with him." Tru thumped his ear again. "That's for getting me all riled up thinking my good friend Holly did me in."

"Oh, so you believe me now, huh?" No sooner than she said it she realized she'd talked to Tru out loud. *Crapola.*

"I didn't say I believed you." Buster picked up his clipboard. "And just between you and me, you're going down for Mr. Stalwort's murder. It's just a matter of time before I connect the dots."

Tru knocked Buster's clipboard out of his hand.

"I'm in no mood for this. I've been robbed," Tru said. "Bob is not here, and Burl says he's not with the saints upstairs. That means he went where I was before." Tru shrugged. "You know. This idiot needs to figure out that Bob pushed me off the roof." Tru glanced back at Holly. "Bob's in Hell now. I checked. But I'm still here. And I don't know why. You've got to help me.

Tru's image flickered just before he disappeared.

# CHAPTER TWENTY-EIGHT

Holly's stomach rumbled. How long had it been since she'd eaten anything?

She opened the refrigerator door and noticed a pile of bacon, egg, and cheese biscuits. *Thomas. How thoughtful.* He was just too busy in the kitchen to notice when all the drama was going on earlier. She pulled out a breakfast sandwich and unwrapped the plastic.

Rhett sat, tail wagging, ready to pounce on any crumbs.

"It ain't fit to eat," Nelda said, as she walked out of the pantry.

"Rhett begs to differ."

"That man moved darned near everything in my kitchen."

"He was just trying to be helpful." Holly took a bite of her bacon, egg, and cheese biscuit. The savory flavor satisfied her hunger. "I think he likes to do things for other people."

"Now, how would you know that?" Nelda shoved a

well-worn cookie sheet under the cabinet. "You don't know that man."

"You're right, but I think I might like him if I knew him." She took another bite of her sandwich. Unless, of course he's the murderer. She had to stop thinking that way. She needed facts.

"I'm tellin' you, he's not what ya think he is." Nelda pulled down the cabinet panel that hid the dishwasher. "I haven't lived on this earth for sixty-five years and not learned how to size a man up." She grabbed a stack of blue willow plates and started loading them on the shelf above the dishwasher. "And that man does not measure up."

"You didn't like him from the first time you laid eyes on him." Holly walked over to Nelda and propped her hip against the counter. "It's not like you to be this way about someone."

"That's why you need to pay attention." Nelda wagged a spatula at Holly before stuffing it in a drawer.

A chunk of egg fell out of the breakfast sandwich and Rhett pounced on it. "I think it's pretty good, too," Holly whispered.

"I heard that." Nelda huffed and carried a large pot to the pantry.

Rhett tore off for his favorite view from the window. He pranced and pounced, then turned to her and whined.

"What's the matter, boy?" Holly crossed the kitchen to the window beside the planter's table.

Jake hurled a big stick in the air for Dog, and she shagged across the yard to fetch it.

"Want to go play, Rhett?" Holly snagged another

bacon, cheese, and egg sandwich, then headed out the door.

"How about a sandwich?" she asked Jake as Rhett and Dog played.

He took the sandwich and bathed her in his warm stare. "Thanks."

If Jake stayed around, would he be considerate and helpful like Thomas or fall into the trap of indifference?

Dog rolled over on her back and Rhett jumped over her. "Wow. That's a big jump for a little dog," Jake said.

"You know, Mackie was worried about Dog not eating enough." Holly noticed eight little teats mounding up on Dog's belly. "You don't suppose she's pregnant, do you?"

Jake jerked his focus from Dog to Holly. "Who?"

"Dog." She pointed to her belly. "Look."

Jake eyed Rhett. "You don't think . . . ?"

"We'll see soon enough."


"That hammering is about to drive me to drink," Holly said. "With three of them up there, the widow's walk should be up to code lickety-split. I can't imagine how loud that is over the attic rooms."

"Well, poor old Bob can't hear it. God rest his soul." Nelda crossed herself. "I'm glad I was out in the honeymoon suite when he passed or I wouldn't have gotten a wink of sleep."

"You needed the rest."

"You got that right." Nelda slathered mayonnaise on toasted French bread for roast beef po'boys.

"The only way I would have slept any better is if I'd had a honeymoon partner with me in that king size."

"Like you tell me, it's never too late." Holly lined the French bread with sliced tomatoes and shredded lettuce. "How's that?"

"Good." Nelda grinned. "That's 'cause you didn't have to cook."

"You know, you've got lots of stuff frozen in the freezer that I can heat up. You don't have to stay here since Buster said you could go. I'd really like you to go home and rest."

Nelda shrugged. "Don't know how I'm goin' to do that. The water's high and my car is broke."

"Call your nephew to pick you up on the other side of the road. Mackie has a pirogue that he can use to paddle you across the high water."

"What ya gonna tell Angel and the rest of 'em?" Nelda piled debris roast beef over the tomatoes and shredded lettuce. "You know they're bustin' to get out of here."

"Yeah, but Buster said you could go and I want you to rest." And after what Tru did to Angel's room, she couldn't chance him putting on a show in front of Nelda. She'd never come back to Holly Grove.

"I could use a change of clothes."

"It's settled then." Holly wrapped a po'boy in butcher paper. "As soon as we bring these po'boys up to the men, you'll call your nephew and make arrangements."

"Is Thomas up there hammerin'?" Nelda asked.
Holly nodded.

"I don't know." Nelda screwed up her nose. "I may

just go take a nap in the honeymoon suite. I might dream me up a man this time."

"Are you afraid to leave your kitchen with Thomas?" Holly asked.

"You wouldn't believe the mess he made in my favorite little skillet. Burnt-on crud that smelled like an ashtray and grass." Nelda elbowed Holly. "And not the kind the Deltas smoke. The kind you mow." She shook her head. "I hear they eat funny out in California, but even Rhett wouldn't eat anything that smelled that bad."

"Okay," Holly said. "Don't say I didn't try to bust you out of here." Holly loaded the sandwiches on a tray then blew Nelda a kiss. "Sleep tight in the quiet."

One way or another, Tru would be moving on tomorrow, according to what Angel had told her about the Devil's roll call. Somehow, she had to break that news to him, because Burl neglected to share the fine print on the trade. It expires after three days, and she wasn't sure how he'd react.

"Hungry?" Holly said when she reached the widow's walk.

"Your cooking or Nelda's?" Jake asked, only half joking.

"Nelda's." She put the tray on top of a piece of plywood resting on two sawhorses. "Dig in."

Mackie, Thomas, and Jake washed their hands under the spigot of a five-gallon water cooler while she checked out their progress.

The Plexiglas panel wouldn't be noticeable from the street, and it blended in pretty well up here. She'd almost decided against it because it wasn't period, but neither were four-foot railings. She sighed. If she'd known what she knew now, she would have put up barbed wire.

"Oh, my." Thomas sopped up the gravy with what was left of his French bread. "I've missed roast beef po'boys so much. Do you think you can talk Nelda out of the recipe? I know she won't give it to me."

"What is it with you two?" Holly propped her elbows on the plywood.

"Yeah, man." Mackie wiped a drip of gravy from his gray beard. "Nelda loves everybody. Especially if they like to eat." He pointed a greasy finger at Thomas. "And looks like you do."

Thomas gave a "don't care" shrug, but his expression didn't match.

Holly caught the glint of the sun reflecting off something metal behind Thomas. "My telescope! You've mounted it."

"It's perfectly level too. You ought to be able to read your horoscope in the stars with that thing," Mackie said.

Wind rippled over the butcher paper and remnants of po'boys. Tru materialized right about where he had gone over the edge. "A little too late for me, huh?"

A sour feeling settled in her gut. She had been so excited about fixing up the widow's walk and sharing it with everyone, but now it felt wrong. As if she was disrespecting the dead.

For once, she wanted to talk to him in front of people. To explain how she felt.

"What's wrong?" Thomas asked.

Holly sighed. "I'm so glad to get this place up to code and the telescope set up, but I feel a little like we're dancing on Tru's grave.

"That's not going to happen." Tru rubbed his fingers along the edge of the Plexiglas. "I donated my body to science."

Holly sighed. "There has to be a way to make this right."

Tru waggled what was left of his eyebrows. "You could name it the Tru View."

"I just got this beautiful idea." She clasped her hands together like she was praying. "We could name it the Tru View." She gave a Vanna White flourish toward the door on the cupola. "And the bronze plaque would be right here."

Tru dug his sooty loafer into the decking. "I'd like that a lot."


The knock on the front door of Holly Grove came at two o'clock in the afternoon.

Holly opened the door to the bluebird day. Buster stood on the front steps with his hat in his hand. "Please step outside."

She cocked her head to the side. "Pardon me?"

"Please step outside." Buster rested his hand on his gun.

"What's going on here?" Thomas asked from behind her.

"Step aside, sir," Buster said as he grabbed Holly's arm and pulled her outside. He spun her around.

Cold steel circled her wrists and the solid click of metal on metal sounded. "Are you arresting me?"

"Yes, ma'am." He spun her around to face him. "You're under arrest for the murder of Truman Jeremiah Stalwort, the third."

"Don't say a word, Holly." Thomas came out on the porch with them. "I've got a good lawyer and I'll fly him here on the first available flight, or even better, I'll get Chris to fly him here."

Buster's smug mug stayed in a tight line. "Are you finished, Mr. Sinclair?"

"What if I'm not?" he said.

"I've got another set of cuffs." Buster fished a card out of his pocket and started reading to Holly. "You have the right to remain silent and refuse to answer questions. Do you understand?"

Holly nodded.

"I didn't hear you," Buster said.

"Yes." A slight quiver crept into her voice. Her stomach churned like a Ferris wheel.

"Anything you say may be used against you in a court of law. Do you understand?"

She nodded then quickly said, "Yes."

"You have the right to consult an attorney before speaking to the police and to have an attorney present during questioning now or in the future. Do you understand?"

"Yes." *Mercy. How can this be happening?*

"If you cannot afford an attorney, one will be appointed for you before any questioning if you wish. Do you understand?"

"Yes." *How much will this cost? Who'll take care of Rhett and Holly Grove?*

"If you decide to answer questions now without an attorney present, you will still have the right to stop answering at any time until you talk to an attorney. Do you understand?"

"Yes." She couldn't wait for an attorney to come all the way from California. *Can my old roommate do criminal law? If she can, would she do it pro bono or on credit? How can I run a B&B from jail? What will this do to my business?*

"Knowing and understanding your rights as I have explained them to you, are you willing to answer my questions without an attorney present?"

"No, she's not." Jake glowered down at Buster. "I hope you know what you're doing, because if you don't . . ."

"Are you threatening an officer of the law?" Buster asked.

"No. I'm making a promise. If this is a trumped-up charge, which it probably is, there will be consequences." Jake leveled an eye at Buster.

Buster grabbed Holly by her wrists and pushed her forward. She would have tripped going down the steps if he hadn't held on to her cuffs.

"Is that really necessary?" Thomas asked, trailing beside them.

"Standard procedure." Buster walked Holly down the driveway.

"For crapweasels like you," Jake said, making long strides to stay ahead of them. "Don't worry, Holly. I've got a call in to the judge."

Buster smirked. "Won't do you any good. He's in the ICU. Had a heart attack this morning."

Holly's stomach churned. That's why Buster was being so bold.

They stepped into a clearing at the end of her driveway where a helicopter waited.

On the bright side, she'd never flown in a helicopter.

"Wait," Thomas called.

Buster didn't. He stuffed Holly in the helicopter and it whirled upward.

Then she puked in Buster's lap.

# CHAPTER TWENTY-NINE

Holly sat on a concrete ledge in a windowless cell. Her one phone call to her lawyer roommate went to an automated message that she was out on vacation for two weeks. *Luck really blooms some days.*

Some poor soul in the next cell was coughing up a lung.

Surely, Jake and Thomas would get here soon. If she'd thought about it, she could have called her good buddy Purvis Cumpton, the lawyer turned bail bondsman. Just because he wasn't a lawyer anymore didn't mean he couldn't represent her on the sly. She'd seen people represent themselves in trials on TV.

*Mercy.* What was she going to do?

"Hey, got a smoke?" Was it a guy? Girl? She couldn't tell from the voice and couldn't see him through the thick jail wall.

She covered her face with her hands and tried to cry to relieve some stress. Even her tears were too tired to come out.

Voices came from down the hall. She recognized Jake's voice and another male voice. Maybe Thomas. Footsteps neared her cell.

The baby-face deputy parked himself next to the wall. Jake and Thomas stood in front of her six-by-eight-foot cell.

She rushed across the cell and laced her hands around the bars. "Can you get me out?"

"We're trying," Jake said. Then he said something under his breath she couldn't hear.

"Don't worry, Holly." Thomas patted her fingers because that's all he could get to, but it was sweet.

Jake's jaw was so tense she could see his veins through his skin. "I can't believe that little twerp did this."

"Why did he?" Holly slumped against the bars. "Did he find more evidence?"

"No. Just more freedom to be a jerk with the judge out."

"Oh . . ." Holly closed her eyes. "I forgot about the judge. Is he going to be okay?"

"Not any time soon." Jake bumped his fist against the bars. "He's under the knife now."

"Open-heart surgery is no fun," Thomas said. "My Chris had it last year. Tough recovery."

"I'm so sorry," Holly whispered. *In more ways than one.*

"Time's up," the baby-face deputy said as he stepped away from the wall.

Holly's eyes welled with tears. This stink just got real.

\* \* \*

A bone-deep chill rushed over Holly. She opened her eyes. Still in the cell. How long had she been there? Twenty minutes or twenty years?

"Fine spiritual guide you are," Tru said as his image formed in front of her.

For once, she was glad to see him. "How did you leave Holly Grove?"

Tru shrugged. "I'm not tied to Holly Grove like Burl was or you are. If I don't have to do the rest of my time down there," he looked at the ground, "I think I can float around anywhere I want to."

"Don't you want to go to heaven?"

"It's more like getting in at the select country club. They may not let me in." He lifted a shoulder. "Anyway, I thought I'd hang out with you a while."

"I really let you down." Holly leaned back against the concrete wall. "You know tomorrow is your last day to get your name replaced on the devil's roll call."

"Yeah." Tru put his hands in his pocket. "I'm kinda hoping for a miracle."

"Me too." Her stomach growled. She put her hand over the rumble. "Maybe Nelda will bring me something good to eat with a file baked in."

"You know, I may be able to bust you out of here."

"Where would I go? Holly Grove is the only place I know. I'd never be happy bumming around from place to place."

"I'd like to try it, but since you've given up on me and all."

"I didn't give up on you." She picked at a piece of lint on her shirt. "I got arrested."

"Well, you getting arrested ends it for me." He sat down beside her. "Who's going to look for the guy or gal who pushed me off a roof when a nice lady who didn't is in jail for it? Lose-lose. That's the way I see it."

"I'm sorry, Tru." She patted him on the back but her hand sunk into chilled air.

"Don't be." He smiled and she noticed he hardly had any soot on him anymore and his hair was only slightly singed.

He shoved off the concrete bench and wind swirled around him as he blew down the corridor. Doors slammed. Crashes, bangs, and a few shrieks.

Yep. He was having fun on his last day. If only she could have been a successful spirit guide for him and he could have had a better afterlife than his life. Regret tugged at her heart and weighted her mind.

# CHAPTER THIRTY

No radio. No TV. No phone. All Holly had were her thoughts, and she'd spun them out to every dark corner.

She paced and fretted.

Holly Grove would be sold and taken apart bit by bit to be reassembled in a subdivision. She wanted to gag at the thought.

There were exactly eight steps from the front of the cell to the back of the cell.

Or the land would be sold off in small lots or worse for a mobile home park. They'd call the subdivision or mobile home park Holly Grove to hang further embarrassment on her and her family.

The portraits of all five generations would be sold along with all the furniture at an auction to pay for her legal fees, and it probably won't be enough. She'd end up with that state lawyer Buster told her about when he read her her rights.

Holly grabbed the bars and rocked back and forth.

Rhett would move in with Miss Martha Jane and her cats, never to see his puppies with Dog.

She rubbed her hands up and down the bars.

Jake would think about Holly every now and then, but he'd never come to see her in prison—that is, if the jury didn't send her to the electric chair, which was still legal and lethal in Louisiana.

Nelda would go to work at Dottie's Diner or at the school cafeteria, and no one would appreciate her like Holly did. She'd never have one of Nelda's pralines again unless she mailed them to her at Angola. *Wait. Angola is only for men.* She didn't even know where to tell Nelda to send them.

She shook the bars.

*Cry me a freakin' river!*

*I'm not going down without a fight.* She pushed off the bars. *Whatever it takes, I'm getting out of here.*

"Hey!" Baby-face came into her narrow view. "Quiet down. You're not the only person in here. Keep the peace."

"I demand to see my lawyer." She pressed her nose to the bar so she could see Baby-face with both eyes. "You can't just dump me in here by myself."

More footsteps came down the hall. "Well, well, well," Buster said. "Didn't take you long to break."

"I'm not broken. I'm lonely. There's nothing but four walls and concrete in here. It's not healthy."

"I could put you in with Bertha, but she's got a nasty cough. Snores like a bear, too."

"Maybe I'm not that lonely." Holly rested her

head against the bars. "I know you don't believe me, but I didn't do it."

"Evidence says you did." Buster tilted his head back. "Want to talk about it?"

Holly shook her head. "Not without my lawyer."

Buster turned around and strolled down the hall.

*Lordy. I'm not cut out to be a criminal. I'm not a criminal. Justice will prevail. Don't go back down that dark path of the bad things. Think positive. The power of positive thinking and all that jazz.*

Holly closed her eyes and leaned against the concrete wall. *I'm walking out through that locked door. I'm walking down the hall. I'm getting my purse back with my gum in it and I'm going to chew the heck out of it. And then I'm going to walk outside into the sunshine a free woman. I see it. It will happen. Mind over matter.*

"Miss Davis." A man's voice bounced off the walls.

"Huh?" She opened her eyes.

A short, bald guy wearing a suit that was too tight and crepe sole shoes stood before her.

"I'm Carver Millworth, attorney at large." He slid a card between the bars. "You're free to go."

"Do you mean someone made bond for me?"

"No. You're free to go. The charges are dropped."

"Woo-hoo!" She would hug the guy, but she'd never seen him before in her life. "How'd you get me out? A technicality?"

He gave a solemn shake of his head.

"Did the judge order it from the ICU?"

The head shake was barely noticeable.

"Hey, I'll take it no matter how you did it. I'm just curious."

"I'm not at liberty to say."


Jake picked Holly up at the jail and he still looked ticked. He hugged her tight, but it was stiff, as though he were made of the same concrete walls she had just been trapped in. Was his anger trapped inside?

"I'm okay." She touched his arm. "It's over."

He gave a tight nod. And kept his eyes on the road.

Fast-food bags littered the floor of the stripped-down Ford F-150, and there were tiny cracks all over the faux leather seats. "Whose truck is this and how did you get out, by the way?"

"One of Mackie's friends. He's going to pick it up at the bayou."

"And then what?" She dusted some crumbs off the seat.

"Mackie is waiting for us with a pirogue." He shifted the truck and the engine gunned down. "He'll paddle you across."

"What about you?" Her insides twisted. Something was very wrong, even though he should be happy she was free.

"I've got some things I need to take care of." He slowed the truck to a crawl and stopped just at the water's edge. Leaning over her, he pushed the car door open for her. "I'll be back before dark."

"You're making me nervous." She held on to his arm. "Tell me what's going on."

"He broke his stone face with a hint of a smile. "I'll tell you when I get home."

*Home.* That had a ring to it, especially coming from Jake.

She slid to the edge of the bench seat, hopped out of the truck, and slammed the door. "See you tonight."

Mackie paddled up in the pirogue, and Holly waded knee-deep to take his hand and step in the boat.

"Thanks," she said, "for getting the truck for Jake and paddling us back and forth."

"No problem." He shoved off. "It's only about two feet deep. You'll be able to drive through it in a couple of hours."

Holly sighed. "That means everyone can leave and someone is getting away with murder."

"Maybe. Maybe not." Mackie looked off into the horizon like the answer was there.

"There's something y'all aren't telling me." She huffed and folded her arms. "And I don't like it."

"Don't blame you," Mackie said and kept paddling.

A few minutes later, they were across the blacktop to her side of Bayou St. Agnes.

She helped Mackie pick up the pirogue and balance it in the back of his truck bed.

Mackie slapped the aluminum hull. "She's sitting there on imagination, but I don't have far to go, and we've got the road to ourselves."

She climbed up in Mackie's truck and nearly sat

on two guns, a pistol and a rifle. "Any reason you're packing today?"

Mackie gave a half-assed grin behind his beard. "Every reason."


Holly Grove never looked so good as when they turned onto her driveway. She closed her eyes and said a little prayer of thanks for being free.

Mackie stopped out front. Nelda, Miss Alice, Sam, and Rhett all poured out of the house and waited on the porch. She got the oozy, warm fuzzies just looking at them. Who says she doesn't have a family?

Holly bounded out of the old truck and ran up the stairs. Nelda wrapped her in a hug first. "I sure am glad I don't have to go to the penitentiary to see ya."

"Me too." Holly hugged Miss Alice, but her oversized purse got in the way.

When Holly pulled back to look at her, Miss Alice sniffed and pulled a tissue out of her purse. She waved the tissue. "Allergies."

"Welcome home." Sam wrapped her in a bear hug. "I sure am glad I didn't have to write the story Buster was selling."

A light breeze dusted across the porch but the chill in it made her wonder if that wasn't a hug too.

"Are you hungry?" Nelda asked as they walked up the stairs together.

"Starved." Holly pulled out of her wet boots at the door. "I swear, I felt like I was already on death row."

She peeked in the parlor but it was empty. She

didn't expect Sylvia, Liz, or Angel to come down to greet her, but she though Thomas would. "Where's Thomas?

"I better get on supper," Nelda said as she scurried toward the kitchen.

Sam avoided looking at Holly, and Miss Alice took her glasses off and let them dangle by the beaded chain around her neck.

"Oh, no." She could barely get the words out. Surely no one else had died at Holly Grove. "Please tell me Thomas is okay."

A man Holly didn't recognize stepped into the entrance hall from the back door, the riverside. *No one comes in that door for the first time. This guy has been here a while.* She racked her brain for a guest scheduled to check in today. *Mercy! And how could he get here without a local connection to get him over the bayou?*

The man continued to walk toward her. He wore a blue suit that looked custom-made and a red tie. His shoes shone like money. He extended his hand. "I've been looking forward to meeting you."

Holly took his hand in hers. His skin was soft and his nails impeccable.

"I'm Chris Sinclair," he said. "Thomas's husband."

# CHAPTER THIRTY-ONE

"It's such a pleasure to finally meet you," Chris said as he sat on the settee next to Holly. "I've heard so many things about you."

His expression was pleasant but there was tension in it.

She smiled to put him at ease. "Thomas told me a lot about you, too. He said you enjoy renovating old houses, building hobby airplanes, and traveling together. Oh, and he says you're a fabulous cook."

He lifted a salt-and-pepper eyebrow. "But he didn't tell you I was a man, did he?"

"Uh, well . . ." And you're supposed to be working on telling the truth. "No."

"I told him that was a mistake." Chris sat a little straighter. "It's always good to start off as you intend to continue."

"Sometimes that's harder than you think." She glanced over her shoulder. "Where is he?"

"He wanted me to talk to you alone." Chris put his hand on top of hers. "Thomas is the most kind and generous man I've ever known, but he avoids difficult conversations."

"Most men do," Holly replied.

Chris sucked a thin breath of air in. "I want to start with the fact that he loves you very much and always has."

"Pardon me?" Holly studied Chris. His hands were relaxed and his eyes warm. Whatever he was trying to tell her came from sincerity if not misguided thought or fantasy.

He kept his hand over hers. "I want you to just listen. I have prepared to have this conversation and Thomas is aware of everything I'm going to tell you. There's a glass of water right there if you need it."

He glanced at Grandma Rose's footed Fostoria crystal goblet, sitting on a linen napkin and filled with crushed ice and water.

"Are you going to tell me he's dead?" she asked around a lump of emotion in her throat.

Chris smiled. "No. I'm going to tell you a love story."

"Your love story with Thomas?"

"Partly." Chris unbuttoned his jacket and leaned back. "A long time ago, Thomas was married to a woman he loved very much. He'd planned to spend his entire life with her. But there was something inside him that he thought was abnormal, and it was for a heterosexual man. But Thomas was soon to find out he was a gay man."

Chris took a sip of water from the matching glass on his end table. "This was in the eighties. You're too young to remember the AIDS epidemic and the paranoia that came with it, but this was the time he chose to tell the wife that he loved that he could not be her husband in good faith. It was traumatic for both of them, but Thomas, being Thomas, sacrificed everything to spare his lovely wife pain or embarrassment."

"I can believe that." Holly rolled her tongue over her dry lips. She wanted to be polite and kind because this was important to Chris, but it was so personal.

"It was about that time that his wife learned she was pregnant." Thomas placed the crystal water glass on a linen napkin on the side table. "He agreed to leave the community and never return or communicate with his family again. It was a different time in our country. Of course, Thomas, being Thomas, paid child support, tuition, lessons, and all the things that go along with being a parent. The only thing he asked was an annual photo and a letter once a month about his daughter. This proceeded even after his beloved first love died. Her mother continued with the letters. And then a trusted friend."

Tears pricked at her eyes. "That's such a touching story."

He pulled an envelope from behind him and handed it to her. "These are the pictures."

With shaking hands, Holly opened the envelope. Dozens of photographs of her slid from the envelope onto the settee. Baby pictures. School pictures. Sorority pics. Wedding pics.

The dad she thought didn't love her or her mother enough to even send a birthday card had never abandoned her. He loved her. Tears streamed down her face.

"I finally convinced him to break the vow he made years ago and to meet his daughter. He wants you to know he always did and always will love you."

"What a blubbering mess." Holly stared at herself in the powder room mirror. Crying always made her blue eyes bluer. And now she knew the man who had given her those blue eyes and he loved her and she loved him, too.

She splashed her face with cold water and patted it dry. Pat. Pat. Pat. Never scrub. That's what her mother had told her. She'd told her so many things but never this. Holly wanted to be angry with her mom, but the way Chris told the story made it hard. It was a love story.

After another big honking nose blow, Holly left the powder room. Maybe Thomas would be waiting for her.

She returned to the parlor but no one was there.

Voices came from outside on the porch. She opened the door and there were Chris, Mackie, and Jake in deep conversation.

When they saw her, the chatter dried up like a September cotton boll.

Holly stepped into the thick of them. "What's going on?"

"I think you've had enough excitement for one day," Jake said.

"It has been an eventful day, but I'll be the judge of what I can handle." Holly hesitated. "As long as you don't tell me someone is dead."

Silence.

"Is someone dead?" she whispered.

"No." Jake said. "No one is dead, but you're not going to like it."

"I didn't like being locked up in the St. Agnes jail for the day either, but I lived." She flopped her arms at her sides. "You're scaring me."

Miss Alice stepped onto the porch. "Tell her."

She must have been listening from the other side of the door. Grandma Rose's trusted friend? Had Miss Alice continued to send pictures and letters all these years? Was that why she kept her nose in Holly's business?

"We were hoping we wouldn't have to tell you," Jake said.

"Tell me what?" Holly searched their faces.

"The lawyer told you today that he was not at liberty to tell you why you were released other than the charges were dropped."

"Yeah." Holly tilted her head to the side to make sure she heard every word. "And?"

"Thomas confessed to murdering Tru," Chris said. "He did it to protect you."

Jake shook his head. "He's in the same cell you were in."

"Oh, good gravy. Why?"

Chris straightened his tie. "I think we just went over that."

"I can't let him do it." She marched inside and grabbed her purse. "Let's go right now and get him out."

"A confession is not something you can just take back." Jake rubbed his chin. "He was read his Miranda rights and waived them. Unless something changes around here, he'll be in jail until his trial."

# Chapter Thirty-two

"I'm surprised you're still here," Holly said when she answered Liz's knock on the door.

"Can I come in?" Liz's face was a road map of misery as she looked everywhere except at Holly.

Holly stepped aside for Liz to enter.

"We've got an app that monitors the roadway hazards." Liz fidgeted with her hands. "The bayou should be low enough to drive a car through sometime within the next few hours."

"Again, I'm really sorry about Bob." Holly gave Liz's arm a quick brush. "I know you and he had a kind of, sort of thing."

"Yeah, well." Liz sniffled a little. "I think that was mostly me with the thing."

"I don't know. He seemed pretty in tune with you," Holly said, stretching the truth a little for a good cause.

"Sometimes." Liz fumbled with her hands again.

Holly didn't remember Liz having that nervous habit. "You okay?"

"Yeah, yeah." She gave a dismissive wave, but it

wasn't convincing. "I just want to get something off my chest. Nothing will probably ever come of it, but it's the right thing to do."

"Okay . . ." *Spit it out already.*

"You know how Bob didn't talk much."

Holly nodded.

"Well, he talked a lot around Sylvia." Liz slumped and blew her nose into a tissue. "If she said jump, Bob asked, 'How high?'"

"Do you think maybe they had a . . . um, romantic relationship?"

"No." The answer came quickly with a bit of an edge. Liz shoved the tissue in her pocket.

"Sorry. I'm a little suspicious of that kind of thing. If Burl hadn't gone down in his plane I would have divorced him for good reason."

"If they did it was a one-off." Liz twirled a few strands of hair around her finger.

"Do you think they did?"

"Here's the deal." Liz hesitated. She seemed to debate going through with saying whatever she was going to say. "The night of the séance, Sylvia was inconsolable. She thought her career was over. She'd never work in TV again. It was B-A-D."

Not Holly's best night either. She knew Tru's video debunking her ghost would mean the end of her business and maybe the end of Holly Grove.

"Anyway, Bob had a bottle of booze in the van and he brought it in to calm Sylvia down." The hair she'd been twirling around her finger snapped. "So, they both get an alibi, if you know what I mean."

Holly nodded.

"The thing is . . . Bob wasn't in there long, because

I saw him creeping up the attic stairs toward his room. It was later, after everything happened—the fall and all—that Bob spent real time with Sylvia." Liz seemed to study the restless movement of her hands as she rubbed them together almost as though washing them without water. "I don't know. Promises may have been made."

"And kept."

"I just wanted to get that off my chest." Liz took a deep breath. Finally, she lifted her head. Her warm brown pupils surrounded by watery whites in a web of fine red lines stared back at Holly. Gone was the playful gleam Holly had first seen in Liz's eyes. "I just can't be sure, but I'd hate for a nice guy like Thomas to go to jail when a guy who is already dead might have done it."

Holly wasn't sure how she could prove that, but it was worth a try.

*Buster knew I'd talk Thomas out of this confession nonsense.* Holly hurled her cell phone onto her bed. That's why Buster had him transferred to the district prison and didn't tell anyone, including Chris, about it. Buster was already counting his votes for catching a killer. But he had the wrong guy.

If only that stolen memory card would show up somewhere. Tru used those glasses constantly. Holly wondered if Tru had more than one memory card. Maybe if she watched the footage, there would be a clue on there. Something Tru may not have thought important at the time.

Once again, she wished she could just ring up a ghost when she wanted one and put them all in a box when she didn't.

Holly walked across the hall to Jake's room, which had been where Tru had stayed. She knocked on the door. When no one answered, she pulled out her master key and opened the door. Maybe Jake wouldn't mind her searching his room for the card.

*Yeah, right.* She'd tried that before and it didn't go over so well. But, hey, the sheets needed changing anyway.

The door clicked back in place and Holly turned a full circle in the room. "Tru. Can you hear me?"

She almost laughed at herself. Calling a ghost was as likely to get results as calling a cat. She'd learned ghosts come on their own sweet time.

It couldn't hurt to look for an extra memory card. No telling what she may find on there.

Too bad Tru didn't have the glasses on when the killer pushed him off the widow's walk.

"Tru. Come on. Make it easy on me."

Holly stripped the bed and felt along the edges of the mattress and deeper. She pulled out gum wrappers.

Wonder if Tru missed chewing gum all the time. He'd never mentioned it.

She fumbled along every edge in the room and didn't find anything except dust.

If Liz was right and Bob was doing Sylvia's dirty work, maybe he stole the memory card.

Holly scrubbed her hand across her forehead as though that would help her think. Bob may have kept it for insurance or blackmail. It wouldn't hurt to look.

She trotted up the stairs to the attic room where Bob had stayed. She combed through the closets, under the rugs, and even checked to see if a memory card had been taped under one of the tables. Nothing.

If he'd been stupid enough or under Sylvia's spell, he may have given it to her. She'd probably destroyed it so it wouldn't come back to bite her if anyone else got their hands on it.

Holly decided to give Bob's room one more pass. This time she checked the ceiling fans, bottoms of drawers, and the back of the headboard. The memory card was so small, but the stakes were high. If there was a video of Bob threatening or menacing Tru, that would help Thomas's case. They'd all seen Bob pin Tru on the dining room table, but in pure Tru style, he'd asked for that. She had to find that card.

Holly crawled around on her hands and knees looking between the cracks in the cypress floor. She found more gum wrappers.

*Wait! Gum wrappers. Why would Tru have been in Bob's room? Hmm. This could be interesting.*

"Tru?" Holly randomly called out his name to see if he would get the message.

Maybe if she went about this systematically, she would have a better chance of finding the card.

She knew it was only a hunch, but it was all she had to get Thomas out of jail.

"Hey, Tru. Could I have some help down here?"

*If we find the card it could be a double. If I can prove for sure that Bob killed Tru, I may be able to put together who killed Bob.*

She'd become convinced that the allergic reaction was no accident. Especially after Liz suspected that Sylvia had had a fling with Bob for special services.

But what if . . .

*What if Sylvia put peanut butter in her mouth and kissed Bob? Lordy. That's one disposable weapon! But how could she keep a big guy like that away from his EpiPen when it was right in the bed with him?*

*Or what if it wasn't there? What if after he'd died, she'd dumped it on the bed?* If Holly was a gambling woman, she'd put money on that. But she needed proof to win Thomas's freedom.

While Holly was thinking, she had been feeling around in Bob's room and found nothing.

She kicked the pile of bedding on the floor. Bob must have been dumb enough to give the memory card to Sylvia if he ever had it.

Somehow Holly had to search Sylvia's room before she packed up and checked out. That meant getting her out of her room. But how?

"Yoo-hoo," Miss Alice called from the hall. "Holly, are you up here?"

A smile pinched Holly's cheeks. She knew just the right person for the job.

# CHAPTER THIRTY-THREE

Holly eased Bob's door open just enough to peek out at the back of Miss Alice's bluish-gray hair as she leaned in and cupped her ear to the door of Thomas's room and listened. Then Miss Alice padded along in her stealth orthopedic shoes, carrying her wonder purse hooked over her arm. Miss Alice stopped at the next door and leaned in. *If her hearing ever goes bad, Heaven help us. She'll turn her hearing aids up to spy level.* "Psst."

Miss Alice casually checked her hair with a quick fluff then turned to Holly. "Oh, there you are."

With a wiggle of her finger Holly motioned Miss Alice into Bob's room and closed the door behind her. "I need your help," Holly whispered.

"Why on earth are you whispering?" Miss Alice said, casing the chaos of the search of Bob's room. A wry grin smoothed out the wrinkles above her lip. "Spring cleaning, dear?"

"Something like that." Although Holly had no

doubt Miss Alice knew exactly what she had been doing.

"You know I always find lost things when I deep clean." Miss Alice lifted up a doily. "Do you?"

"I'm not that lucky. Maybe you could help me."

She patted her wonder purse. "I've got a few cleaning supplies right in here."

"It's not exactly the cleaning I need help with."

"I know, dear. But you do need help and so does your father."

"You knew, didn't you?" Holly's throat tightened. "It was you who sent the letters and pictures after Grandma Rose died?"

Miss Alice nodded.

"How did you not recognize him when he checked in?"

"Oh, I did, or I thought I did. It had been thirty-two years since I saw him. He had a full head of hair, tight skin, and muscles then. It was the name that threw me off. I sent the letters to his given name."

"But you . . ." Holly's voice cracked and her eyes stung, "you knew the whole story."

"Not until Rose was on her deathbed. She kept the secret because she'd promised your mother." Miss Alice dug a tissue pack out of her wonder purse. "And I promised Rose."

Holly swallowed back a lump in her throat. Mama, Grandma Rose, and Thomas. They'd all loved her in their own ways. She missed them all so much. "I can't lose Thomas. He's all I have left."

Miss Alice plucked a tissue out of the pack and handed it to Holly. "You've got me, the Deltas, Nelda, and Sam. For better or worse."

And she'd had both from them and given it, too. She blew her nose in the tissue, then told Miss Alice her suspicions and what she was trying to do. "All I need is for you to get Sylvia out of her room for thirty minutes. Can you do it?"

Miss Alice took a tissue and cleaned her glasses while they dangled from a beaded chain. "Is the Pope Catholic?"

"Amen." Holly took a deep breath. "Can you do it now?"

"Give me thirty minutes. I may need to draft Nelda to help." Miss Alice slid her glasses on her nose. "And you need to do one thing."

"What's that?"

"Search Thomas's room," she said in her no-nonsense nurse tone.

"Why?"

"If he was willing to confess to killing someone he didn't for you, he could be willing to kill someone for you. He knows how much this place means to you and what was at stake with that debunker."

"Thomas would never kill anyone."

"I'm not saying he did, I'm just saying he loves you that much and that's motive." She dipped her chin down and peeked over her glasses. "If you don't do it, I will. You need to know."

Miss Alice was right. Holly didn't know her dad, but she knew Thomas. He couldn't be a murderer. Could he?

She opened his suitcase. Neatly folded khakis, jeans, knit polo shirts, and T-shirts filled the inside.

Holly took everything out and checked the lining and then rifled through every pocket. The whole time she prayed she wouldn't find the memory card. After she turned the last pocket inside out she glanced skyward and mouthed *thank you*.

Twenty minutes later, she'd stripped the bed, checked every crevice on it, and combed through the armoire. She'd also looked under the bed, the antique rug, the Empire chest, the mahogany pie-crust table, and the bed steps. All she'd found was dust and evidence she and Nelda needed to step up their cleaning a notch.

Holly stood and studied the room. She had touched everything except the French doors. After she pulled the bed steps over so she could stand on them to reach a little higher, she noticed the lining on the back of the drapes had a hem too. She picked up the fabric and felt along the hemline. She felt something hard. Actually, several disc-shaped things. She stuck her finger in the hem, loosened the stitches, and pulled out a washer-looking thing made of lead, probably to weight down the hem.

The only place left to look was the bathroom, and her confidence was high that a tech guy like Thomas wouldn't put anything that went in a computer in a damp bathroom. She dropped the end of the drapery and something fell out. She blinked as though her eyes were lying. There on the floor a flat rectangular memory card lay among a sprinkling of dust.

Her stomach sank as she climbed down the bed steps. She kneeled, picked up the memory card, and closed her eyes to a flash of a memory from after the séance.

Thomas had picked up Tru's glasses after Bob knocked them off during their tussle. Thomas could have taken the card then. It had all of Tru's debunking video from the séance on it. How many times had Thomas told her he thought everything was going to be okay? He knew that card would never be seen. She clutched the card in her fist and pressed it to her chest. If Thomas had the card, he had no reason to kill Tru.

A scream she knew too well erupted from the hallway. Holly jumped to her feet. "Nelda!"

# CHAPTER THIRTY-FOUR

Holly threw open the door and ran into the hallway just as Nelda let out another Hollywood scream. She waved a broom over her head and whacked it on the floor.

Rhett yapped and bounced with each swat of the broom.

"Did you get it?" Miss Alice yelled trotting behind Nelda and aiming an old-school revolver at the floor.

"Missed." Nelda swung the broom again, then let out another slasher-movie-worthy scream.

Rhett zigzagged, nose to the floor, like he was hot on the trail of something.

And they were chasing something, but Holly couldn't see it and neither could Rhett. And mercy, what was Miss Alice doing with a gun? "What is it?"

Sylvia's door flew open and she poked her head out. She wore glasses, a Holly Grove white bathrobe, her hair in a towel, and not a stitch of makeup. Her ten status dropped a few points, evening her perfect ten to a pleasing five. "Are you people crazy?"

"There it is!" Miss Alice pointed the revolver near Sylvia's feet.

Sylvia jumped out of her Holly Grove slippers and slammed the door, but Nelda stuck the broom in the gap and pried it open.

Nelda jogged in swinging the broom with Miss Alice and Rhett behind her. "They's a whole family of mice in here, and if we don't kill 'em, they'll be a hundred in a month."

Poor Rhett ran in circles. He knew they were after something and he wanted it, too.

Holly clamped her hand over her mouth to keep from laughing as she stood in the doorway.

"Where is it?" Sylvia stood on a chair and frantically scanned the floor for a nonexistent mouse.

Miss Alice pointed the toy gun under Sylvia's perch and squinted. "I don't see it. It must be going up the backside of the chair leg."

"There it is!" Nelda pointed to Sylvia's feet.

Sylvia launched off the chair like a long jumper and nearly ran Holly over getting out of there.

Nelda doubled over holding her stomach and her laugh in, then lifted her hand to Miss Alice for a high five.

Miss Alice slapped Nelda's hand, then turned to Holly. "Is the Pope Catholic?"

"Amen." Holly raised her hands for her high fives from her accomplices.

"Whew!" Nelda, said holding her side. "That hurts. I shoulda let that laugh out in the wild."

"I'm gonna go downstairs and make Miss Inquiring Minds a hot chocolate and tell her there's still one or two mice kickin' up here and y'all are gonna let us know when you get 'em all."

"That should buy us at least half an hour." Miss Alice dropped her toy gun in her bottomless purse. "Did you find anything in Thomas's room?"

Holly pretended she didn't hear Miss Alice. Should she tell the mouth of the South that Thomas stole the memory card that probably caused Tru's murder? She crawled across the floor with her head buried behind the drapes. Maybe she'd get lucky again and find something in the hem. So far they hadn't found anything in Sylvia's room.

"I know you're not as deaf as Sam." Miss Alice pulled the drape away from Holly.

"Uh." Holly blinked. How could she get out of this one without lying?

"Well?"

"Nothing that would prove him guilty or innocent, so no." That was her opinion and she was sticking to it. Holly got up off her knees and dusted herself off. "What haven't we checked?"

"Why don't you climb up on that dresser and check the top of that?" Miss Alice pointed to an aged mirror with a cluster of acorns at the top of the heavily carved frame.

"I think I can reach that." Holly stood on her tiptoes but couldn't quite reach the top of the frame, so she kicked off her ballet flats and hefted herself on top of the dresser. As she ran her fingers across the rough wood on the back side of the frame, she pulled out a spiderweb. Every fine hair on her arm jerked to attention as an eerie tingle raced up her arm. She slung her hand and nearly lost her balance.

"My word." Miss Alice huffed as she steadied Holly and pulled the spiderweb from her fingers. "We don't have time for any more broken bones, Hurricane Holly."

Holly groaned under her breath. "I was thirteen the last time I broke a bone. I'm not that clumsy anymore." She wiped her hand across her pants but couldn't shake the feeling something could crawl up her arm at any moment. "Anybody would freak out a little bit if they stuck their finger in a spiderweb. I didn't fall, did I?"

"Only because you're young and limber. You've got to get a grip on things like that as you get older." She eyed the cluster of acorns at the top of the mirror. "Check there."

*Oh, crapola. There is probably more of the spiderweb back there.* Holly shivered but she reached over the top of the carving anyway. She felt around the rough wood, and then her fingers glided over something smooth. "There's something here."

"What?" Miss Alice asked, leaning around the chest. "Is it the memory card?

"It's feels like plastic." She stretched a little harder to get her fingers around the thing. "It moved."

Holly gave one more stretch and pulled the thing free. She turned it around in her hand.

"What in the world is that?" Miss Alice adjusted her glasses. "It looks like a fat chip clip with a tail."

Holly wiggled the tail and it stayed wherever she

bent it. The flat backside of the thing stuck to her fingers. "It was stuck to the back of the mirror with this sticky stuff."

"Let me see that thingamajig." Miss Alice squeezed down on the clip and it opened. She released it and it closed. "If it's not a chip clip it would make a good one."

"One thing is for sure. Someone put it here for a reason, and I don't think it was for a midnight snack." Holly climbed off the chest with as much grace as she could manage. "Let me take another look at the thingamajig."

Holly held it up to the light and rotated it. The tail had a little ball on the end. On the side of the clip there was a slight indentation and an arrow. She pushed up on the indentation and a little door opened. Her breath caught. Out popped a memory card.

"Did you break it?" Miss Alice said from over Holly's shoulder.

"No." Holly lifted the little door. And pulled out the memory card.

Miss Alice slid her glasses up on her nose. "Is that what we were looking for?"

Holly nodded. "This clip wasn't just a hiding place for the memory card. It's a camera."

Miss Alice took a long gander from the mirror to the bed. Her eyes widened and her jaw dropped. "Oh. My. Word. We've got to tell Sylvia . . ." Miss Alice's hand fluttered to her neck. "Unless she put it there."

*Ew.* That creepy-crawly feeling came over Holly again, but it had nothing to do with a spider. "Miss Alice!"

The old dame straightened. "Well, either she knows or she doesn't. It's a matter of fact."

"But we don't know. For right now, don't ask her or tell anyone about this."

Sylvia loved the camera, but Holly couldn't imagine that her ego would allow anyone to videotape her in her natural state. She certainly wouldn't do it to herself.

But Tru might. After all, he'd videotaped them all with his spy glasses. Why wouldn't he plant a camera? Could he have slipped it into Sylvia's room?

Holly and Nelda usually prop the door open when they clean the guests' rooms. Maybe he slipped in and hid the camera while they were cleaning the bathroom or getting fresh towels.

Somehow she had to ring up her reluctant ghost to find out if he had hidden the camera in Sylvia's room. *And if he did, why didn't he tell me? Something is not right at all about this.*

Still no Tru. What could he be doing that was more important than finding out who was responsible for his death? Didn't he want to be set free? She needed to know if he hid the camera in Sylvia's room and why he did it.

Holly was no techie, but she'd tried the memory card from Sylvia's suite in every slot on her computer. It wouldn't fit in any of them. Neither would the card Thomas had stolen from Tru's spy glasses. Her laptop was probably ancient, so she called Jake to bring his computer to her room. He was the only person she could trust with the memory cards.

Where was Jake? He said he'd come right over. Rhett watched her pace from his perch on her bed. Nelda could only keep Sylvia out of her room for so long. After her experience with what she'd believed was a family of mice, she'd waste no time packing up. Time was running out.

Rhett let out a low growl.

"You look rough," Tru said floating into the room. The soot had mostly worn off and his hair seemed a little less singed since it had finally returned to its reddish-brown color.

"Now you show up?" Holly flopped her hands at her sides. "Where have you been?"

"Thinking," he said with a shrug. "You know today is my last day until they send me," he glanced at the floor, "back."

"Well, think about this." She folded her arms. "I found a hidden camera in Sylvia's room."

Tru cocked his head to the side and crunched his brows together. "Huh?"

"Don't huh me. You were the one recording everyone with your spy glasses." She waved the memory cards in front of him. "Is there something in here you don't want me to see? Something that will prove you deserve to burn?"

He huffed. "Now that's low. Even I wouldn't put a camera in someone's bedroom. I was trying to debunk a ghost, not get blackmail on her."

"Blackmail . . ." Holly remembered what Liz had told her about Bob and Sylvia. Could Bob have been planning to blackmail Sylvia? Maybe taking out a little job security insurance.

A knock sounded at her door and she rushed to answer it.

"Charged and ready." Jake filled her doorway as his chocolate gaze zapped her right in the heart.

*Charged and ready. Crapola. How does he do that to me?*

"What ya got?" he asked as he strode into her room and put his computer on her bed.

*I've got a world of trouble if I let my guard down again with this man. That's what.* "I found a camera in Sylvia's room—hidden behind a mirror and pointed right at her bed." She handed Jake the memory card.

"Whoa." Jake opened up his computer. "This could be interesting."

"See," Tru said. "Why else would anyone put a camera in front of a bed?"

"Depends if it helps me figure out who killed Tru and maybe Bob." Holly stood beside Jake. "Tru thinks someone put it there to blackmail Sylvia."

"Totally possible." Jake looked around. "Is he here now?"

Holly nodded.

He fired up his computer and slid the memory card in. In a few seconds, a jumpy video of the ceiling filled the screen. Then a hand covered the camera.

"There's no sound," Holly said.

Jake clicked a few keys. "It was recorded without sound."

"You don't need sound if you're just going to put up a nude video of a celebrity," Tru said on the other side of Jake. "Blackmail. I told you."

The video flashed back to the ceiling and a hand again. Then the hand pulled away slowly as though someone was testing to see if the camera was secure on the mirror. As the hand pulled away, Bob's face and bare chest came into view. He adjusted the camera one more time and then opened a bottle of wine on the dresser. In the background, Sylvia walked into the picture and sprawled across the bed in a silky nightgown. "Uh-oh. This may be something private."

"Blackmail." Tru pointed to the computer.

Holly cringed. "We shouldn't watch this."

"Someone may have to take one for the team," Jake said.

"I'm in." Tru rested his elbows on the bed and Rhett growled.

Holly rolled her eyes. "You're such a man."

"We've got to know what's on here, right?" Jake asked.

"Yeah, but . . ."

"Actually, I've had to watch all kinds of things for surveillance with ICE. It gets old fast." He pointed to the screen. "Hey, there's a time stamp on the video."

Holly squinted. "That's before Tru was killed."

On screen, Sylvia downed her glass of wine and rolled to the side of the bed. Holly watched through her fingers because she didn't know what she may see next.

Sylvia's shoulders shook as though she were crying. Bob sat on the edge of the bed and rubbed her back as he talked to her. He nodded, then left the room.

"So much for Bob's alibi with Sylvia for the time of the murder," Jake said.

"I know that guy pushed me now." Tru pointed

toward the screen. "I just don't know why I didn't get my pass out of here when he checked out."

No sooner than Bob was out of her room, a smile slid across Sylvia's face. She poured another glass of wine and disappeared from view.

"Did you see her play him?" *Maybe she's a better actor than I gave her credit for.* "No way, she'd let him see her take off that mask if she knew she was on camera." Holly looked from Jake to Tru. "If y'all are right and Bob was trying to get some . . . Let's just say candid videos to blackmail Sylvia with, he didn't get it."

"He got proof they both lied about their alibi," Jake said.

"Yeah," Holly said. "And he didn't live to destroy that evidence."

"No kidding, Sherlock," Tru said. "I'm still dead though, and so is Bob."

"You know how Bob and Liz always set up two cameras for the *Inquiring Minds* shoots?" Holly asked.

"Gotcha." Jake's dimple in his chin deepened. "A cameraman always has more than one angle. I'm thinking somewhere private like his room."

"One way to find out." Holly dangled her master key from a chain.

A few minutes later, Holly had found another camera hooked onto the back of an Audubon print in Bob's attic room. Jake inserted the memory card in his computer as he balanced it on his knees. He'd wedged himself into the oak rocker that had rocked generations of the Lane family babies. *I might*

*as well dust away thoughts of rocking the next generation.*
*Lordy. Why did I even think of that with Jake in the rocker?*

She needed to think about Thomas and proving who the real killers are so he can get out of jail and Tru can stay out of Hell.

"Is your ghost still hanging out with us?" Jake asked.

"Barely," Tru said. He looked pale, even for a ghost.

"For now." Holly watched what looked like a still-life of the attic bedroom until Bob opened the door and came inside. He leaned against the door like the weight of life was just too much to carry.

Jake fast-forwarded the video until Bob gives a chin check at the camera and then answers the door.

Sylvia is wearing a Holly Grove guest bathrobe but is still decked out in full makeup. She wraps Bob in a hug and kisses him at the door. As they walk by the camera he looks right at it. Holly tapped the screen. "See how he checks in with the camera. Now look at Sylvia. She totally ignores the camera, which is not natural behavior for her."

"Nope," Jake said. "That confirms she doesn't know she's being recorded in either place."

While Bob is in the bathroom, Sylvia takes something wrapped in a napkin out of her robe pocket and takes a bite.

Bob comes out of the bathroom wearing his pajama pants and a wife-beater T-shirt. He carries a glass of water, which he gives to Sylvia. She sets it down and pulls him in for a kiss. Seconds later, he's gasping for breath. She takes the glass of water back into the bathroom and comes back out with Bob's pants and a washcloth. He's now sprawled on the floor beside the bed. She uses the washcloth to take the EpiPen out of his pants pocket and tosses it on the bed.

"That's one cruel woman." Tru shook his head. "She killed him with a kiss."

"I've got enough." Jake stood. "You keep watching. I'm going to make sure Sylvia doesn't leave before Buster can get his posse over here."

# CHAPTER THIRTY-FIVE

Holly slipped another memory card into Jake's computer and waited for it to load. *Why oh why, when I am in a hurry does that little beach ball just bounce all over the freakin' computer screen?*

Finally, the memory card from Tru's glasses loaded. Holly sat at the planter's table scrolling through the images. She scanned for Sylvia's and Bob's faces. She sped them up and slowed them down over and over again.

Tru had recorded practically everything that had happened since he arrived at Holly Grove. How could she ever sort through all this fast enough for it to make a difference to Tru—or Thomas?

Holly sighed. It would be so much easier if the DA could depose the ghost of Tru the departed.

Two hours into Tru's recordings, Holly watched a close-up of Sylvia's very angry face as she threatening to ruin Tru. Three hours later, she's trying to blackmail him.

Holly called Jake and asked him to get her to the sheriff's office and help her make Buster understand he had the wrong man. And the woman responsible for it all was about to get away.


"You've got the goods," Jake said as he walked with Holly down the hall at the St. Agnes Parish Sheriff's office.

"Yes I do." Holly patted the computer bag strapped across her shoulder. "Thomas is coming home with us."

"Just tell them your story." Jake opened the door and they stepped into Buster's office.

Buster stood and shook their hands, then reared back in his chair and put his feet on his desk. "You're going to be hard-pressed to beat a full confession on video tape, but, hey, knock yourself out."

Jake settled in one of two standard-issue office chairs in front of Buster's institutional desk.

Holly stood so she'd be taller than Buster. A little leverage never hurts. "I'll start with the history and how and why murder came to Holly Grove.

"First, I'm going to tell you what happened and then I'm going to show you the evidence."

Jake leaned forward. "It's quite a story. Old Sam is going to have this story on the front page of the *Gazette,* whether you decide to let Thomas Sinclair walk today or not. I'm sure he's interested in a juicy story that frees an innocent man."

"We'll see." Buster crossed his arms. "Let's hear it."

"I'd had some success with Holly Grove B&B after we got a lot of good publicity from a YouTube video that went viral. Then *Inquiring Minds* shot an episode that proved Holly Grove was haunted. It proved to be the most popular show of their season." *Thank you very much, Burl Davis.* "It was good for my business, Sylvia's *Inquiring Minds,* and Angel's psychic services."

"Is this relevant?" Buster's police-issue shoes scraped across his desk as he repositioned his feet.

"Enter the stirrer of stink." She threw a photo of Tru on the table. "On live radio, he challenged Sylvia Martin of *Inquiring Minds* to pick any show she'd done and he could debunk it. She took the challenge and chose the most popular episode of the year, 'Ghost in the Grove.' Shot right here in Delta Ridge at Holly Grove."

Buster looked at his watch.

"But there's a kink in the works," Holly said. "My ghost goes into hiding." *In the promised land.* "When the Ghost in the Grove is a no show, the debunker smells chum in the water."

"Sylvia doesn't want to lose her reputation. Angel doesn't want to be named a fraud. And I just want to keep my rooms rented, and a haunted house helps in the B&B business. Do you see the conflict?"

Buster didn't respond.

"Anyway, enter one Tru Stalwart wearing superspy glasses he bought on the Internet. He recorded everything with them and no one knew." She pointed at Jake's computer on the table. "I'll play a few for you shortly. Remember, we don't have a ghost on duty but need one."

"A ghost or lack of one is not going into evidence." Buster eyed Jake. "I can promise you that."

Jake nodded. "Stay with her."

"Let's just say some faking went on at the séance,

and Tru caught us dead to rights. He told us he'd recorded it all with his spyglasses. He won. He's going to expose us all as frauds all over the World Wide Web. It got a little crazy, and Bob slammed Tru over a table and knocked his glasses off. But in the dark and while everyone is all riled up, one of us steals the memory card right out of his glasses."

"I'm aware," Buster said. "Tru reported the theft."

"That's right" Holly held her index finger up. "The rest of us there, including Tru, don't know that until later. Tru still thinks he has the proof to debunk the Ghost in the Grove and expose us as frauds. Tru goes up to his room to view his handiwork and he realizes one of us stole the memory card."

"You said that." Buster checked his watch again. "I've got an appointment in ten minutes. Can you just show me the evidence?"

Jake lifts his hand in a halting position. "Give her a minute, Buster. She's almost finished."

"You come." Holly eyes Buster. "Tru is already dead, right?"

"I was there, Holly," Buster said.

"Everyone is a suspect, right?"

Buster nodded.

"Sylvia sweetens the pot with some very personal attention for Bob, who has secretly been in love with her for years. All she wants is for him to make this all go away and he's willing. They buddy up on an alibi and Bob makes Tru go away by tossing him off the roof."

"While we're all freakin' out thinking Tru fell to his death, Bob jimmies the lock on Tru's room and finds more memory cards, and some of them could

make Sylvia look very guilty, so he hides those away
for insurance. Unfortunately, he doesn't get to cash
in because Sylvia tags Bob with a poisonous kiss, for
him anyway, because he's allergic to peanut butter.
So Sylvia gets Bob to throw Tru off the roof and she
gets rid of the evidence by killing the killer. Make
sense?"

Buster slid his feet off his desk. "Look, this is all a
good story, but it's speculation, and that doesn't
beat a confession. You need evidence."

"You're so right, Buster." Holly unzipped the computer bag. "How about videos?"

"Where did you find those?" Buster sat up straight.
"My men covered every inch of that place."

"They didn't clean it." Holly smiled. "I had a little
help too. It occurred to me that Tru probably had
lots of memory cards because he'd recorded everything for days. And what do you know? I found
something else. Bob the camera guy had a hidden
camera in his room, but it wasn't of the séance. Will
that do?"

Buster leaned forward and put his elbows on his
desk. "Depends what's on it."

Holly pulled out flash drives loaded with copies of
the videos. She held them up and described them
one by one. "Here's Sylvia and Bob all lovey-dovey.
Here's Sylvia threatening Tru. Here's Bob man-
handling Tru. Here's a time-stamped video of Sylvia
alone at the time Tru was murdered, which blows
Bob's alibi. Here's Sylvia watching Bob die while she
withheld his EpiPen. She thought she'd destroyed
all the evidence, but sometimes the dead speak."

Buster fingered a flash drive. "I'll take a look at all this and get back to you."

"While you keep an innocent man in jail?" Jake asked.

"He confessed."

"Thomas Sinclair lied." Holly leaned over the desk. "He did not kill Tru. He lied because he's willing to go to jail for me. You know why?"

She didn't wait for him to answer. "He's my daddy and he loves me. Always has. Thomas is innocent, and I demand that you look at this evidence right now and release him."

Jake stood. "Yep. Old Sam would love to solve a double murder between the pages of the *Gazette.* I bet he could stretch that story out all the way until the election"

"I'll get my deputies on this right away." Buster eased out of his chair.

Holly lined the flash drives up across his desk. "We'll be waiting right outside."

The siren blared as Holly and Jake raced behind Buster's patrol car back to Holly Grove. Jake had left Mackie in charge of making sure Sylvia couldn't leave and he didn't care how he did it.

When they turned down the gravel driveway covered with an oak canopy, she spotted Mackie sitting on the front porch of Holly Grove with Nelda. Sylvia was nowhere in sight. Holly's heart fell.

Sure, the police would find her eventually, but Tru needed that closure. He needed an arrest to go with the name he provided to the devil. He needed the satisfaction that justice was done so he could rest in peace. And so could she.

They piled out of the car and Holly rushed to Mackie. "Where's Sylvia?"

"That woman ain't goin' nowhere except to jail," Nelda said, poking one foot from under the hand-made quilt on her lap. She gave the porch swing a good push and glided backward.

Mackie grinned and thumbed toward the chicken coop.

Buster sauntered that way and everyone else followed except Nelda.

"How'd you get her in there, Mackie?" Jake asked as they walked across the side yard.

"I didn't." He eyed Dog. "She did. Herded that lady right in the coop. Pretty good, considering she's carrying a litter.

Jake grinned. "I bet Dog has some border collie in her mix too."

"Good dog." Holly had never thought she'd say that and mean it about Dog.

"Thank God you're here," Sylvia yelled. Her fingers curled around the chicken wire so tightly they'd nearly turned purple. The winter wind had whipped her Bergdorf blond hair into a string mop. She jerked against the chicken wire and rattled the whole coop.

Dog leaped to her feet and let out a low, nasty growl while Rhett backed her up with a barrage of sharp yaps.

Sylvia jumped back and pointed at Mackie. "That man is holding me against my will."

"Ma'am, it's called a citizen's arrest, and I didn't put a hand on you." Mackie stuffed his hands in his pockets. "Heck, I didn't even latch the chicken coop. You could walk right out."

"At your own risk." Holly folded her arms and stood in front of Sylvia. "How do you feel about starring on prison TV?"

"Don't harass my prisoner," Buster said, removing his handcuffs from his utility belt. "Don't worry, Ms. Martin. The good news is Louisiana hasn't executed a woman since 1942."

"What?" Sylvia snapped.

"That's right. You'll have the rest of your life to wait to go straight to hell." Holly drilled Sylvia with a stare. "I have it on good authority that your name is on the list."

Cuffs in hand, Buster opened the chicken coop door.

Sylvia's stilettos sunk into the dirt as she tried to back up. "You can't put those on me!"

"Yes ma'am, I can." Buster wrangled Sylvia into the handcuffs. "You're under arrest for the murders of Bob Morris and Tru Stalwort. You have the right to remain silent—"

"I have an alibi, or are you so daft you forgot I was with Bob when *Thomas* threw Tru off the roof? And Bob died of anaphylactic shock. That is a medical condition. Not murder." She shook her wayward hair off her face.

"Watch your step, ma'am." Buster guided her toward his patrol car.

"Not only am I *not* going to be executed, I'm going to sue Holly Grove and this rat trap you call a town for everything you've got."

"You know I speak to ghosts, right?" Holly said as she trotted beside Sylvia and Buster, leaving Mackie and Jake behind with the dogs.

Sylvia threw her head back and laughed. "So *now* you're on speaking terms with your Burl."

"Nope." Holly trotted alongside Sylvia. "Tru is my new ghost, but he won't be here long now that his murder is solved. Bob didn't come back as a ghost, but he left you a message."

"Really?" Sylvia gave Holly a side glance. "Some sort of woo-woo ghostly message. Yeah, right."

Buster put his hand on Sylvia's head and guided her into the backseat of his patrol car.

"It was more of a video message." Holly pasted a sarcastic grin on her face. "He set up hidden cameras in your room and his."

Sylvia turned ashen.

"And I gave the memory cards to our chief deputy sheriff here, and Tru is going to give your name to the devil."

The wind caught the door, slamming it hard.

Holly looked skyward. *My sentiments exactly.*

# CHAPTER THIRTY-SIX

Holly turned to go inside Holly Grove and walked right through the icy cold aura of Tru. She shivered and brushed herself off.

"Wow." Tru grinned. "That was like a hug. Can we do that again?"

"What? I mean no." That was like an ice bath to her. She looked over her shoulder to see if Nelda was still on the front porch. The empty swing barely moved in the breeze.

Tru followed her gaze. "They're all inside."

"Didn't you get the memo?" Holly let out a breath like a pressure release valve. "Sylvia was arrested for Bob's murder and accessory to *your* murder."

"Yeah." Tru dug his loafer across the grass. "I heard."

"What are you still doing here?" Holly held her hands palms up. "Aren't you happy?"

"I guess," he said with a shrug.

"You get a choice of eternal fire or heaven. You got heaven. And you *guess* you're happy?" Holly rolled her eyes. "Let me give you a little hint. Heaven is the happy part."

Tru nodded but didn't look up at her. "Remember, I told you I'd been thinking."

"Yeah." Holly dragged out the word. "And . . ."

"When I was a little kid, my grandfather died suddenly of a heart attack." Tru finally looked up at Holly. "He and my grandmother had taken care of me while my mother worked since I was a baby. He was the only best friend I ever had and he was gone forever. It was a huge deal."

"I'm sorry, Tru, but now you can go be with him."

Tru shook his head. "He's not there. I checked."

"Where is he?"

"I'm getting to that." Tru looked out in the distance as he spoke. "When I was little, Grandma said she knew how to visit him. Every week she'd go to a medium and pay her to call Gramps up for a visit."

"Did it work?"

"At first, I thought so. I felt like he was there, but I couldn't see him." Tru gave a sheepish look. "But Grandma did. After a while I quit going, but Grandma never did. Even when she was in the nursing home the medium would come and call up Gramps. Then Grandma ran out of money. Every time I'd visit her, she wanted me to pay the medium. It made her happy, so I did it for a while. I decided to check out this medium. She lived on gated acreage and was loaded, but she made a woman in a nursing home pay her last dime to pretend to talk to her dead husband. I decided I would never let anyone take advantage of someone like my grandmother again. It took years, but I took that medium down, and I've been doing it ever since. I thought I was the good guy."

"I'm sure you did take down some frauds."

"And probably some legit mediums," Tru said.

"You didn't know any better, but now you do."

"Yeah. That's why I want to find my grandfather. When Grandma stopped paying, they lost touch before she died. She went on to Heaven and he's stuck in between."

"Like you were?"

"That's what I've been thinking about. I have another choice. I can stay in between and help the people everywhere like Grandpa find their way. Like you do."

Holly swallowed hard. "You think I help?"

Tru nodded. "Other than Grandpa, you're the first real friend I've ever had."

*Jeez. He's going to make me like him after all.* "Thanks, Tru."

"I've got a lot of work to do in faraway places, so I don't know when I'll see you again. If you ever need me, call me."

"But . . ."

Tru faded into a misty gray.

Debunker to spirit guide. She didn't see that one coming. *Good-bye, Tru. Maybe I'll see you on the other side one day.*


Miss Alice's pale blue Cadillac eased down the driveway as Buster's patrol car motored toward the blacktop highway. The gravel crunched under the whitewall tires of the Cadillac until it idled in front of Holly.

When she spotted Thomas in the backseat, something twisted in her as though every missed birthday and holiday had been wrung out of her. She'd only just begun to know her father, but she now knew he loved her without bounds.

Chris climbed out of the car first and opened the door for Miss Alice. Thomas kept his head down for a moment before he opened the door. When he stepped out, he covered his mouth and stared at her with watery eyes.

A lump she couldn't swallow lodged in her throat. She didn't know what to say, but she did know what to do. Holly walked to Thomas and wrapped him in a hug.

Neither of them said anything for a moment. They just held each other tight and let the tears flow.

Thomas took a step back. He held her at arm's length and looked into her eyes. "I'm not good at talking about this kind of thing, but I want you to know I'm sorry I wasn't there for you when you were growing up. I can't change that, but if you're willing I'd like to be here for you now.

"I'd like that." Holly took a big breath of a new life. "We have a lot of time to make up for."

They walked in the house and joined Chris, Miss Alice, Nelda, and Jake for celebration Sazeracs.

"I knew who you were when you walked in my kitchen," Nelda said as she sidled up between Holly and Thomas. "But I was still mad at you for leavin' Holly's mama brokenhearted. Mind you, I didn't know the rest of the story. Everybody who knew but Miss Alice are dead and gone." Nelda crossed herself. "God rest their souls. But when you marched yourself up to the jail and took the blame for Holly, I scratched off all the mad I ever had at ya."

Thomas clinked his Sazerac glass to Nelda's iced-tea glass. "That means more to me than you know."

Holly caught a glimpse of Jake stepping out the back door with his phone pressed to his ear. "Yes, sir." Jake listened for a minute or so. "Normally, I'd do it, but I need to spend some time back home. I've made promises to myself and others I need to keep. I'll see you in about three weeks."

She smiled at Jake as he crossed the porch and leaned against the banister next to her.

"Think you can spare a room for three weeks?"

"Sounds promising, but we'll see."